CW00865003

SPITFIRE

gina glass

iUniverse, Inc.
New York Bloomington

Spitfire

iUniverse books may be ordered through booksellers or by contacting:

iUniverse
1663 Liberty Drive
Bloomington, IN 47403
www.iuniverse.com
1-800-Authors (1-800-288-4677)

ISBN: 978-1-440-10846-4 (pbk)
ISBN: 978-1-440-10847-1 (ebk)

Printed in the United States of America

iUniverse rev. date: 11/14/2008

To all of you who I have met, talked with, worked with, played with, or crossed paths with, you have my sincerest heart-felt thanks!

To the fans that wouldn't let the flame of Spitfire die out - thank you! It's because of your belief in Dillon & Ashley, and the story of their love, that has brought us all together again! You are all so important, and I appreciate every one of you!

To my family and friends, thank you for your love and support! You realize what this dream meant to me, and you've encouraged me to follow it!

To my parents, your love and support tells me I'm doing the right thing! I love you!

To the great ladies who have helped to make Spitfire beautiful, both inside and out: Giulia, Michele, CC, Lori, Judy, Kerry & Kim. You are awesome Thank you for having my back!!

To Marnie Alton, button your soul and love for life is inspiring! Thank you for being a part of Spitfire. I'm thrilled that you're the one to give Ashley her voice!

To Cathy DeBuono. C, you have been there since the day I brought Spitfire to you! You have embraced Dillon, not only bringing her to life, but also to bringing her to a new level! It's been an honor to work with you on this project! Thank You!!

Show Your Support!

http://www.myspace.com/spitfire_themovie
http://www.spitfire08.com/Spitfire.htm
http://www.myspace.com/gglass_author
http://www.myspace.com/cathydebuono
http://www.cathydebuono.com/index.html
http://profile.myspace.com/marniealton
http://www.myspace.com/krrrr

The smoke grew thick and heavy. Dillon knew that there wasn't much time left to find the boy trapped inside. She turned her air pack on and grabbed her halagan.

"Get out of my way!" she yelled to her crew as she passed them. Her best friend and partner, Jack, grabbed a pick and followed.

The eerie creaking of the collapsing apartment rang loud in Dillon's ears; she hated this part of the job! She wanted to find the boy and get out! She and Jack dropped to their knees and began the search for the missing boy. She heard a loud pop. Her instincts told her to move, as part of the ceiling came down. Looking back, she saw that Jack had moved out as well. They headed down the hall crawling, checking every room. They came to a room with the door shut. Dillon jumped to her feet to open it. It wouldn't move. Jack moved in and tried to break the door down. Dillon took her halagan and started to hack away at the door until there was a sizable hole in it. A mans body lay across the doorway blocking access to the room. Dillon climbed over him and looked around. She reached down to check his pulse. There was none. She spotted the boy in the middle of the room. She knelt down by him and took her air mask off.

"Spit! What the hell are you doing?" Jack yelled at her. "It's grab and go!"

Dillon placed her air mask over the boys face and lifted him into her embrace.

"Do you ever follow procedures?" Jack asked her as she walked by him.

"Grab and go, Jack!" She said as she stepped over the dead body with the boy still in her arms.

Dillon and Jack stopped in the living room. Dillon felt the smoke starting to get to her.

They stepped through the piles of flaming embers and walked to the door. Part of the ceiling came crashing down, driving the firefighters back into the living room.

Dillon started to cough.

Jack pointed to a broken window, and they moved to it. Jack cleared the glass from the window and climbed out.

Dillon took the air mask off the boy and passed him through to Jack. As she was about to climb through, the floor gave away. She moved to her left and was blindsided by a beam crashing down. She lay lifeless as the flames came closer to her.

1

The ambulance rolled into the E.R. Dillon was still unconscious. An EMT was checking her vitals as the other two drivers unloaded her. They wheeled her into E.R. and into a room.

"She hit her head" the EMT explained. "Got hit by a falling beam saving a boy. She's taken in a lot of smoke. There's a couple of broken ribs and possible traumatic pneumothorax. Pulse is rapid, breathing shallow."

Dillon came to, still groggy and coughing. "The boy. Need to get him."

Dillon tried to sit up but the pain and the hospital staff pushed her down.

The nurse hurriedly put a sedative in Dillon's IV. It had a quick affect on her.

"The boy," was all she could get out before she drifted back off.

"Is the boy she's talking about the one from the apartment fire?" the nurse asked the EMT.

"Yeah, she went back into the apartment to get him. You should have seen it. It was a fricken' inferno she ran into. Two guys from her crew pulled her out. She's damn lucky to be alive."

Rhonda Harris, one of the head E.R. nurses, walked into the room, grabed the chart and started to read. "Spitfire?" She looked at the firefighter lying there, her face covered in soot, hooked up to an oxygen mask.

"You know her Rhonda?" The duty nurse asked.

"Everyone knows Spitfire. She always follows in, especially the kids." Rhonda said.

"She pulled the boy in bed two out of a burning apartment. She was hit by a beam in the process." The duty nurse explained.

"That doesn't surprise me." Rhonda added "Is she stable?"

"Shortness of breath, rapid pulse, possible traumatic pneumorthorax," The nurse said.

"Well, what are we waiting for? Come on people; let's get a move on! Let's get her into x-ray A.S.A.P!"

A male orderly came running in. "Rhonda, there's been a huge crash. A metro-link train hit a bus. They're transporting here." He yelled.

"Wonderful." Rhonda rolled her eyes. "It must be a Wednesday. Steve, call for all available floor doctors, stat!"

"All ready done." Steve said.

Rhonda left her team with instructions and walked back to the nurse's station.

"Hey Rhonda," a female's voice called out. Rhonda turned around smiling. She knew the voice of her friend.

Dr. Ashley Wilkerson came walking up to her with her arms open.

She was a beautiful woman, all five foot six inches of her. Her soft blonde shoulder length hair shined, with radiant blue eyes that danced when she laughed. All the women envied her natural beauty; all the men wanted her in bed.

Ashley was a very private person, and only her closest friend, Rhonda, knew anything about her.

Ashley recently became one of the staff doctors at Mount West-L.A.

It was all very nice - the promotion, the money. But inside, Ashley felt alone. After the promotion dinner, she came home to find her girlfriend in bed with another woman. It took Ashley a few months to get over the shock. Her relationship with Giavanna was an extreme surge of ups and downs. They continued living together for rents sake. Now six months later, Ashley was finally earning enough money that she had asked Gia to move out. Gia stalled Ashley's request by saying, "I'm working on it".

"I got the page. How can I help?" She asked her friend.

"Didn't you hear about the apartment fire?"

Ashley looked blankly at Rhonda.

"Apparently not." Rhonda continued, "Five people dead, two are in surgery now. Some jealous boyfriend tried to barbeque his girlfriend and kids!"

Ashley looked at Rhonda. She never understood how people could try to make light in such a tragic situation.

"Who survived?"

"The mother is in ICU, not expected to live, and her nine year old son, prognosis is good, burned with some smoke inhalation. He's very lucky to be alive. There was one firefighter hurt - concussion, smoke inhalation, fractured ribs, and possible traumatic pneumo of the right lung. They're popping pictures of it right now. Then, to add to the excitement, a metro-link hit a bus. They're transporting here."

"Oh God." Ashley said.

The commotion was loud. Being in L.A. they were used to the media frenzy that would follow every time something of a large magnitude occurred.

"Right on time." Rhonda looked at her watch. "Here, these are yours." She handed Ashley some charts. "The top one is the most serious. Have fun." She winked at Ashley.

Ashley shook her head and chuckled. Rhonda could be a little much at times, but she was a great friend. Ashley opened the chart as she heard Rhonda yelling at the media in the lounge. She laughed, then turned her attention to the paper.

"Dillon McCabe." She read further then closed the chart. "OK, Mr. McCabe. You keep your slimy firefighter hands to yourself, and I won't kick your ass," she said under her breath. Ashley walked into the room and stopped dead in her tracks. She froze, staring at the firefighter who lay peaceful in the bed. She had beautiful black hair, with strong features. "*Wait a sec.*" Ashley thought. She opened the chart again; there it was in black and white. Sex F. Ashley smiled. "Well, good for you."

She moved closer, taking all of the firefighter in. Her arms were muscular. Ashley felt a shiver up her spine. She looked around for a possible draft. Nothing. She slowly placed her hand on the firefighter's wrist to check her pulse. The touch sent chills through both of them.

Dillon's eyes opened. "Am I dead?" Dillon asked in her now raspy voice.

"Sssh. You'll live," Ashley said as she looked down at her watch. "But you need to be quiet." Ashley looked up and their eyes met. Ashley had never seen such a rich shade of brown staring at her. Those eyes were amazing.

Dillon became flushed at the stare of the gorgeous blue-eyed doctor.

Becoming flushed was a trademark of Dillon's since she was a little girl. A trademark she wished she could trade in.

Growing up Dillon was a tomboy, always picked first for the sports teams, playing with stinkbugs as opposed to Barbie dolls. With age also came the decision to push away any feelings and crushes she had on the girls and female teachers she had at school. She told herself that it was just idolizing, that she longed for a sister, instead of the cruel hearted older brother she ended up with. Her mother forced her to wear a dress on Sundays, and by senior year she was mostly a loner on campus, having only made a few friends along the way. Dillon was pushed into going to her senior prom with Tommy Nichols. Their mother's played tennis together. Tommy was nice enough, but he was known for his wandering hands. On the way home from the prom he put his hand on the inside of Dillon's thigh. "I'm gay!" she proclaimed, much to both of their surprise.

From that second on, Dillon knew her life would change. With just three days until her high school graduation, she came out to her family. She was eighteen and felt she couldn't live the lie any longer. Her mother went into theatrics about failing as a parent and never being able to show her face at her Thursday night bridge game again. Her father grounded her until she was eighty. Her brother laughed at her and called her a "Dyke," and left with his friends.

The night of her graduation, her father lifted her restriction so she could be with friends for the annual "all night party". Instead, that night Dillon drove down to Long Beach. She had been there once before and felt right at home. She went to the Executive Suite and played pool and even danced for a bit with a cute blonde that kept rubbing up against her. At about 1:00 am, Dillon drove home. As she turned left onto her street, there were four fire trucks, paramedics, police, countless news crews and onlookers. Dillon's home was ablaze. She pulled over and tried to head up the street on foot past a huge crowd that had gathered by the police caution tape. Dillon tried to stop a few people, but no one would talk to her. She made her way to the policeman guarding the barrier.

"Sorry, miss. We need you to stay back."

"That's my house!" Dillon yelled. "My family! Where are my parents?"

The officer quickly grabbed a woman in jeans and a leather jacket. She turned to Dillon.

" Is this your house?" she asked Dillon

"Yes! Yes! Here." Dillon fumbled in her pocket for her ID. She handed it to the woman.

"Please follow me." The woman lifted the police tape for Dillon to go under.

Dillon stared at the woman's eyes. They were caring and soft. The kind that you could get lost in. The kind that were staring at her right now.

"Hi." Ashley smiled.

Dillon couldn't believe it. Yep, she must be dead cause there was nothing truly as lovely as this vision in white that stood in front of her.

"Hey." Dillon mumbled and coughed. She grabbed her side. "What happened?"

"Well, you got hit by a beam in a burning house. Your partner and another crew member pulled you out. You broke some ribs, you have a concussion, and a traumatic pnumothroax. Good job Ms. McCabe."

"Great." Dillon tried to find a comfortable position. "The little boy? Is he ok?" Dillon grimaced.

"Ben will be fine. He's in surgery. I'll keep you posted."

Dillon smiled. "Can I go now?"

"Ah, you're not going anywhere anytime soon." Ashley said sternly.

Dillon looked at Ashley. Ashley gave the look right back. She knew she was staying.

The duty nurse came in.

"Let's get her prepped for a chest tube." Ashley told the nurse.

"Chest tube?" Dillon said groggily. She started to cough. She struggled for her breath.

The duty nurse put the oxygen mask on Dillon.

Ashley took out her stethoscope and put it on Dillon's chest. "We need to put that chest tube in stat. Let's go."

The staff started to prep Dillon, and Ashley went to scrub up.

Dillon struggled to watch Ashley as she slowly faded into a deep sleep.*The fire completely destroyed Dillon's home. She was left only with the clothes on her back. The lead detective on the case, Kris Bryant, brought Dillon to the station. From all accounts, they were blaming the fire on a gas leak. Dillon was in shock. She lost her entire family, everything.*

"If you need a place to crash, I have an extra room." Kris offered to Dillon. Dillon took her up on her offer and stayed for three years. It turned out that Kris was a lesbian, which made Dillon feel even more at home. She really opened up with Kris and shared her thoughts, her fears. Kris hooked Dillon up with some EMT's and soon Dillon tried out for the fire academy. She'd made a promise at her family's memorial that she would honor them by becoming a firefighter.

On her graduation from the fire academy, Dillon had two offers for local firehouses; she chose Engine Co. # 31. That night, Kris took her dancing. It was magical for Dillon! She danced with many of the women there, but especially liked the slow dance with Kris. They drank and partied the night away. When they got home, Kris took Dillon to her bedroom and did a striptease for her. Dillon couldn't believe it. Kris had a fabulous body! They had sex many times that night. It was Dillon's first time. She was scared and excited all at once. Kris was a good teacher. She showed her everything.

The next morning, Dillon awoke to an empty bed, and a note on the pillow from Kris. It read: "I think it's best if you move out." Dillon was a confused mess. She called her new fire station to see if she could start immediately. She went into an extreme workaholic mode. She knew that if she stopped, she would think, and that would make her depressed. She decided that it was indeed her fault that she was gone. After Kris, Dillon turned her heart off. She now knew what her life would entail. She was incapable of loving someone the right way, so she accepted her fate of living a solitary life.

For the next two years she excelled at being a firefighter and becoming one of the guys. She was a highly respected firefighter. She would be there for Wednesday's poker night, and was always willing to pick up a shift no matter what.

Dillon's memories woke her from her anesthetic. She tried to sit up, but the pain overtook her and she let out a howl. Ashley was nearby and heard her. She bolted through the door, followed by a nurse.

"It's ok." Ashley's smooth voice and deep green eyes had a soothing effect on Dillon. Ashley could tell that Dillon had been having nightmares. She was in a cold sweat from the pain.

She quickly took her pulse.

"You wanna talk about it?" Ashley offered.

"No." Dillon said flatly "What I want are my clothes so I can get the hell outta here! I'm on duty tomorrow!"

"Hmm, well, Ms. McCabe, it seems you will be joining us here for a while."

"What?" Dillon looked at Ashley. "And it's Spit."

"You have some blood that has collected behind that punctured lung, ...Spit."

"Great." Dillon said groggily. "I have to go to work."

"I talked to your Captain and explained that you'll be here for the next week or so, and your recovery will take six to eight weeks. He said, 'see you when you get better' and not a moment before. So, I don't think you have any pressing engagements."

"Six weeks?" Dillon sighed heavily. "What the hell am I gonna do sitting around for six weeks?

"Rest comes to mind."

"What's next?" Dillon grumbled.

"You rest. You have a pretty nasty concussion too."

Dillon rolled her eyes. "My head is fine, my ribs are fine. I've busted them before, and I don't need a tube."

Ashley knew that Dillon wasn't going to be an easy patient. "I hear Ben is recovering, and I'm sure he would like a visitor." Ashley offered.

Dillon smiled.

"Oh my gosh, she smiled and her face didn't crack! I'll have to note that on the chart." Ashley winked at Dillon.

Dillon started to laugh which made her cough, sending her into a coughing spasm which made her ribs hurt even more.

Ashley turned on the oxygen. Dillon breathed deeply. She finally settled down. "Easy, there." Ashley smiled.

Dillon looked into Ashley's blue eyes. *She is so beautiful,* Dillon thought.

Ashley took the oxygen mask off. "You feel better?" She asked.

Dillon shook her head.

"I'm going to see about getting you into a room." she said, walking to the door.

"No! Wait."

Ashley, with her back turned to Dillon, was smiling. She turned around. "Can I get you something?" She walked back to Dillon's bedside.

Dillon tried to take in Ashley's scent, but all she could smell was smoke. She bet she smelled beautiful. The doctor was stunning and her skin was flawless. A true lady, very classy. Dillon thought that the lucky man who was with her didn't know what he had. Dillon always dreamed of Ashley's type. She was the kind fairytales were made of.

"Ah, just, thanks." was all Dillon could get out.

Ashley reached down and gently squeezed Dillon's arm. Both women felt the energy between them. Both got goose bumps.

"Just doing my job." Ashley winked at Dillon. She didn't want to leave the dark haired firefighter. She was so attracted to her. It scared her a little and excited her too. She really wanted to get to know her.

Dillon watched her go, not wanting her to leave. She felt like the good doctor was flirting with her. *"Who are you kidding?"* Dillon told her self *"You know what happens, you fall for them, they dump you. Nope, never again."*

But, through all of Dillon's doubt, she kept feeling that Doctor Ashley Wilkerson was different, very different.

2

Ashley made her way through the cafeteria. She'd always loved food and never gained an ounce. Her Daddy always called her the bottomless pit. She searched around the food picking up two slices of pizza, lasagna, a salad, bread sticks, ice tea, chocolate cake and a carton of milk. She paid for her meal and found Rhonda sitting at their usual table.

"Girl, I swear you could eat any man under the table!"

Ashley smiled proudly.

"I put on six pounds just looking at it." Rhonda shook her head.

Ashley laughed. "Hey, how's Ben doing?"

"Better. ICU says he opened his eyes."

"Wonderful!" Ashley smiled. "What about his mother?

"Not so good. They've called in social services."

"What a shame."

"Yes, it is. By the way, word has it that you've spent quite a bit of time in recovery with a certain firefighter."

"Word travels fast here." Ashley said as she continued to eat.

"Yes, it does girl. So, what's the scoop?" Rhonda looked at Ashley to see if she could tell by the look on her face. Many years in the closet had given Ashley the upper hand of showing no emotions.

"There is no 'scoop'. I'm her doctor, that's all."

Rhonda looked at Ashley.

"What?" Ashley stared back. " I swear Rhonda, don't turn this into something it's not."

Rhonda continued to stare at Ashley. There it was, as plain as day.

"Girl!..........You are falling for Spitfire!"

Ashley shot Rhonda a look. "Will you keep it down." She looked around to make sure no one else had heard Rhonda's outburst.

"You so know I'm right." Rhonda smiled triumphantly.

"Oh, please. I just met her three days ago. Don't go picking out bridesmaid's dresses."

Rhonda started to laugh.

"What?" Ashley asked.

"It's nothing really. I was just trying to imagine you and Spit together. That would be like oil and water!"

"Well, I happen to think she's interesting." Ashley said matter of factly. "I was even thinking of offering her a ride home."

"Well, before you send for the limo missy, let me give you the 411 on Ms. Spitfire McCabe." Rhonda settled in to tell her tale. "She's a loner Ash, keeps to herself. She let's no one past that stone cold heart of hers. Trust me Ashley, find someone else."

"How do you know all this?" Ashley asked.

"Word gets around. You know, firefighters and EMT's talk n' shit."

"So, you're basing your whole opinion of Dillon on a bunch of talk n'...shit?"

Rhonda stood up. "Look, I need a ciggy. You now know what I know. You make your own call, but don't come crying to me when this one turns you off like a floor lamp!"

"Well, thanks Rhonda, I'm glad to know you care this much about who I date."

Rhonda looked at Ashley in the eye. "I do care what happens to you. I don't want to see you hurt again." Rhonda kissed Ashley on the top of her head and walked out.

Hurt again? Ashley thought. *"I'm the world record holder for getting hurt."* Ashley stopped to think. *Since coming out twelve years ago, she had gone through at least five different girlfriends, thinking each new one was 'the one.' Luckily, she had the support of her parents. All her mother wanted was for her to be happy and to give her a grandchild. Ashley tried to explain to mother all that it entailed, but her mother was persistent. She never had the heart to tell her parents about the last year she and her girlfriend Gia tried to reconcile. They decided that a baby would bring them closer. Ashley was artificially inseminated. Gia calmed any doubts that Ashley had by saying that this baby would solve all of their problems. After Gia missed Ashley's first ultrasound, Ashley found out that Gia was sleeping around again. The stress and shock of the whole ordeal sent her to the hospital, where she miscarried.*

The page of Ashley's name over the intercom brought her back from her thoughts. She looked at her watch. Three more hours and she was off. She could hardly wait; she knew she had some unfinished business to take care of.

Ashley quickly made her rounds, saving the firefighter's room for last. She kept asking herself why she was so drawn to her. She couldn't give herself any kind of logical reason. She checked in at the nurse's station and walked over to Dillon's room. She slowly opened the door. Dillon was sound asleep. Ashley sat in the chair and watched, as the firefighter lay peaceful in her bed. She thought she would watch her for a few minutes. It turned into two hours. Ashley couldn't take her eyes off Dillon.

* * *

The California sun was bright. Its rays danced off the stark white walls of Dillon's room. She sleepily took one of her pillows and held it to her face.

"Good afternoon, sunshine."

The familiar voice sent chills through Dillon's body. She took the pillow from her face. There, standing before her, was an angel.

Ashley was smiling. She was in tight blue jeans, which curved at all the right places, a tank top and a denim shirt. Dillon thought she looked perfect.

"Do me a favor?" Dillon pointed to the window at the bright ball beaming into her room. "Turn that off."

Ashley chuckled and walked over to the window and pulled the curtains.

"You gonna lay around here all day?" Ashley teased.

"You gonna let me go home?" Dillon looked hopeful.

"No, not yet, but, you don't have to lie around like 3rd base either. You can get some air you know."

"Well, thank you, warden." Dillon looked smugly at the doctor. "But I'm not walking around this place with my ass hanging out of this thing." Dillon slowly pulled herself up a bit. Her head felt like the end of a fire hose had hit it. Her pain was still evident to Ashley.

"Your head?" She asked.

"I don't know what hurts more." Dillon finally admitted.

"Well, I guess that means no marathons for you." Ashley moved close to Dillon to look into her eyes.

Dillon froze as the doctor gently cupped her chin in her hand. Dillon breathed in, she could now smell Ashley. It was just what the firefighter imagined - clean, and natural.

"Well?" Dillon asked, not wanting the doctor to stop.

"I don't know...."

"What?" Dillon looked concerned

"You're going to live." She reached down and picked up a bag. "Here." Ashley lightly tossed the bag to Dillon.

Dillon opened the bag to find a pair of sweats, some house slippers and a robe. Dillon grinned. She looked up at Ashley. "Thanks, Doc."

"Ben said he would like to meet you. So if you're up to it...."

"Cool."

"He's still a little weary, but he'll be fine. He's out of I.C.U."

"I'm there."

Dillon reached for the blankets and pulled them back. Her lean muscular legs took Ashley's breath away. A devilish grin came to her as she wondered what it would be like to have those legs wrapped around her.

"Ah...?" Dillon nodded at Ashley. She wouldn't get dressed in front of her, doctor or not.

"Sorry." Ashley blushed. "Didn't know if you needed some help." She quickly turned around.

"I think I can manage." Dillon said shyly.

Dillon slowly sat up. She moved one leg at a time until both were dangling over the bed. She scooted to the edge of the bed and stood up.

Ashley could hear her grunting, her determination to help herself.

She was a bit wobbly at first. Dillon tried to reach back to untie the hospital gown but couldn't.

"Damn!" Dillon grabbed her side at the stabbing pain.

Ashley wheeled herself around seeing Dillon wince in pain.

Dillon quickly grabbed Ashley's shoulder for balance.

"Easy." Ashley tried to lower Dillon back on to the bed.

"Just a little wobbly I guess." Dillon tried to put up a front for Ashley. The cold sweat that beaded on her hairline gave her away.

"I think you need a bit more bed rest. No sense in pushing it." Ashley suggested.

"No way. The sooner I'm on my feet, the sooner I get the hell outta here!"

"You need to take it easy, Spit."

Dillon looked at Ashley. She liked the way it sounded when Ashley said Spit. "I can rest at home as well as I can here."

"Maybe, but I don't believe for a second that you would be resting." She looked at Dillon.

Damn! Dillon thought *She called me on that one.* "Look, I'm feeling better now." Dillon tried to hide her pain.

"You are?" Ashley asked.

"Yeah, but could you please untie it?"

Ashley slowly untied Dillon's gown. She wanted so much to stare at the firefighter's firm body, but she behaved. She had seen female bodies before, but Dillon was different. She was drawn to Dillon. So much so, it started to scare her. She wanted to ask Dillon out, but knew that it would end like all the others. It had only been three days, and all she knew was that she wanted Dillon McCabe in her life.

"You know I finished first in med school for this." Ashley said.

Dillon chuckled. "Good to know."

Ashley slowly helped the firefighter off with the gown. Ashley shivered as she saw Dillon's broad shoulders. They were toned with biceps to match. They were perfect.

Dillon tensed up at the silence. Ashley noticed the scar on Dillon's shoulder blade. Unknowingly, she traced the scar with her finger. It startled Dillon.

"Hey!" She yelled as she shrugged Ashley's hand away.

"Oh, I'm sorry." Ashley was embarrassed. "Ah, I'll get a wheelchair and be right back."

Still embarrassed, Ashley left the room without looking at Dillon.

Dillon watched her leave and looked down. The hair was standing up on her arms. "*Why is this happening?*" She thought. There was no way in hell she was falling in love with Ashley. She didn't do that anymore. And there was no way that Ashley would fall for her. She was beautiful, incredibly beautiful. *"She's probably married and has a slew of kids!"* Dillon tired to talk herself out of it. She was letting Ashley get to her. She had to stop.

The pain was excruciating, but Dillon's firefighter instincts told her to keep going. She somehow managed to get dressed. The cold sweat and dizziness overtook her as she sat back on the bed.

Ashley walked in with a wheelchair. "Your limo awaits!" She smiled as she looked up at Dillon.

"I don't feel so hot, Doc." Dillon admitted.

"Come on Spit, you need to lay back down." Ashley moved to her and helped her back into a laying position. "This is ridiculous, you're in no way ready to be up and about."

"I'll be OK." Dillon tried to ease Ashley's worry.

"Look at you! You're as pale as a sheet!" Ashley walked into the bathroom and came back with a cold wet cloth. She laid it across Dillon's forehead.

The coolness felt good to Dillon.

Ashley walked over to Dillon's chart and started writing in it.

"What are you doing?" Dillon asked, as the color started returning to her face.

"I am keeping you here longer. I was thinking about releasing you in a few days, but there is no way now." Ashley was very business like.

"No way?" Dillon was heated. "I told you I was just a little wobbly. I just needed to get my sea legs."

"Spit, you can't even move around on your own. I can't do it, and I won't do it."

"This is crazy." Dillon stared at Ashley "Let me talk to a doctor!" Dillon's anger started to surface.

"I am your doctor."

"No, I want a real doctor!" Dillon blurted out.

Ashley had had it. She could take the wall Dillon had thrown up, but no one ever knocked her as a doctor. She got into Dillon's face, her green eyes on fire.

"Look sweetheart, I am one of the head doctors here. You are darn lucky I came this far with you! If you don't like me, then fine, I'm outta here!" She walked to the door. She stopped and turned around. "I really thought you were special. Silly me." Choking back a mixture of anger and tears, Ashley left.

Dillon was stunned. No one had ever called her special before. Ashley was a tough little cookie. Dillon tried to laugh it off, but the feeling of guilt wouldn't let her.

Dillon McCabe didn't need anyone. She'd been on her own and a lone wolf for some time now. People didn't care about her, with the exception of Jack. Then why did she feel so strange when Ashley walked out the door? Like she had suffered a huge loss.

She looked around for her nurse buzzer and pushed it. Within minutes an older gray-headed nurse came in. "One push is all it takes." she told Dillon sternly as she took the pager away. "What can I get for you?"

Dillon looked at the nurse. They could have at least sent that cute redheaded Amy back in. "I need to speak with my doctor. " Dillon said flatly.

"Sorry, but Dr. Goldstein called in. He's running late. Flat tire." The nurse looked at Dillon.

"Dr. Goldstein?" Dillon looked puzzled. "No, my doctor is Dr. Wilkerson. Ashley Wilkerson."

"Not anymore. Dr. Goldstein is your doctor."

"Wait a sec!" Dillon thought she must have been dreaming. "She was just in here."

"Well, sorry. Can't help you out there. All I know is what they tell me, and after thirty years, I still don't understand half of them." the salty old nurse said. She turned toward the door. "If you need anything else, just ring….once." she said without even looking over her back.

Dillon watched the nurse leave. She sat there stewing. *Fine!* She told herself. *"I don't need to get involved with a hothead like her. I'm just fine alone!"* She folded her arms in protest and gave herself a shot in the ribs. It took her breath away as she tried to slowly move herself back down into bed.

* * *

A week passed and Dillon was recovering nicely. Dr Goldstein thought it best to keep Dillon and let her heal in the hospital. They wanted to keep an eye on her lung. It was fine with Dillon. It would give her a chance to run into Ashley. She spent a lot of time talking and playing with the kids in the pediatric ward. Kids had always loved Dillon. She spent most of her time with Ben, the boy she had saved from the fire. Dillon was sad; Ashley was nowhere to be found. Dillon didn't want to admit it, but she missed her. A lot! But as usual, she held her feelings back and pushed people away. She had put up quite a wall to keep people out. That way, she wouldn't get hurt when they abandoned her.

After five games of chutes and ladders with Ben, he looked up at her.

"Hey Spit?" he asked.

"Yeah buddy?" Dillon started to put the game away.

"Why are you so sad?" He looked into her eyes.

Children could always see into your heart. Ben was no different.

"Well, Ben, I'm kind of getting stir crazy in here. I wanna get back to work."

Ben smiled coyly at her.

"What?" Dillon looked at Ben.

"Why don't you go see Doctor Wilkerson?" Ben chuckled.

Dillon looked at Ben in amazement.

"You know you want too."

"How did you know?" Dillon asked.

"I just do. Besides she was here yesterday asking about you."

"She was?" Dillon perked up.

"Yep."

Dillon had an idea. She got up and patted Ben on the head.

"See you later, Ben. I have to make a phone call."

Dillon walked to the hall and found a phone. She quickly dialed a number. She couldn't believe she was actually doing this, but somehow it just felt right.

* * *

Ashley walked into the nurse's station to start her shift. She had been moping all week since the fight with Dillon. How could she possibly care so much about a stranger she just met a week ago? She kept trying to talk herself out of her feelings. "*You can't reach someone like Dillon McCabe.*" She told herself. She would be better off just walking away. But her heart wouldn't let her. It told her that this was indeed worth holding on to, that fate had brought them together for a reason.

"There you are! I've been looking all over for you." Rhonda's voice brought Ashley back to earth.

"Hey, Rhonda." Ashley tried to smile

"Now if that isn't the saddest face I've seen around here! Girl, what's wrong with you?" Rhonda put her hands on her hips.

"I'm just a little tired." Ashley replied.

"Un huh. Well, if you ask me -"

"Rhonda, please." Ashley cut her friend off.

Amy, the cute redheaded nurse, came walking in carrying a huge bouquet of yellow roses. She set them on the desk.

"Dr. Wilkerson, these just came for you." She handed Ashley the card. "I don't know who he is, but he has my vote!" Amy smiled at Ashley.

Ashley looked at the card.

"Well, aren't you gonna open it?" Amy asked excitedly.

"Ok Miss Busy Body, you need to shoo. Didn't your momma ever tell you it wasn't nice to mess in someone else's business?" Rhonda looked at Amy. "Now you get along missy."

Ashley smiled as Rhonda walked Amy out.

She slowly opened the card. It read: "Doc- I'm an Ass! Always, Spit." Ashley smiled. She replaced the card back into its envelope and stuffed it into her pocket.

Rhonda came back in "Well?" She looked at Ashley.

"Well what?"

"Who are they from?"

"Rhonda you just gave Amy a lecture about getting in other people's business."

"Yes, that's right. But you are not other people. You're family. It's OK to get into other family members' business, so tell me who sent the flowers?"

Ashley looked at Rhonda and smiled. That said it all.

"Oh Lord, they're from Spitfire." Rhonda said.

"Could you please put them in my office, Rhonda? I'll be right back." Ashley grinned.

Rhonda shook her head as she watched Ashley head towards the elevator.

Dillon was flipping through the channels. She hated T.V. Nothing was ever on. She could hardly wait to get out of here. The doctor told her two more days. She was anxious to get on with her life. She did promise Ben that she would visit often; she would miss seeing him on a daily basis. She missed her work too, even though Jack called or came by with daily station updates.

She stopped on a movie. That Whoopi Goldberg was a scream. Dillon loved her work and thought she was one of the most intelligent women in the world today!

There was a soft knock at the door. Dillon muted the sound.

"It's open, come in." Dillon called to the knock.

Ashley walked in smiling. Dillon's heart skipped a beat. *Man, she's beautiful.* Dillon thought.

"What's up, Doc?" Dillon grinned.

"Hey, Spit." Ashley came and sat on the edge of the bed. They stared at each other.

"So, I hear you'll be free in a couple of days." Ashley tried to make conversation, when what she really wanted to do was to curl up in Dillon's strong embrace.

"Yep. Can hardly wait," Dillon smiled.

"Look Spit, I need to apologize to you."

"No, you don't."

"Yes, I do."

"No, you don't."

"Spit, I do! I just let myself get too sensitive. It's just that I worked my tail off to get where I am, and it wasn't easy. It's just when someone pushes my buttons I get....

"Pissed off? It's OK, you can say that." Dillon grinned.

Ashley looked into Dillon's beautiful brown eyes. "I'm sorry."

Dillon snickered. "It's cool, Doc. Don't go losin' any sleep over it."

Ashley laughed. "And thank you for the roses. Yellow are my favorite."

"I'm glad you like them."

"They're beautiful. Just like you."

The rush of red to Dillon's face was in record time! "I need to apologize too. I shouldn't have said those things to you. You're a great doctor!"

Ashley smiled. "Well, at least we got our first fight out of the way."

Both of the women broke out in laughter.

"So, hey, how about lunch tomorrow?" Ashley asked.

Dillon thought long and hard. "Well, now, that all depends." She grinned.

"On?" Ashley played along.

"Where are you taking me?" Dillon asked.

"It's a great French place Le Café..teria."

They laughed.

"Well, I better get back to work." Ashley got up and walked to the door. "I'll see you tomorrow, Spit."

"Have a good one, Doc." Dillon smiled as she watched Ashley leave. For the last week Dillon had dreamed about what it would be like to kiss her lips. Dillon was sure they were soft and sweet. She could easily hold her in her arms all night long and make love to her. But as Dillon thought, she realized that these were fantasies, just tucked away in the corner of her mind, out of harms way, and behind the wall. Dillon turned the sound back up on the TV and drifted off to sleep.

For the next two days that Dillon was in the hospital, she and Ashley spent all of their free time together. They visited with Ben, they talked about their work and their friends. Both women knew that they would always have a friend in one another. Both secretly wanted more, but knew that it wouldn't happen.

* * *

Ashley wheeled a chair in at 10:00 am. She wanted to get to Dillon early. She had promised the firefighter a ride home. She wanted to stop and pick up a few things for her so she could settle in at home and continue to heal. Ashley opened the door to Dillon's room.

"OK, you win. They're kicking you out." She smiled and looked around to find that no one was in the room.

The duty nurse walked in.

"Hello Dr. Wilkerson." The nurse smiled.

"Hi. Hey, do you know what happened to Ms. McCabe?"

"Spit's in pediatrics seeing Ben. She's always up there."

"How's his mother doing?" Ashley asked.

"She's brain dead. They're gonna place Ben in foster care if they can't find any relatives."

Ashley shook her head. "What a shame." She remembered her long talks with Ben; he was a smart kid with a lot of potential.

"Would you like me to page Spit for you, Doctor?" The nurse smiled at Ashley.

"No, don't bother. I'll go up myself. Thanks for your help, Kim."

The pediatric ward was empty except for Ben. He loved all of the attention he got from the staff at Mount West, but it was Spitfire he looked forward to seeing the most every day.

Dillon told him stories about firefighting. She had some of the guys come over from her station to meet Ben. They brought him a huge fire truck that had all the bells and whistles on it. They both loved sports. Dillon found out that Ben was a huge fan of the Dodgers. She promised to take him to a game just as soon as he was better.

Ben was healing fast, but would require a few more skin graphs before he could completely heal.

Ashley stepped off the elevator and looked around. She frowned when she saw the orderly, Dan Jenkins, walking her way. It only took him a second to radar in on Ashley. He was a jerk. All the women hated him. He bothered Ashley, even scared her a little. His slimy advances would make any woman's skin crawl. She was caught alone with him once. He made it very clear what he wanted from Ashley. She wanted to turn him in for harassment, but she knew of a nurse that had tried and her life at the hospital became such hell that she quit and moved out of the state.

"Hey babe, I thought that was you." Dan smiled.

Ashley felt the unpleasant churn start in her stomach.

"What brings you by the BBQ Pit?" Dan chuckled at his own joke.

"You're such a pig." Ashley's voice was loud as she looked at him. She didn't care who could hear.

Dillon did. She was sitting in Ben's room playing fish, when her ears perked up. She thought that she had heard Ashley's voice. She looked at the clock.

"Come on, Ashley." Dan slowly moved closer into her personal space. "We both know you want it." He slowly licked his lips.

"We both know that you're full of it too." Ashley started to get a little scared.

Spit looked up again. That was Ashley. "Hey partner, I'll be right back." Dillon ruffled Ben's hair lightly. She slowly moved up to the doorway and peeked around the corner.

Dillon couldn't believe she was seeing this creep advancing in on Ashley. She quietly came up behind him, so quietly even Ashley didn't know she was there.

Dillon lowered her voice some. "I only hope for your sake that you're getting something out of Dr. Wilkerson's eye."

Dan froze. He felt the firefighter's breath on the back of his head.

Ashley was relieved. She smiled at Dillon, who returned a wink to her. Then she put a finger to her lips.

"We were just confirming a few things." Dan said calmly. He didn't recognize the voice, but he knew that this guy had to be big.

"Well now, lets see here." Dillon placed her large hand on Dan's wimpy shoulder. "It looks like you were trying to get into this lady's pants. Can we confirm this?" Ashley nodded as she tried with all her might not to break out into laughter. Dan was shaking! Beads of sweat covered his hairline.

"No! Hey!" Dan tried to get out of it. "I just asked her if she'd like to go out, that's all."

Dan felt the grip of the firefighter's hand intensify.

"Sounds fair enough." Dillon smiled. "Young lady, would you like to go out with him?"

"No." Ashley looked Dan in his beady eyes.

"Well buddy, I guess that confirms things. I suggest you leave her be and get going."

Dan took off like a shot out of a gun, not even trying to turn around to get a look at Dillon. He kept walking faster with each step. Ashley and Dillon watched until he was out of sight. They both started to laugh.

"My hero." Ashley stood on her tiptoes and planted a kiss on Dillon's now flushed cheek.

"It was nothing." Dillon said, trying to play it down.

"Well, it was to me. That guy always gives me the creeps."

"Are you saying he's done this before?"

"Yeah. He tries to pick up all the women here." Ashley said.

"Doc! You have to turn him in. That freak isn't safe to be around." Dillon looked concerned.

"Spit, we can't turn him in. He's one of the good ol' boys. Kisses up to everyone he can. He had one nurse so freaked out, she turned him in, and then she was harassed by him even more."

"What happened to her?" Dillon questioned.

"She finally quit and moved."

Dillon shook her head. Dan was lucky because she wanted to rip his head off when she saw the way he was coming on to Ashley. He'd better be careful.

* * *

Ashley pulled up to Dillon's home in West Hollywood. The outside was subtle, but nice. The lawn was immaculate and every flower trimmed to perfection. The rose bushes were beautiful as they lined the path up the walk. Their rainbow of deep, rich hues, and big hearty blooms, were the sign of a true green thumb. Ashley was impressed. The firefighter was quite an intriguing woman.

"Spit, your roses are beautiful."

"Thanks." Dillon smiled. "It's a family thing I guess. My mom loved them."

"Well, I'm impressed." Ashley smiled. "I have such a brown thumb, I can kill silk plants."

Dillon laughed.

Ashley loved the way Dillon's eyes would soften every time she laughed.

"Well, thanks for the ride, Doc." Dillon opened the car door.

"Wait." Ashley pleaded. "I.... I.... kind of thought that I could pick up a few things for you at the store. You know, since you're supposed to be relaxing and all."

"Thanks for the offer, but I can manage." Dillon smiled.

Ashley was confused. "*What was that about?*" she thought. "*We had this thing going back and forth at the hospital and now suddenly you want to close the door and bam, it's over? No way, babe!"* Ashley told herself. She was too determined to breakdown that almighty wall of Spitfire's!

"Hey, how about lunch? I'm starving?" Ashley tried.

Dillon shook her head "No, thanks. I'm a little tired. I'm just gonna go on in and rest." Dillon smiled.

Ashley reached into her purse and pulled out her business card. She grabbed a pen and scribbled on the back of it.

"Ok. Here's my cell number, my pager number and my home number."

Dillon took the card and laughed. "Did you forget any?" She winked.

Ashley chuckled. She wanted so badly for Dillon to invite her in. Take her into those big strong arms of hers so she could melt away. She wondered what Dillon would do if she kissed her?

"Doc?" Dillon called her for the third time.

"Huh?" was all that Ashley could say as she came back from her fantasy of Dillon.

"Thanks again." Dillon grinned at Ashley.

"Thank you, Spit, for saving me from Dan. I don't know who I can call for help now that you won't be around." Ashley smiled at Dillon.

Dillon looked into those magical green eyes of hers. She thought about asking Ashley out on a date. The urge was strong from the first day Dillon laid eyes on her. *Hell, who was she kidding? She wanted Ashley to move in and live happily ever after. But she couldn't put herself through the rejection that she knew would be sure to follow if she let Ashley too close.* Then something came out of Dillon's heart, humming through her vocal cords, then out of her lips. "You can't get rid of me that easy."

A slow grin spread across Ashley's face. In an instant a good foot of that wall around Dillon's heart came crashing down.

"I don't intend to." Ashley put her Volvo in gear and rode off with Dillon looking after her.

* * *

Dillon set a goal for herself for next week. She would work hard at getting herself back in shape. She wanted to go back to work and move on with her life. She would exercise to the point of exhaustion, then clean up and head over to see Ben. She carried Ashley's card with her all the time, but she never got the courage to call. She made the excuse that she would only be setting herself up for rejection. What was the point of going back there? Kris pulled one over on her, and she couldn't trust another woman not to do the same. Although she did admit to herself that Ashley felt different, not like any of the girls that Dillon rushed to sleep with after Kris. It just got to the point where Dillon just stopped that part of her life altogether. She hadn't slept with anyone in well over a year. Why should she? It was all meaningless in the end. She'd meet a girl, sleep with her, then right on cue, she would dump Dillon. Ashley's beautiful face filled Dillon's thoughts. She made Dillon laugh and she felt so good to be around. Dillon made a bet with herself that the next time she ran into Ashley, she would suggest a dinner and a movie. Only as friends of course. Dillon would like to see her again. It seemed that every time Dillon went to the hospital Ashley wasn't there. She pulled the card out from her wallet and fingered the raised lettering of Ashley's name. She picked up the phone and started to dial the number. All of the old feelings of doubt and insecurity came flooding back. Dillon slammed the phone down. "*What's the use?*" Dillon asked herself out loud. She talked herself out of it once again. She looked at her watch and grabbed her leather jacket. Ben had his final checkup today and Dillon promised him she';d be there. She jumped on her Triumph, put her helmet on, and headed for the hospital.

* * *

It had been five weeks since the accident and Dillon was feeling top notch. She planned on stopping by the station tomorrow. She missed the guys, just as much as they missed her. She also wanted to ask her Captain when she could start working again.

Dillon parked her bike and took her helmet off. Her hair was always wild and had a mind of its own. She tried to brush it in some sort of hairstyle, but settled for just out of her face! She looked down at her watch as she entered the hospital. She still had time before Ben was expecting her. She went up to the reception desk to sign in.

"Hey, Spit!" The older gentleman behind the desk smiled.

"Hey, Gabe. How are you today?" Dillon returned his smile.

"I'm alive." Gabe retorted. He handed Dillon a visitor's pass.

"Well, that helps the workday go by faster doesn't it?" She chuckled. "Hey, where's the social services office here?"

"Right on the bottom floor, next to E.R."

"Great. Thank you, Gabe. Have a good one."

As Dillon made her way down the elevator, she leaned back and thought. She exited and looked around. Rhonda spotted her.

"Hey there, Spitfire." She walked over and gave Dillon a hug. "How are you feeling?"

"Much better, thanks." Dillon smiled.

"Well, that's great to hear! If you're looking for Dr. Wilkerson, she's not on duty for about another hour."

Dillon looked surprised. Did Rhonda know?

"Actually, I was trying to find the Social Services office."

"Oh." Rhonda looked deflated. "It's just down the hall, third door on your right."

"Thanks." Dillon said coolly. "It was nice to see you again."

"Come on, Chicken!" Dillon yelled at herself *"Tell her the truth! Tell her that you have fallen big time for the good doctor and that you want to be with her. Tell her that you want to hold her in your arms and caress her smooth flawless skin. And how you could never, ever, want to stop making love to Ashley Wilkerson!"* .... Nope not this time. Dillon swept the feeling back in.

"Nice to see you too, Spit." Rhonda smiled back at the tall firefighter. She watched her as she walked down the hall. She shook her head "If these two don't get together soon, they'll spontaneously combust."

"Ms. McCabe? Mr. Harris will see you now." The cute receptionist smiled at Dillon.

"Thanks." Dillon smiled back. That gal is a real flirt! Dillon thought. *She goes to tell Mr. Harris I'm here, then comes out with her blouse unbuttoned by two.* Dillon kept her head buried in the magazine she was reading. She caught the blonde staring at her out of the corner of her eye, licking her lips. She was nothing compared to Ashley. But, according to Dillon, who was? Before she met Ashley, she would have flirted with the blonde, maybe even asked her out. Now she was saving herself for a woman she could never have. That made a lot of sense. A tall, well-built gentleman, of fifty, greeted her. Dillon was surprised. She never expected a social worker to look like that.

"Dante Harris." The man held out his hand to Dillon.

"Dillon McCabe." She took his hand and shook it.

Dante wasn't surprised by the strength in Dillon's handshake.

"Please, come in and have a seat."

Dillon followed Mr. Harris into his office. He shut the door behind her. Dillon took a seat in the soft leather chair across from Mr. Harris' desk.

"So, Ms. McCabe, what can I do for you?"

"Well, it's about Ben. Ben Wright."

"Oh yes." Dante pulled the file off his desk. "The child from the fire." He continued to read the file. "A charming young man." He flipped the page. "Wait, are you Spitfire?"

Dillon chuckled. "Guilty as charged." She smiled.

"Well, I guess you're a hero Ms. McCabe. Or, do I call you Spitfire?"

"Please, Spit is fine." Dillon grinned. "Mr. Harris, what's going to happen to Ben?"

"Well, he'll be here for a while, depending on his mother's outcome. We either have to make an effort to find his next of kin, which we've been doing, so he can be with his family, or we have to put him in foster care, where he'll eventually be put up for adoption. Frankly, Spit, at his age, it's not likely that will happen.

"Do you have any info on the adoption process?" Dillon looked him in the eye.

A smile came over his face. "We sure do. Just ask Tina for the info kit on the way out. So you're thinking about adopting Ben?"

"I sure am." Dillon said proudly.

"Well Spit, I need to be honest with you. You're in for a long battle with this."

"Why is that Mr. Harris? You just said that nobody would want him."

"Please, Spit. There are other factors."

"Such as?" Dillon was growing impatient.

"Such as your job." He looked at Dillon

"I make good money, Mr. Harris. I'm a firefighter."

"Money is only a small piece of the pie. We need to know that the child would be safe. That he would have his parents there for him. And that's another issue." Dante stared at Dillon. She knew what he meant.

"Are you saying I can't adopt Ben because I'm a lesbian?"

"No, Spit, I'm not saying that at all. We have gay couples adopt all of the time. But it's not easy, and frankly, with his mother still alive, the only thing we can do is wait."

The only thing Dillon hated more than that word was doing it. It wasn't what Dillon wanted to hear. But she knew it would be an uphill battle. Why did she let herself get attached?

She stood up. "Where do I enlist for the battle?"

Dante could see Dillon meant business. It was nice to see. "I'll have Tina get you the proper paper work. Fill it out and bring it back here. We'll get the ball rolling."

"Thank you, Mr. Harris." Dillon smiled and held out her hand.

"No, thank you Spit, for opening up your heart." Dante shook her hand.

Is that what she was doing? It felt right. More importantly, it felt good. Maybe things were looking up after all.

3

The bar was crowded, but Dillon didn't mind. It felt good getting her life back. She did miss Ashley. Most of her thoughts were about her. She knew she blew it by not calling her. But if she had, she was sure Ashley would have been like all the rest and turn her down.

Dillon's buddy Jack came walking up with a bottle and a glass.

"One club soda on the rocks." He handed it to Dillon.

Dillon smiled as she took the glass. "Salute, Jack."

They clinked their glasses and took a swig.

Dillon looked around. "Where is everyone?"

"I told them you weren't feeling well. Kind of wanted to hang with you by myself." Jack smiled at his friend.

"Aw man that's sweet!" Dillon hugged Jack gingerly. She was still sore.

"So Spit? Who is she?" Jack looked Dillon in the eye. He never questioned Dillon's sexuality.

"Who's who?" Dillon always knew Jack could read her like a book.

"C'mon man. This is Jack you're talking to."

Dillon looked into Jack's eyes; they were so understanding, so wise. She could tell him anything. Jack's wife Marie was sure lucky to have him. And Dillon was lucky that Marie shared her husband with her. She loved them both dearly.

"That obvious?" Dillon looked up.

"Yeah, Spit, it is." Jack grinned.

"It's the doctor I met at the hospital. I mean I thought she might be interested in me, she gave me her number and all."

"Did you ask her out?"

"No, Jack. She wouldn't want to be with me."

"Spit, you're so full of shit, I may need my hip-waders to continue this conversation!" A serious expression came over his face. "Yes, I said full of shit. You let one woman you slept with destroy your whole life? Hell, it took me three marriages to finally find Marie. You won't melt from one date."

Dillon looked at Jack. Her first thought was to throw up a defense. How dare he say that to her. He had no clue what happened with Kris. Kris was supposed to be the love of her life. Her first and only! She made big time promises to her that night on the dance floor. All she ever told Jack was that she was burned. The problem was that Dillon was pissed that Jack could read her emotions and call her on it.

"And before you throw up that wall that you're so famous for Spit, let me tell you this. You're a good friend to my family, and to me. I've always been there for you, and will continue to be. I want you to find your happiness Dillon, and I have the feeling we both think that is with the same woman."

Dillon's eyes welled up. She didn't want to cry right here in the middle of a damn sports bar! She grabbed Jack and hugged him "Thank you for being you Jack, for being in my life." She whispered in his ear.

Then she saw her. It looked like her. She stayed locked on the figure in the tight blue jeans and navy blue blazer. Could it be?

Ashley plopped down in the chair. "So why are we here?" She asked her friends who sat down next to her.

"We need to find us some men!" Her friend Jody giggled.

Oh great! Ashley thought. *Another Friday night spent dodging the advances of the breeders!* She didn't know why she always let herself get talked into these things. They were old college friends, getting together for their once a month girls night out. Ashley had nothing in common with them anymore. She shook her head. The waiter came over to take their order.

"Welcome beautiful ladies. What can I get for you?" He winked at Ashley.

"We'd like five sex on the beaches, and the combo nacho platter." Rachel smiled at the waiter.

"Excuse me." Ashley smiled. "Could you make mine a club soda with a lime please?" Her friends looked at her.

"I'm on call." Ashley explained.

"For you, doll, anything." The waiter smiled again and left.

"Whoa, Ash, I think he likes you." Susanne smiled.

"You should go for him Ash." Maria chimed in.

"Uh, hello? He's a little young!" Ashley tried to get them to stop. She hated this.

"There's nothing wrong with a young stud in your stable." Cathy laughed.

Ashley looked down at her pager, hoping she would get called in. Then she felt it, a burning throughout her body. The same feeling she felt the first time she saw Dillon. "I'll be right back." Ashley excused herself.

She looked around the bar. For what, she didn't really know, but something inside told her she had to. It was dim and hard to tell who was who. It was all a mesh of alcohol, clinking glasses, loud voices, and bodies coming together. She started to walk back toward the pool tables, ignoring the whistles and the catcalls. She was on a mission.

"Doc?"

The familiar voice was music to Ashley's ears. She turned to see Dillon approach her.

"Doc! Hey, it is you." Dillon unknowingly threw her arms around Ashley.

There in the bar and for an instant, Ashley melted in Dillon's warm embrace. She tried quickly to make an imprint. Her scent, her heartbeat, the feel of her body next to hers.

Dillon broke away first. "So what brings you here? Are you checking up on me?" Dillon grinned.

"Ah well…." Ashley was still in a daze. "I met some college friends here for happy hour."

"Cool. Hey, ya got a minute, Doc? I'd like you to meet someone."

"Sure, Spit." Ashley had a sick feeling come over her. Was this it? Was she going to meet Dillon's girlfriend?

Dillon led her to the bar. "Doc, I'd like you to meet my partner, Jack Thomas. Jack, this is Doc. Oh...um Dr. Ashley Wilkerson"

Ashley stuck out her hand to receive Jack's. "Hi Jack. Nice to meet you." Ashley smiled.

Jack could see why his partner was all caught up in her. She was stunning. "The pleasure is all mine, Dr. Wilkerson." Jack smiled back.

"Please, call me Ashley. Everyone does. Except Spit." She winked at Dillon.

"Can I buy you a drink Ashley?" Jack smiled.

"No, thank you, Jack. I'm on call."

Jack shot Dillon a look as if to say what *in the hell are you waiting for?*

Dillon caught it but she couldn't speak. Ashley was in front of her, and she couldn't do it.

"Well, I guess I should get back. Jack, it was a pleasure meeting you. Dillon, nice

seeing you again. Take care."

"Thanks Doc, you too." Dillon couldn't believe she was letting Ashley walk away. She stared at Ashley as she made her way back to the other side of the bar.

"Man, you're crazy!" Jack turned to Dillon.

"What?" Dillon looked at Jack.

"Shit. Spit are you that blind? She's in love with you!"

"Shut up, Jack!" Dillon started to laugh. "Not possible my friend."

Jack looked into Dillon's eyes. He could see the doubt, and the fear. "Look Dillon, I know how things used to be for you, but she's the real deal! Don't lose her!"

Jack never called her Dillon unless he was serious. *Damn!* Why was she so confused? She wanted Ashley so bad that it hurt. But she was terrified. She looked at Jack. She couldn't move.

"Damn, Dillon! Don't make me kick your ass!"

Jack was getting angry. Dillon took a deep breath. She grabbed her leather jacket and moved toward Ashley's direction. She stopped and turned around. "If you're wrong about this Thomas..." Dillon held up her fist.

"You'll be thanking me tomorrow!" Jack called after her.

Dillon spotted Ashley talking to a waiter. She had just finished and was walking away. Dillon hurried her pace and caught up with her.

"Doc, wait a sec." Dillon grabbed her arm.

Ashley spun around. "Spit? What's wrong?" Ashley looked into her eyes.

"Um............" That queasy sick feeling of doubt came washing over her.

"Yes?" Ashley asked

"Would you...do you.........damn!" Beads of sweat were starting to form on her hairline. *It was now or never,* she told herself. "Could we go somewhere and have some coffee...or talk...or maybe both?" She did it and she was still standing. But just barley. Now she geared up for the big let down. She held her breath.

"I'd love to. Let me get my bag and ditch my friends. I'll meet you out front."

Dillon stared as Ashley went back to her table and made her excuses. Dillon couldn't believe it. Dillon looked around. A few eyewitness accounts would be nice. Dillon looked back at Jack. She gave him the thumbs up and smiled! She was grinning from ear to ear as she headed for the exit.

She waited only a few minutes before Ashley made her way out of the bar.

"I'm all yours." Ashley smiled.

The rush of heat sent color to Dillon's cheeks immediately. "Where would you like to go?" Dillon tired to play down her blushing.

"Well, I'm on call, so someplace not too wild."

"How about my home, my bed, my life?" Dillon thought. "How about the coffee grinder?" Dillon said instead.

"Great!" Ashley said. "You want to drive?"

"Great, I'll get my motorcycle."

"Wait a sec...Lets take my car." Ashley winked at Dillon. "If I get called in, I might look a bit funny with bugs in my teeth."

Both women laughed.

"Shall we?" Dillon asked

"Yes." Ashley smiled, as they walked to the car.

The coffee grinder was empty. Ashley sat at a table while Dillon bought their drinks. Ashley smiled as the tall lean firefighter came walking up holding two cups.

"One tall, decaf, triple chocolate, mocha, frappy, crappy, sissy foo-foo drink, with soy milk."

Ashley laughed. "Very cute. And what did you order?"

"Well Doc, I'm not on call so I went all out and got an earl gray ice tea, my favorite. I'll be up till next Tuesday.

"Livin' on the edge huh?"

Ashley sipped her drink. She looked up at Dillon. She had some whipped cream on her nose.

Dillon chuckled. "You.....got a little..." She reached for Ashley's nose.

"Oh."

Dillon carefully wiped the whipped cream off Ashley's nose. She looked for a napkin, but instead, licked it off her finger.

"Good?" Ashley smiled.

"Very."

"Maybe you should try the whole thing next time."

Dillon stared into Ashley's eyes. "Maybe I will."

Ashley grinned. Dillon shifted her weight.

"So do your folks live nearby?"

Ashley thought about not letting Dillon out of this one, but she did. "Yeah, in the valley. Do you have any other family out here?"

"Nope. Just me. I have some family back in New York, but they can't be close to someone who's, and I quote "Chosen the sinning lifestyle."

"Oh geeze."

"I know. I do however have an awesome cabin up on the Kern River. It was my grandparents."

Dillon stopped for a second and watched Ashley. She was so easy to look at. Pure and graceful. She needed someone to pinch her to make sure that this was real.

"I've been camping up there," Ashley said. "What a small world. Ok, tell me Spit, have you ever had the burritos at that truck stop on Weed Patch Highway?"

"I love those!" Dillon grinned as she rubbed her stomach. "Made myself hungry."

"Not to change the subject, but how are your ribs?" Ashley asked concern.

"Gettin' better everyday."

They sat for hours and talked. After the shop closed, they walked over to an all night cafe so they could talk some more. Dillon couldn't believe how easy she found it to talk to Ashley. She said nothing of Kris, and Ashley told Dillon very little of her past relationships. Especially Giavanna. Then came the sound that neither woman wanted to hear - Ashley's pager went off.

"Excuse me I have to call in." Ashley reached for her cell phone.

"No problem." Dillon smiled. She stood up and went to the dessert counter.

"Two maple oat nut bars please." Dillon couldn't take her eyes off of Ashley. She only hoped that Ashley wouldn't be called away. Jack was right about her. Dillon wanted to ask her out, officially, on a date. But, she knew she couldn't.

"Here you risk your life walking into houses engulfed in flames, surely you would survive asking the good doctor out." She told herself.

Dillon took the bag and put the change in her pocket. She walked back over to Ashley, her face said it all.

"Ya have to go in huh?" Dillon looked disappointed.

"Yes, I do." She stood up and squeezed the firefighter's arm. "I'm so sorry. Please believe me, I would have rather stayed here and talked with you some more."

"Really?" Dillon smiled. "Maybe another time?"

"Yes. Hey! I'm off tomorrow, let me make it up to you" Ashley asked.

"OK!" Dillon smiled.

"Come on, I'll drop you off at your bike." Ashley said.

The ride back to the bar was too fast for both women. There was a confirmation of tomorrow, but that was it for talking. Their arms both touched one another all the way back. Neither woman moved them. Both smiled as they felt the heat radiate in their bodies.

Ashley put her car in park. "Spit, I had a nice time, thank you."

"Yeah, me too." Dillon smiled.

They stared at one another. Ashley leaned in. She wanted to kiss Dillon since the first day she saw her.

Dillon spooked. "Ah, thanks again. I'll see you tomorrow."

Ashley took the hint and let her off the hook. "Six o'clock, your place." Ashley reminded Dillon.

"See you then. Drive safe, Doc "Dillon shut the car door. She froze. She couldn't believe she had just said that. She stood watching as Ashley drove off with a smile on her face. A smile no one could remove.

* * *

Dillon didn't sleep much. She was way too nervous, although, deep in her heart, she felt that Ashley was the one. Her inner demons kept their vigilant reminder of her past, and the failure that this relationship would also have.

Dillon tried hard to push the voices away. The phone rang making her heart jump into her throat. She looked at the clock. 8:30. Was Ashley calling to cancel already? She slowly reached for the phone.

"Yeah?" was all she could say.

"Spit?" The soft warm tones echoed in Dillon's head, forcing a smile, even though she was about to get dumped.

"Hey Doc." Dillon answered tentatively.

"Did I wake you?"

"Nope, just lying here." Dillon held her breath, ready for the big blow off.

'Well, good, I wanted to call -"

"Great, here it comes". Dillon thought.

Dillon was so sure about Ashley calling to cancel, that she didn't hear her ask if she wanted to spend the day together.

"Spit?" Ashley brought Dillon back to reality.

"What? I'm sorry what did you say?"

"I said that it was such a beautiful day today, I was wondering if you wanted to spend it together? But if you're busy?"

"No! I…I...I… mean yes...I.... mean!"

Ashley smiled at the thought of the firefighter blushing on the other end of the phone. "I'll take that as a yes." Ashley chuckled.

"What time?" Dillon smiled.

"See you in an hour!"

Before Dillon could answer, the phone went dead. She smiled. She lay there for a moment listening to her heart race. This lady really had an affect on her. Dillon wanted to scream she was so happy. She just didn't want to jinx it.

Ashley finally hung up the phone. She couldn't believe she was actually going out on a date, let alone being the one who asked. She had grown to like Dillon more each day.

There was a knock on Ashley's bedroom door.

"What?" Ashley asked.

Gia opened the door. She stood in a pair of men's boxers and a tank top. She had been working on her tan and had been working out.

"Hey baby...oh man you're already dressed." She fell onto Ashley's bed.

"What do you want?" Ashley asked coldly.

"Well for starters, you, naked, on top of me." Gia laughed.

"You wish. Look Gia, you need to get your life together, and get on with it. It's time for you to grow up."

Gia got up and walked over to Ashley. She slowly wrapped her arms around Ashley's waist.

"I got it together babe, and I was kind of hopin' that we could make a comeback. Whatta' ya say we start right now?" She pulled herself up close to Ashley. She was swaying back and forth, grinding her hips into Ashley's.

"Baby, where are you?" The faint voice came from the other room.

Ashley pulled Gia's arms away.

"You're sick." Ashley said. She started for the door.

Gia blocked her way. "Come on, Ash, say the word and she's gone."

Ashley pushed her aside. "What word do I say so you'll be gone?" She walked out leaving Gia standing there.

Why did she let this woman get to her? She was like a drug. She knew which buttons to push to play on Ashley's emotions. They hadn't slept together in over a year, although Gia kept trying. Once or twice Ashley did think about it. But that was also the time when Gia showed her true colors.

She remembered bringing Gia home to meet her family. Her parents never liked her, but they kept quiet, for the sake of their daughter's happiness. Gia used to make Ashley feel guilty whenever she wanted to go and see them.

So Ashley quit going. She couldn't believe that she let herself fall for Gia's head games. Her folks were so happy when Ashley told them that they broke up.

The ring on her cell phone brought her back to reality. "Hello?"

"Hi baby girl, this is Daddy," the soft loving voice said on the other end.

"Hi Daddy, how are you?" Ashley asked as she started her car.

"Just fine. How's my girl?"

"Great Daddy. I'm on my way out."

"Oh, working?" he asked

"No." She giggled. "I have a date."

"Really? It's not with Gia I hope?" He sounded concerned.

"Daddy. I told you. It's over between us. This is someone I met at the hospital."

"A Doctor?" The familiar female voice chimed in. "Are you seeing a doctor?"

"Hi Mom. And no, she's not a doctor."

"A nurse then?"

"For goodness sakes Mary, give her a chance to tell us!" Bill said.

Ashley giggled. Her folks were so cute together and still in love! It was nice to see.

"She's a firefighter." Ashley told them.

"Hey, now that's not bad." Bill said.

"When do we get to meet her?" Mary wanted to know.

"Take it easy you two. It's only our second date."

"Well honey, I can tell by the sound of your voice, that she must be someone special." Bill was always so encouraging.

"She is Daddy. Very special."

"Does she have any children?" Mary asked hopefully.

"No, Mom." Ashley rolled her eyes.

"Does she want to have any?"

"Mary, please!" Bill reprimanded her lightly.

"OK, I've got to get going, I'm gonna be late."

"Ok honey, have fun. Give us a ring when you get home."

"Thanks Daddy. I love you."

"Ashley take your mace just in case." Mary said.

"Oh mom. I love you both. Bye."

Ashley shook her head and laughed. She was truly blessed with two wonderful parents.

She came out to them upon her graduation from med school. Her mother went into dramatics about having failed as a parent. She claimed that she would never again be able to face the world. She said that she would have to go away for a while. It took her two weeks to come around. Her father took her into his arms and said he already knew, and that his love for her would not change. Ashley felt a huge release and relief.

Dillon was a wreck. She had already tried on six different shirts and hated every one of them. She had never had trouble throwing on a pair of jeans and a t-shirt. Now she felt like she was trying to dress for a meeting with the royal family. She decided on the black jeans. They were snug and showed off her toned legs and ass. She went with a black tank top and a purple shirt. She stared at herself. *"Ugh!"* she thought. *Look at that hair!* She was blessed or cursed, as Dillon thought, with the McCabe family hair. She ran to the bathroom and raked the brush through it. *Couldn't it just behave for one day?* When she was semi-happy with her hair, she ran to the kitchen.

It was spotless except for today's coffee cup and cereal bowl. But to Dillon, it could never be clean enough. She did a quick wipe down of the sink, then looked around. There. It was perfect for Ashley.

The knock at the door released the butterflies in Dillon's stomach. This was it. Today was either going to be the best day in Dillon's life or the worst.

She stopped to take one more look at herself in the mirror. She took a deep breath.

"*This is it.*" She said to herself as she opened the door.

"Hey." was all that Dillon could say. Ashley, standing there on her doorstep, took her breath away.

"Hi, Spit." Ashley smiled. She too was nervous and the sight of Dillon in her tight jeans excited her. Couldn't she just jump her now, so they could get on with their lives and live happily ever after?

"Ah... sorry. Come in Doc." Dillon felt like a fool staring at Ashley. She hoped she didn't notice.

Ashley giggled and stepped inside. The house was very warm and inviting. Very rustic and outdoors....very Dillon. The river rock fireplace in the living room was beautiful. The whole place gave Ashley a feeling of safety and warmth.

"Spit, your home.............it's wonderful." She turned and looked into the firefighters deep brown eyes. "Very inviting." She smiled.

The doctor always knew the right words to make Dillon blush on cue. Ashley loved it. She thought it was adorable.

"Thanks." Dillon managed to get out.

"Oh Doc if you only knew." Dillon thought. *"This place, my heart, my soul, all of my love, it's yours for the taking. Just say the word."*

"Well, should we get going?" Ashley asked.

"Ah, yeah, sure." Dillon opened the door for Ashley. "What's on our agenda?"

"Hmm. I was thinking maybe Laguna Beach?" Ashley smiled.

"Great! A beautiful day for it."

"Well, if you want, I have two tickets for Pageant of the Masters. I thought we could walk around the Sawdust Festival, and then catch the show. Have you ever been?"

"No, I haven't. I hear it's great though." Dillon grinned.

"Well then, off to Laguna we go." Ashley smiled as Dillon locked up her house.

"You wanna take my bike?"

"You are kidding, right?"

" I have two helmets." Dillon tried to keep a straight face. She could see Ashley horrified at the thought of riding on a motorcycle.

"Funny, Spit! Get in, sit down, buckle up and hang on" Ashley looked dead serious at Dillon.

Both of the women started to laugh. It was the start of a great day in the making.

* * *

The drive to Laguna Beach was inspiring for both Dillon and Ashley. They talked about a lot of things, music, movies, actors, singers. Ashley was pleasantly surprised by what a bookworm Dillon was. Dillon was equally amazed by Ashley's love of the outdoors. Neither was surprised by the lack of information either was willing to give on their past relationships.

Laguna Beach was postcard perfect. The sun was playing hide-and-seek as it dodged in and out of the clouds. It was breezy and cool for August. The town was abuzz with tourists for the annual Festival of Arts, a showcase and sale of Laguna's finest and brightest local artists.

Ashley loved Laguna. It was such a carefree town. She came a few times with Gia. Those were not memorable times for her. They argued over where to eat and what to do. Gia thought the Pageant of the Masters show was a bore. Why would anyone want to look at people replicating paintings and statues? Especially when there was a great gay bar just down from there. She wanted to sit on a bar stool, drink and check out all the local hotties.

Ashley learned her lesson after that weekend. She decided it was useless to do anything cultural with Gia. She would either take Rhonda or go by herself. She never knew what she ever saw in Gia in the first place.

They met at the local gym one Saturday night during a power cycle class. Giavanna Regitti. She was very Italian, with sharp exotic looks. Ashley was attracted to her immediately. Gia wanted her, and wined and dined Ashley until she got her into her bed.

They moved in together after two weeks of dating. Ashley had to admit that sex with Gia was exhilarating. She was creative, that was for sure, but that was all it was. Sex. There was never any emotion, or tenderness. Ashley thought for sure that she could change Gia. She soon found out that leopards don't change their spots.

She knew that Dillon was different. Shy, but with a hint of attitude. So sure of herself and what she wanted. Ashley knew that she wasn't in her league, but her heart told her to try.

"Have you ever been to Laguna?" Ashley asked as they parked the car.

"Yeah, once, a long time ago."

Dillon remembered the last time she was in Laguna. *Hand in hand with Kris. How she fell asleep in Kris' arms, in the hotel. It was also a week before they slept together and Kris pulling the rug out from under Dillon's heart.*

The Sawdust Festival was already crowded. People moved about like slow moving cattle, grazing on everything the local artists had to offer.

Dillon promptly pulled out her wallet.

"No way, Spit! It's my treat." Ashley looked at Dillon.

"Come on, Doc. You drove. It's the least I can do." Dillon raised her eyebrow.

Ashley giggled. "Ok, thank you."

Dillon paid for the tickets as Ashley shook her head. *Wow!* She thought. *Gia would have never offered to pay. She would have just looked around in a daze and waited for Ashley to pull out her money.*

They joined the crowd as they walked from vendor to vendor, admiring their fine works. They came across a jewelry stand. The artist had beautiful gold and silver jewelry.

"Spit, look at that!" Ashley said, pointing to a stunning gold necklace. The pendant was like a pear shaped cage and in its enclosure was a perfect black pearl.

"That's nice, Doc. It looks just like you."

"Care to try it on?" The stocky female artist asked Ashley.

"Oh, no thank you. It is beautiful though."

Dillon looked at Ashley. She couldn't understand why some people drooled

over things but never bought them.

"Excuse me, I need to use the restroom."

"I'll wait for ya here." Dillon smiled.

When she was sure Ashley was out of sight she turned toward the artist. "How fast can you wrap that up?" she motioned to the necklace.

"This will look great on your girlfriend." The artist said as she put it in a little gold box.

Dillon grinned as she paid for it. *Man that sounded good.... my girlfriend... I only wish.*

It was expensive, but well worth it to see it hanging around Ashley's neck. She thanked the artist and slipped the gold box into the inner pocket of her jacket. She went over to the restroom and met Ashley who was just coming out.

"Much better." Ashley smiled, "Are you hungry?"

"Yeah, I could eat." Dillon looked at her watch. It was already noon. The day was flying by and she didn't want it to end.

They walked up Pacific Coast Highway to the Cottage Restaurant. There was a wait, but neither one cared. They were so into each other, that a bomb could go off next to them and neither one would notice.

"So where did you get the nickname Spitfire from? " Ashley finally broke the silence.

"You know the sound water makes as it hits a fire? That sort of spitting sound? My buddy Jack gave it to me. Company 31's Spitfire. Of course it stuck and now everyone calls me that."

"That's cute." Ashley smiled.

"Cute, huh?" Dillon chuckled. "What about you? No nicknames?"

"Nope, not a one." Ashley said

"Oh wait a sec! You answered way too fast Doc. Hmmm, must be an embarrassing childhood nickname." Dillon stared at Ashley. For the first time it was Ashley who was now blushing. "There it is! See! OK, c'mon give it up."

"No, really, it's nothing." Ashley tried to play it down.

"Yeah, sure." Dillon grinned.

"Just you calling me, Doc."

The waiter came and called them to their table.

"Saved by the bell," Ashley laughed as she looked at Dillon.

"It's never over. I have ways of making you talk."

Ashley smiled. She wanted to see every one of them.

They were seated in the back at a nice cozy table for two. Dillon pulled out the chair for Ashley. She smiled as she took her seat.

Dillon took her jacket off and carefully hung it over her chair. She grabbed the menu and looked at it. "Wow it all looks so good," she said.

"It is." Ashley smiled. "I love it here. Big portions."

Dillon laughed.

The waiter came to take their order. Dillon ordered the chicken fried steak and eggs. Ashley went for the chicken chili omelet with tofu cheese.

"Tofu?" Dillon crinkled her nose. "Are you sure you aren't one of those crunchy tree hugger type gals?"

Ashley burst out laughing. "I can assure you that there is nothing crunchy about me! I am one hundred percent smooth."

They spent the next hour and a half laughing, flirting, and joking with each other. Both found out about a mutual love of horses. Dillon told Ashley about her dream to one day own a ranch. Ashley smiled in agreement.

"The picture over your fireplace. Have you been there?" Ashley asked.

"Yes, that was my grandparent's cabin. The one I was telling you about. It's up on the Kern River. Hey! Can you get some time off?"

"I guess so, I do have vacation coming."

"Well, I'm going up there on Thursday and coming back on Monday. Would you like to go?"

"I would love to." Ashley said excitedly.

"Really?" Dillon asked.

"Yes, really. Let me see what I can do."

"Cool." Dillon said as she looked down at her now sweaty palms. "Well, shall we join the masses again?"

"Lead the way."

Dillon quickly grabbed the bill and put the money down.

All Ashley could do was smile. In fact, she was beaming.

Time seemed to fly by as the girls explored Laguna Beach. They went to see the Pageant of the Masters. The sunset and the cool breeze came sweeping through the canyon.

Dillon kept reaching in her jacket to feel the little gold box to make sure it was there. She knew that Ashley had caught her a couple of times, but never asked her.

They made their way into the bowl. Ashley had two great seats right in the middle. Dillon frowned as she slid into the much too tiny seat. She felt sorry for the sardines packed in the cans. But they at least had oil! She put her arm over Ashley's chair to give herself more room.

Ashley smiled and as the house lights dimmed, she slid close to Dillon.

The show was incredible. Dillon had never seen anything like it. The fact that these volunteer performers could freeze and perfectly depict a painting or a sculpture awed her completely.

Dillon stood up and stretched. "Wow! That was awesome Doc."

"I know. It's pretty cool." Ashley smiled. She was pleased that Dillon was at least showing some appreciation for it.

"Thank you so much for taking me." Dillon grinned.

They started to follow the mass of people leaving the venue. Ashley took Dillon's hand as not to get lost. She looked at Dillon for approval. Dillon smiled. They held hands all the way back to the car.

Dillon looked at her watch. It was almost 11:00 o'clock. "You in a hurry to get home?" Dillon asked her.

"Are you kidding? I'm having a great time!"

"You wanna shoot some pool? I know a great place in Long Beach."

"You are so on!" Ashley grinned as she dug her keys out of her pocket. "Be prepared to get your butt whopped." She looked at Dillon.

"Is that so?" Dillon played along.

"Yep." Ashley chuckled.

"Well darlin' you got me shakin' in my boots."

"Really?" Ashley looked at Dillon.

"No. You're toast." Dillon grinned.

Ashley tossed the keys to Dillon, "You drive."

Dillon smiled as she walked to Ashley's side and opened the door for her. She looked at Ashley. There was a look in both women's eyes. It was deep and it meant more than any one word that was said the entire day. Ashley shivered.

Both knew from that moment on, without ever saying a word, that they would never be apart.

* * *

Dillon drove up to Long Beach. It was a nice ride up the coast. She drove to her favorite pool hall and parked the car.

Ashley got out and looked around. The smell of the ocean filled her senses. It was just steps away.

"Hey Spit, would you mind if we skipped the pool?"

"You OK? You wanna go home?" Dillon asked.

"No, not at all. Can we take a walk on the beach?"

Dillon smiled, "of course."

They walked along the beach for a while. They saw the lights from the oil refinery and the Queen Mary. The moon was full, the stars were out, and the night was perfect. Ashley again took Dillon's hand as they walked. They had the beach to themselves.

"It's so nice out here." Ashley remarked. "I could stay out here forever." She stopped and turned to Dillon. "Thanks." She stood on her toes and placed a soft kiss on the firefighter's cheek.

"What was that for?" Dillon asked.

"For such a wonderful time." Ashley smiled.

"Well, it takes two. So, I thank you too."

Ashley moved close to Dillon. She leaned on her hoping the firefighter would take her in her embrace. Dillon happily obliged. Dillon's ribs were still sore. She grunted as Ashley fell into her.

"Oh Spit! I'm sorry, I forgot." Ashley tried to pull away. Dillon held her there.

"It's ok Doc. I'm fine. Just a little tender."

Dillon loved the way the moon lit up Ashley's beautiful face.

"Spit, look." Ashley lit up at the sight. "The ocean, it's glowing."

Dillon turned. "It's the phosphorus."

"That's amazing." Ashley said.

"It's a plankton that blooms in the ocean that causes it to glow." Dillon remembered.

Ashley watched amazed by the ocean glowing in the dark.

Dillon looked around. "C'mon. We can see it better from up there." She pointed to the lifeguard tower. She took her hand and led her to the ladder. Ashley climbed up first. Dillon tried hard not to watch the doctor's fine assets as she climbed the tower. Lucky for her it was dark outside.

Dillon climbed up next. "Now look," Dillon told her and turned her toward the water.

"It looks like lights being turned on from the ocean floor." Ashley said amazed.

Dillon sat against the tower and watched Ashley. She saw her shiver.

"Doc, are you cold?"

"A little," Ashley admitted.

"Come here." Dillon took Ashley's hand and led her down to sit between her legs. She unzipped her bomber jacket. Ashley leaned back slowly, careful not to lean against Dillon's ribs. When she was settled in, Dillon wrapped her arms around Ashley.

"Oh that's nice." Ashley let out a huge sigh. "Spit, look at all the stars."

"This is nothing. Wait till you go up to the cabin. You won't believe it."

Dillon tried to take everything in as she sat there, holding this beautiful woman in her arms. She wanted to remember this night, the sights, the smells, the laughter. She had to keep this memory because she knew that in the morning she would wake up and it would have all been a dream.

* * *

Dillon pulled up to her house at 3:00 am. She was tired and sore. She was running on pure adrenaline. Ashley had fallen asleep on the ride home. Dillon looked at her as she soundly slept in the seat next to her. She unbuckled Ashley's belt and got out of the car to open the passenger side. She knelt next to her.

"Doc." She whispered, not wanting to startle Ashley. "Doc, we're home."

Ashley sluggishly opened her eyes. She looked at the firefighter and smiled.

"Home already?" She asked, trying to wake herself up. She looked at her watch. "Wow, I'd better get going."

"No, it's too late. Why don't you just stay here?" She wasn't about to let Ashley drive home now.

"Are you sure?" Ashley smiled.

"Positive." Dillon stood and held her hand out for Ashley. Ashley grabbed her things and took Dillon's hand. They walked to the front door as Dillon fumbled for her keys.

"Thanks for driving back." Ashley smiled.

"No problem." Dillon said as she put the key in the lock.

"Guess I got a little too relaxed out on the beach."

Dillon opened the door for Ashley. "With all that snoring going on, I thought you were bored with me."

"Oh no, Spit, I snored?" Ashley looked horrified.

Dillon chuckled. "It's ok, you were tired."

"I am so embarrassed." Ashley looked at Dillon. "Trust me , it wasn't the company."

Dillon led Ashley into the dark house, through the hall and stopped at her bedroom door.

"Oh shit!" Was all that came from Dillon's mouth.

"What's wrong?" Ashley asked.

Dillon remembered that in her quest to find the perfect outfit this morning, her room was now littered with clothes.

"Look Doc, I need to tell you something."

Ashley looked at Dillon. What was she going to say? *She had a girlfriend sleeping in there?* She thought. "What?" Ashley swallowed hard.

"I.... I had a little clothing dilemma this morning, my rooms kind of-"

Ashley burst out laughing. "Are you serious?" She chuckled.

The familiar flush came to the firefighter's cheeks.

"Tell you what" Ashley let her off the hook. "Point me to the guest bathroom."

Dillon pointed down the hall.

Ashley looked at Dillon. "Ya know, you're awfully cute when you blush." She giggled and walked down the hall.

Dillon shook her head and opened her bedroom door. She moved as fast as she could, grabbing her clothes and throwing them into the closet. *"Why Me?"* She thought. *"Why can't anything go smooth?"*

She went to her armoire and pulled out a clean pair of flannel pants and a sweatshirt. She knew these would swim on Ashley's small petite frame, but it was the only thing she had.

"Can I come in now?" Ashley asked just outside the door.

"All clear."

Ashley stepped into the room. It was warm and cozy, like the other parts of Dillon's home. No one would ever think that a place so rustic could be smack dab in the middle of L.A.

"This is nice." Ashley commented. "I love your sleigh bed."

"Thanks, my Grandpa and I carved it for a birthday gift for my Grandma. I brought it back down from the cabin when…" She stopped herself. She pushed the memory away. "A few years back." She looked at Ashley. "Here ya go. They're kind of big." She handed Ashley the clothes. "Oh and...." She ran into the bathroom and brought back a new toothbrush for Ashley. "Toothpaste is on the counter."

"Thanks, Spit."

"You just make yourself at home and settle in. Sleep well."

Ashley was a bit disappointed. *After all, she was standing in the woman's bedroom. She wasn't going to try anything? Not even a kiss? Maybe I'm not her type?* Ashley thought.

"Can I get you anything else? Dillon asked.

"No this is great. Thanks."

"Thank you again. I had a wonderful time."

"Me too Spit, thanks." Ashley walked over to Dillon.

Dillon's mind was racing. *Should I kiss her? Should I just thank her again and shake her hand? Maybe she just wants me to leave her alone.* The doubt came knocking at Dillon's inner door. She chose the latter. "Well, good night, Doc," she said as she closed the door behind her.

Ashley sighed and started to undress.

Just outside the bedroom door, Dillon stood silently, listening to Ashley's movements. She looked down, watching, until she saw the sliver of light from underneath the door go black. She reached inside her jacket pocket and pulled out the small gold box. She opened it and fingered the necklace she had bought for Ashley. Maybe some day she's get the chance to give it to her. She closed the box and returned it to the safety of her jacket pocket. She kissed her finger and gently touched the bedroom door. "Sleep with the Angels," she whispered and walked away.

4

Dillon woke up fast. She was sore and stiff. She spent the night on the couch, mostly waiting for sleep to find her. It did in spurts. She thought maybe Ashley would come to her senses and leave in the middle of the night.

She rubbed the sleep from her eyes and tried to move her neck around. She really overdid it yesterday and she was sure feeling it this morning. She didn't care. She had the most amazing day of her life yesterday with Ashley. She would cherish it always. She pulled her jacket off the end of the couch. She felt inside her jacket pocket for the box. *"Yep, it was there. This wasn't a dream after all,"* she told herself. The smell of frying bacon and fresh brewed coffee filled her senses. She got up holding her side and slowly walked into the kitchen. She smiled at the site before her. Ashley was leaning against the sink reading the paper. She was wearing Dillon's sweatshirt and nothing else. Dillon felt the heat rush through her. Only this time it wasn't to her face. She got a queasy feeling deep inside. Was she finally falling in love again? That thought scared Dillon.

"Morning." Dillon smiled rubbing her side.

"Good afternoon, sleepy head." Ashley giggled.

"What?" Dillon looked up at the clock "12:30! Oh man, I'm sorry."

"It's fine Spit, I've only been up a bit myself."

"Did you sleep OK?" Dillon yawned.

"Like a log!" Ashley smiled and grabbed a piece of bacon. She walked over to Dillon. "Hungry?" She asked, teasingly. She held the piece of bacon to Dillon's lips. They locked in a stare. Dillon slowly opened her mouth and tenderly bit into the bacon. Ashley popped the rest of it into her mouth.

"Pretty good huh?" She turned back to the stove. "I had a great time yesterday."

"Me too. It was a blast." Dillon smiled.

"So what are your plans today?"

"Um, well I thought I'd shower, then go see Ben."

Ashley turned toward Dillon. "Spit, I was wondering, if you don't have any plans tonight, would you like to have dinner?"

"No, Doc, I don't." Dillon said.

"What?" Ashley looked at Dillon.

"No, I mean I don't have any plans.... Yes, I would like that very much. Where would you like to go?"

"I was thinking I could cook."

"You cook more than just bacon?" Dillon grinned.

Both women laughed. Ashley's pager screeched from the other room.

"Yes I do Spit, and not just in the kitchen."

She ran to the other room to retrieve her pager, leaving Dillon speechless.

Dillon was scared. She was falling hard for Ashley and she knew it. She had to push her feelings aside. This would only lead to heartbreak for her.

Ashley came back dressed in her clothes from last night.

"I'm sorry, I have to go in." Ashley was upset.

"I understand."

"Are we still on for tonight?" Ashley looked hopeful.

"Sure. What time?'

"About seven?"

"I'll be there."

"Great."

Dillon walked Ashley to the door and opened it for her.

"Sorry about breakfast." Ashley offered.

"Not a problem." Dillon smiled.

"How about a rain check?" Ashley winked.

Dillon blushed.

Ashley reached for Dillon and kissed her on the cheek.

"See you later." She turned and left.

Dillon watched from the doorway as Ashley jumped into her car and drove off.

"Shit!" Dillon yelled. "You forgot to get her address!" She slammed the door. Well she could have her paged at the hospital when she went to see Ben.

Ashley hung up her phone. She turned her radio up. After surfing the channels, she put her CD on. Melissa Etheridge's "Kiss Me" came on. Ashley turned it up and sang along. She knew her heart was falling in love with Dillon. She wanted to tell her how she felt, but wasn't sure how the firefighter would take it. She didn't want to seem pushy, especially if Dillon only wanted to be just friends. But if she waited around to see if Dillon would make a move, they would both be too old to act on it!

Ashley clouded over as she thought about last night, sitting in Dillon's strong embrace up on the lifeguard tower. Surely Dillon felt something too, and as she got into Dillon's bed last night, she could have sworn Dillon was standing outside of the door waiting for her to fall asleep.

Ashley pulled into the doctor's parking lot. She thought about tonight. She would just play it cool.

"Oh crap!' Ashley said out loud. She grabbed her cell phone and dialed her house. She got the answering machine. "Gia this is Ashley, I'm having company over for dinner tonight and you need to get lost. Thanks."

* * *

Dillon walked into her bedroom. Ashley had made the bed and had the clothes she borrowed folded neatly on the corner of the dresser. Dillon picked up the sweatshirt and held it to her face. She took a deep breath and smiled. It still smelled like Ashley. She would never get tired of that smell. She walked to her closet and opened it. All of the clothes she had piled up when Ashley came over were now neatly hung in place. Dillon spotted a note. She read it. "I always clean up my messes and I'm house broken too." Dillon laughed out loud. She loved Ashley's sense of humor. The phone rang.

"McCabe." She said in her usual firefighter way.

"Ms. McCabe, this is Dante Harris."

"Oh hey, Mr. Harris what's up?"

"I'm sorry to bother you, but I wondered if you might be able to come down?"

"Is it about Ben?'

"Yes. Can I expect you'll be here then?"

"On my way, Mr. Harris." Dillon hung up the phone.

She grabbed her things and headed for the shower.

Dillon pulled her bike into the visitor's space. She removed her helmet and tried to make some semblance of her hair before she went in. She walked in through the hospital hoping to possibly catch a glimpse of a certain adorable doctor. As she walked through, she was greeted by a couple of cute nurses. At one time Dillon would have stopped to flirt with them, but since Ashley came into her life just a short time ago, no one else now existed. She stopped and reached into her pocket, the gold box was still in its hiding place. Dillon only hoped that she would have the nerve to give it to Ashley.

She walked into the social services offices. Dante Harris was waiting for her. He moved to greet her.

"Ms. McCabe, thank you for coming in on such short notice."

"No problem." Dillon looked at Dante.

"Please have a seat."

"Just cut to the chase, Mr. Harris."

"I know your interest in Ben and your intentions. I thought you should hear this from me."

"What?" Dillon's heart sank.

"We found Ben's Aunt and Uncle. We put the info out to the media and they contacted us yesterday. Yes, Ms. McCabe we had them checked out. We have to."

"Oh." Was all that Dillon could say.

"Ms. McCabe, I don't want you to think for a second that we were not thinking of considering you. It's just that we have to follow policy and do everything in our power to find next of kin."

"No..... I understand." Dillon smiled, trying to hide her feelings.

"Ben's Aunt and Uncle are upstairs with him now. They asked if you would be so kind as to go up there and meet them."

"Sure." Dillon forced a smile.

"I know it's hard when you become attached."

Those words rang in Dillon's head. It was the same words that Kris told her the day she moved out. "Yeah, well, thanks Mr. Harris." She swallowed hard, trying to keep her emotions in check. She shook hands with Mr. Harris.

"I only wish that there were more like you who cared."

Dillon smiled and nodded.

She closed the door and turned right into Rhonda.

"Sorry." Dillon grabbed Rhonda so she wouldn't fall over.

"Hey, Spitfire." She smiled. "How are you?"

"Fine, thanks. Have you seen Doc?....tor Wilkerson?"

Rhonda leaned in. "Just between you and me Spit, I know you two went out. You can call her Doc."

The flush came straight to Dillon's face.

Rhonda smiled. "Yep, Ashley was right. You are cute when you blush."

Rhonda chuckled as Dillon changed two shades.

"If you see her, can you please tell her I'm upstairs with Ben? They found his Aunt and Uncle."

"Oh Spit, I'm sorry, honey."

"It's OK. I mean, he should be with his family." Dillon looked at Rhonda.

"I'll be sure to give her the message."

"Thanks."

Dillon turned and walked toward the elevators.

* * *

Dillon made her way to Ben's room. She made a promise to herself: no tears. She kept telling herself that this was for the best. Ben needed to be with his family! Family was everything.

She knocked on the door and peeked inside. A man and woman were sitting on chairs next to Ben's bed. They looked like an Aunt and Uncle should. Warm and caring. Ben was in bed laughing and to her surprise Ashley was sitting with him.

"Spit! You came!"

Ben's delight in seeing her pulled at the firefighter's heartstrings.

"Hey, buddy, how are ya?" Dillon smiled at Ashley "Hi Doc."

"Spit, this is Ben's Aunt and Uncle, Lee and Henry Lake." Ashley looked at Dillon.

"Hi. It's a pleasure." Dillon shook their hands.

Lee stood up and hugged Dillon. "Thank you so much for saving Ben's life."

"I was just doing my job ma'am." Dillon tried to stay focused. She was thrilled to see Ashley here. She wanted to thank her for her support.

"I'm sorry for your loss." Dillon found herself saying.

"Thank you." Henry said. "It took us awhile to find out about this. We only saw it on the news a few days ago."

Dillon looked at the man. She wasn't satisfied with that answer. It had been over a month and now they are now just finding out about it?

"Ah, sir, may I speak with you outside?"

"Of course." Henry stood.

"Excuse us a moment." Dillon smiled at Ashley.

"Spit, when you come back I got a card trick to show you."

"Cool Ben. I'll be right back."

They walked into the lounge and shut the door.

"What can I do for you?" Henry looked at Dillon.

"Well for starters Mr. Lake, how come it took you so long to find out about this? It happened five weeks ago. Didn't you know where Ben was?"

"My sister was not a smart woman Miss...."

"McCabe." Dillon said flatly.

"Ms. McCabe. My sister was the type who would con you out of every last cent you had, then take off. We would go years without hearing from her. My family is large and we have all tried to help her. Especially when we found out about Ben. She was heavily into drugs, and didn't know who his father was."

Dillon cringed and shook her head. She hated the drug part!

"Ms. McCabe, I promise you that Ben will have a good life. He has many cousins he hasn't even met yet. He's a bright boy, who deserves a future."

Dillon didn't know what to say. Yes, Ben did deserve a future, and she knew it had to be with his family. She grabbed a napkin and a pen. She scribbled something on it.

"Mr. Lake, if there is anything I can ever do for Ben or your family, please call me." She handed him the napkin.

He smiled. He could see the feeling that Dillon had for the boy. He too wrote something down on a napkin and handed it to Dillon.

"You're welcome in our home anytime. Please feel free to visit Ben.."

Dillon looked at the address and phone number. She folded it and put it in her pocket.

"I want to thank you for caring so much about Ben. Mr. Harris told us that you were looking to adopt him."

"Yeah, but Ben should be with family. It's important."

"You'll always be family to us Ms. McCabe."

"Thank you, sir."

Dillon was taken aback by Mr. Lake hugging her. Her heart felt at ease. She felt good about things now.

As they walked back into Ben's room, Dillon was thrilled to see that Ashley was still there.

"Spit, Doctor Wilkerson and I are playing fish."

"Watch out Ben, she cheats."

They all laughed.

"Well, this cheater needs to get back to work." Ashley stood up. "It was so nice to meet you Mr. and Mrs. Lake." She shook their hands. "Ms. McCabe, may I speak with you outside?"

Ashley sounded so official; Dillon tried hard not to laugh.

"Of course, Dr. Wilkerson."

They excused themselves and walked out.

"What's up Doc?" Dillon smiled.

Ashley pulled out her prescription pad and tore the sheet off. She handed it to Dillon.

"Are you gonna medicate me?"

Ashley laughed. "Maybe on the next date. It's my address. For tonight. Oh, and about the weekend….." Ashley looked at her

"Oh. OK." Dillon looked disappointed.

"No, I can go." Ashley grinned.

"Really?" Dillon beamed.

"So I'll see you tonight?" Ashley asked.

"Yep, I'm looking forward to it."

Ashley smiled. "Me too. I'll see you later."

Dillon watched until Ashley was out of sight. She smiled at the thought of their weekend at the cabin. She chuckled to herself and then walked back into Ben's room.

* * *

Dillon pulled up to the address Ashley had given her.

It was a nice little West L.A. complex. She took her helmet off, and, as always, tried to make her hair look passable. She opened her saddlebag and pulled out the bottle of wine she had purchased on the way over. Not being much of a wine drinker, Dillon had no clue which wine went with what. She left it up to the cute sales clerk with the fake boobs. She provided more than just wine tips. She flirted with Dillon, and wouldn't let her go until she took her phone number, which Dillon promptly disposed of when she was out of view.

"Just my luck!" Dillon thought. *"When I was in my wild dating years, I had no one. Now that I've found Ms. Right, the women throw themselves at me!"*

Dillon found Apt 4C. She took a deep breath, and knocked on the door.

She grew anxious as she heard the footsteps approach the door. The door opened. Dillon was surprised to see Gia. *Wow* she thought. *What a beauty.*

"Ah…. Is Doc around?"

"Who?"

Dillon stepped back and looked at the number on the door. It was 4C. "Ah, Dr. Ashley Wilkerson?"

"Oh yeah. Come on in." Gia said flatly. "Hey babe your friend Saliva is here!" she yelled to Ashley.

"Dang it, Gia!" Ashley came from the kitchen ready to lay into Gia. She saw Dillon and stopped. She looked beautiful. She smiled. "Hello, Spit." She walked to Dillon and hugged her hard.

Gia just watched, then cleared her throat.

Dillon didn't want to leave the embrace, but she stepped back.

"I see you met Gia." Ashley shot her a look. "Who was just leaving!"

"No, it's cool" Gia smiled. "I have time."

Dillon started to feel sick to her stomach. *Was Ashley using her to get back at Gia?* She wanted out!

"Hey, if this is a bad time?" Dillon looked at Ashley.

"No, it's fine. Please, have a seat. Gia is leaving." She looked at Gia.

Gia knew that Ashley was getting upset. She smiled. "Well hey, it was nice to meet you Saliva."

She stuck out her hand. Dillon shook it reluctantly.

"I'll be home in a bit doll." She winked at Ashley. "Call me if you need me."

She took her leather jacket and left.

"I'm sorry." Ashley said. "She was supposed to be gone an hour ago."

"It's OK Doc." Dillon said, though it wasn't. She remembered the bottle of wine she had in her hand. "Oh, I brought some wine. I hope it's ok?" She handed it to Ashley.

"Hmmm 1983, a very good year!" She smiled. "It's perfect. I hope you like pasta?"

"It's my favorite." Dillon smiled.

"Then take off your jacket and stay awhile."

Dillon smiled as she slid out of her leather jacket. She was wearing a tight black muscle shirt.

Her toned, tanned biceps were on display. Ashley noticed at once.

"Dinner is just about ready Spit." Ashley said all flustered.

"Can I help you with anything?" Dillon asked.

"Sure, you can open the wine." Ashley smiled. "Follow me."

"You got it." Dillon grinned as she followed Ashley into the kitchen.

She could tell that the kitchen was Ashley's domain, everything in its place. It was very white and very sterile. You could tell a doctor lived there. She watched as Ashley pulled the bottle opener from a perfectly straightened drawer.

"Smells wonderful, Doc." Dillon grinned as she took the opener from Ashley.

"Thanks," she smiled back.

They locked into a stare for what seemed like forever. Then Ashley broke it off.

"I can't wait until Thursday! It's all I've been thinking about!

"Yeah, it should be fun." Dillon agreed.

"Do we have to wait until Thursday? I mean, can we leave after work tomorrow?"

"I guess so. It's a long drive, you sure you won't be too tired?"

"No. I'm way too excited! I'll be fine." Ashley grinned

"OK, but we need to go to the store and pick up some food, and you need to pack."

"I'm already packed." Ashley announced proudly.

"Wow, you are a fast one." Dillon chuckled.

"I just want to get out of here so bad."

"I know the feeling." Dillon smiled. "Hey maybe we could do some grocery shopping after dinner."

"Great!" Ashley smiled.

She had thought of nothing but Dillon and their day in Laguna. She had fallen hook, line and sinker for the tall firefighter. She had decided to let her know of her feelings once they got to the cabin. She planned to spend the weekend in the arms of Dillon McCabe.

The pop of the wine cork brought Ashley out of the clouds. She grabbed two wine glasses and handed them to Dillon.

"Let's eat!" Ashley smiled.

Dillon followed Ashley into a dining area. It was a bit small, but Ashley really knew how to make it cozy. The table was set in a white tablecloth with blue place mats, and matching napkin rings. The yellow roses that Dillon gave her were at the center of the table. They were now wilting but still there. Dillon smiled.

"This is a nice place you got here." Dillon said.

"Well thanks. It's OK I guess. Gia makes it less attractive everyday."

Ashley walked back into the kitchen.

Dillon thought about possibly giving Ashley the necklace. She hesitated. *"Why give her something if you're being used?"* she told herself. She grabbed the glasses and started to put some wine in each.

Ashley came back with two plates filled with pasta, grilled chicken, sun dried tomatoes and artichoke hearts.

"Oh, Doc this looks great!" Dillon smiled. This sure beat the frozen food dinners she was used to having. Ashley made one more trip to the kitchen and came back with a salad and garlic toast.

Dillon handed her a glass of wine. "What should we drink to?" she said, leaving the question opened-ended.

"Ah, how about to us and our new friendship?" Ashley wanted to shoot herself! *What a moron!* she thought.

Dillon clinked her glass and sipped her wine. She looked at everything and started with the main course. *Well, now you know where you stand!* Dillon's little doubting voice told her.

Dillon knew what she had to do. Gather up all of her feelings for Ashley and sweep them under the rug! There was no reason to pretend anymore.

* * *

After dinner Ashley gave Dillon a tour of the rest of the place. Dillon rolled her eyes as she passed *The Love Goddess Lives Here* sign on Gia's door. *Some Goddess you are! You don't even know how to treat a woman.* Dillon thought.

"And this is my room." Ashley opened the door.

Dillon was surprised. It didn't seem like Ashley at all. It was very white, and very plain. Not many things around, just a TV, DVD player, a stereo, and her dresser. It almost looked like Ashley was moving out.

"It's nice..........very..........."

"Bland?" Ashley offered.

Both women began to laugh. They looked into each other's eyes. Ashley wanted so much to kiss Dillon.

Dillon wanted her too.

Neither acted on their impulse.

"Maybe we should get to the store." Dillon said.

"I'll get my bag." Ashley looked deflated.

Dillon met her at the door. She put her jacket on and felt the little gold box in her pocket.

They stepped out onto the porch as Dillon watched Ashley lock the door.

Ashley turned to see Gia walking up. She grabbed Dillon and brought her close. Before Dillon knew what happened, she and Ashley were engaged in a kiss. Ashley's soft lips were expertly moving over Dillon's. Her knee's weakened at the doctor's touch. She wasn't about to stop, even if she passed out right there!

"Well, this is quite the sight."

Gia's voice pierced through Dillon. She broke off the kiss.

Dillon was flushed. She had a tidal wave of emotions crashing through every inch of her.

Gia slapped her on the back. "Seems like dessert is being served out on the porch."

Ashley scowled at Gia. "You're home early."

"Yeah and it looks like I was just in time too." Gia smiled and walked up to Ashley and softly touched her cheek. She winked at Dillon and went inside.

"I think I should go." Dillon said. She started to walk away.

"Spit, wait!" Ashley pleaded.

"Thanks for dinner, Doc." Dillon tried to smile, her heart broken.

Ashley could see the hurt in her eyes "Please, Spit, wait a sec!"

Dillon stopped. She kept her back to Ashley so she wouldn't see the tears welling up in her eyes.

"It's ok." Dillon tried to play it down.

"No, it's not, Gia is a..."

"A bitch?"

"Yes."

"Maybe so, but it's plain to see that she still has feelings for you." Dillon's stomach was churning. She wanted to run, but her legs were frozen.

"I don't care about her feelings." Ashley felt her own tears reaching the surface. "I care about yours."

Dillon wanted to turn around and take Ashley in her arms. But she couldn't.

"Please say something." Ashley begged.

"What do you want me to say? I don't want to get in between you two."

"You're not Spit."

"Look, I need to go." Dillon just wanted to hop on her bike and ride.

"You don't have to, you know." Ashley's voice cracked holding back the tears.

Dillon turned to her. "Yeah, I do." She tried to smile. She slowly reached out and wiped a tear from Ashley's cheek.

Ashley searched Dillon's eyes for anything; they were cold and dull. She never wanted to hurt her.

"It'll be OK." Ashley offered.

"Will it?" Dillon looked Ashley in the eye.

"I promise you. It will."

Dillon leaned and kissed Ashley on the forehead. "I want to believe you, Doc." She looked into Ashley's eyes. "I'll see you tomorrow." She turned and walked away.

Ashley watched as she got on her bike and left. Relief came to her. She had another chance with Dillon. This time she wouldn't blow it. Gia had to go!

She marched back into the apartment, only to find Gia sitting on the couch in boxer's and a tank, eating pasta and sipping wine.

"I gotta give credit to Saliva. She has pretty good taste in wine."

"Gia, you need to move out!"

"Honey, come on now." Gia shook her head.

"That's it! Just stop it, Gia! I've put up with enough of you. I want you out!"

"Hey Ash, baby, just chill." Gia tired to calm her down.

"Don't tell me what to do!" Ashley felt the heat rise in her face. "I am not about to let you screw this up for me!"

"What? Her?" Gia laughed. "Now I know you can do better. Course when you've had the best..........." She winked and sipped her wine.

"Please, Gia, give the world a break!" Ashley barked "You could take lessons from her!"

Gia set her food down and walked over to Ashley. "I thought we were gonna get back together. Remember we talked about it?" She tried to put her arms around Ashley.

Ashley pushed them away. "You are kidding?" she said.

"No, baby, I'm serious." Gia looked at her.

"Why should we? So I can sit around and watch you sleep with the remainder of L.A.'s lesbian community? No Gia, it's over. I want you out of my house!"

"Correction. Our house." Gia smiled. "My name is on the lease too."

Ashley hated when Gia was right. "Fine! I'll move!" Ashley went into her room and slammed the door.

Gia smiled and went back to her dinner.

* * *

Dillon turned the light off and slipped into bed. Although it wasn't a pleasant end to their evening, Dillon was still lost in Ashley's kiss. Her lips were incredible, so warm and soft. She hated what went on there tonight. Ashley's stupid ex almost ruined it for them. Dillon wanted her out of the picture, and now! She didn't like Ashley in the house with her alone. Gia couldn't be trusted. She stopped to wonder about what happened after their kiss. Had Ashley only kissed her because Gia was coming up the walk? *"Oh great!"* Dillon thought, *"Now you're a toy in some jealousy game. Why were you so stupid to let your heart get attached?"* She looked at the clock on the DVD player. It was 12:30am. She wondered what Ashley was doing? Wondered if the kiss they shared meant the same to her. Dillon had to find a way to tell Ashley how she felt.

A noise caught Dillon's attention. She sat up and looked around. She quickly walked into the hall and listened. There it was again. She moved to the entry hall, in front of the door. She watched as the knob slowly started to turn. Dillon slowly unlocked it, then opened the door. She flipped the porch light on.

There stood Dillon's future. She was in jeans and a sweatshirt, suitcases on either side of her. Dillon thought it was the most beautiful sight she had ever seen.

"Doc? What the hell?"

"You scared me." Ashley grabbed her chest.

They stood looking at each other.

"What are you doing here?"

"I needed to talk to you."

Dillon took Ashley's hand and brought her into her embrace. Ashley fell willingly into it. She sighed.

"Are you ok?" Dillon stroked her hair softly.

"I am now." She held tighter. "I wasn't sure you would ever talk to me again after what happened."

Dillon chuckled, "I don't blame you."

"You should. I should have told you what to expect." Ashley said, still holding tightly onto Dillon.

"Why didn't you?"

"Would you still have come?"

Dillon squeezed Ashley tighter. She wanted to tell her exactly how she felt, but the words wouldn't come out. "Come on. It's late and you need to sleep."

Dillon grabbed Ashley's bags, shut the lights off and locked the door. She took Ashley's hand and led her to the bedroom.

"Sweet dreams, Doc." She smiled as she walked to the door.

"Spit?" Ashley asked.

"Yes?"

"You can stay you know. If you want to?" Ashley looked at Dillon.

Dillon wanted to very much. She wanted to take Ashley in her arms and make love to her all night. But she was frozen. The inner demons left by Kris were running rampant through her. She replayed that scene with Kris in her mind a thousand times.

Dillon softly touched Ashley's cheek. It was soft and beautiful. She delicately kissed Ashley on the head. "Sweet dreams Doc." Dillon smiled and closed the door behind her.

Ashley tossed and turned. She wanted to tell Dillon how much she loved her. She needed to be close to her. She slowly opened the bedroom door and walked to the living room. Dillon was on the couch sleeping. "Spit?" Ashley whispered. There was no answer from the firefighter. "I guess you're asleep. I just wanted to tell you… geeze listen to me, blubbering like a stupid schoolgirl with a crush. But this isn't a crush… Dillon, I'm falling in love with you." She waited to see if there was any sign from the couch. "Well, good night." Ashley said, as she walked back into the bedroom.

Dillon lay there quietly waiting until she heard the bedroom door close. She rolled over. She heard every word Ashley had said. She closed her eyes. She tried to sleep but there were too many things rushing through her mind. Ashley proclaimed her love to her and now she would be forced once again to wake up and find Ashley gone.

* * *

Ashley's internal alarm clock woke her up. She focused on the VCR clock. 5:30am already? She sat up and turned the light on. There was Dillon sleeping in the chair next to the bed. Ashley smiled and walked over to her. She never heard her come in. She lightly kissed her head. She quickly made the bed and went into the bathroom.

Dillon woke up. She looked around. The bed was empty. Her heart dropped into her stomach. Panic overcame her. So much so that she didn't hear the shower running. She knew it was a dream. It had to be. She could never get someone like Ashley Wilkerson. She stood up and tripped over Ashley's bag. Falling to the floor brought her back to reality and the sound of the shower running.

She thought about going in to surprise Ashley, but she thought better of it. Twenty minutes later, Ashley came into the kitchen to find Dillon eating toaster waffles and reading the paper.

"Boy, I'm sure glad I'm not your last patient today." Dillon chuckled.

"Ha ha! I need coffee." Ashley looked at Dillon.

"One cup o' Joe coming at you." Dillon got up and poured her a cup.

"Hey, Spit. I was thinking. Maybe you can drive me to work and take the car. I know we need food and all, this way we can leave right at six."

"Great idea." Dillon smiled. "Give me a second to change." She ran toward the bedroom. "Hey Doc, I know it's not bacon and eggs, but there are a couple of waffles for you in the toaster." Dillon yelled. "I don't know what you want on them but there's stuff in the fridge. Help yourself."

Ashley smiled and shook her head. Gia would have never made her breakfast, even if it were toaster waffles. She opened the fridge and laughed. Dillon had made her a lunch. It was in a soft cooler with a white piece of sports tape across it. Doc was written on it and there was a smiley face. Ashley melted.

Dillon came running in "OK, I'm ready.... did you find everything ok?"

"Yes, I did." Ashley smiled as she held the cooler up.

"Oh, well, I thought you might get hungry, so I made ya a lunch. It's turkey... I hope its ok?"

Ashley set the cooler down and walked over to Dillon. She kissed her on the cheek.

"A kiss just for making lunch?" Dillon winked.

"Wait till you see what happens if dessert is involved."

Dillon chuckled "You're going to be late."

"This is the best reason I can think of for being late." Ashley giggled.

Dillon wanted to tell Ashley that she, too, had fallen in love with her. The words just wouldn't come out. "Come on, you." Dillon looked at Ashley. She grabbed Ashley's lunch and her purse.

"Yes, dear." Ashley giggled as they headed for the door hand in hand.

* * *

Ashley walked into the cafeteria carrying her cooler. She was exhausted but she didn't care. She was on cloud nine. She spotted Rhonda and went to sit by her friend.

"Well if it isn't Ms. Happy!" Rhonda chuckled.

"Yep!" Ashley plopped down.

"Bringing your lunch now?" Rhonda looked at the tape and noticed "Doc" written on it. "Hey, wait a sec. You were late for rounds, you brought your lunch, goofy grin.........Did you and Spitfire?"

"Shhhhhhhhh! Rhonda keep it down." Ashley looked at her.

Rhonda looked around. "Details, I want details."

"What's to tell? I'm having a real nice time."

"Nice time? You call a lunch bag with Doc written on it just a nice time?"

"Oh, Rhonda. Dillon is wonderful!" Ashley beamed.

"Dillon? Good Lord child you're in love with her."

"Head over heels. She makes me feel so alive."

"Well, I must say, I haven't seen you smile this much ever!"

"Rhonda, I have a feeling this smile is here to stay."

"So when do we get to meet her?"

"You already know her Rhonda."

"Girl, please! I don't mean walking past her in a hospital hallway. I mean bringing her over and meeting us."

"We will Rhonda, after this weekend." Ashley took a bite of her sandwich.

"What's this weekend?"

"Spit and I are going to her cabin on the Kern River. We leave after work tonight."

"Ashley, hold on. Dating is one thing, but you can't go off with this stranger for the weekend."

"Rhonda, Dillon is kind, gentle and loving. She's everything I've ever wanted."

"I understand all of that Ash, but you're not thinking clearly... The sex is clouding your judgment. You're going to a cabin on a river with some possible psycho firefighter that might kill you?"

Ashley laughed out loud. "You are kidding right?"

"You may think it's funny now missy, but you won't be laughing when they find little pieces of you floating in the river."

"Rhonda, stop. I'm a big girl and I can take care of myself. And if you must know, we haven't slept together... yet."

Rhonda shook her head, "Even worse!" She reached into her purse and pulled out a black leather case. "Here at least take this with you." She handed it to Ashley.

"Pepper spray? Rhonda, c'mon."

"Take it! You can never be too safe."

Ashley took it to appease her friend.

"You'll thank me later," Rhonda said looking at Ashley.

Ashley was hurt. Why couldn't Rhonda revel in the excitement with her? Why did she have to put those thoughts into her head? She knew that Dillon was different from anyone she had ever met. The eyes never lie and Dillon's told Ashley everything she ever needed to know.

"You'll be apologizing later."

"I hope I am."

She dropped the can of pepper spray into her purse and watched as Rhonda smiled.

"So what about Gia?" Rhonda asked next.

"What about her? It was over a long time ago. You knew that. In fact, I asked her to move out last night."

"Whoa this is serious. What did she say?"

"She refused."

"And?"

"I'm gonna move."

"In with Spitfire?"

"I hope to."

"Ashley Wilkerson! Have you completely lost your mind?"

"I'm telling you Rhonda, she's the one."

"That's what you said about Gia, and Cathy, and Audra and-"

"Ok! Ok." Ashley stopped her. "This feels different Rhonda, real different. I know in my heart she's the one."

"Well, we'll see about that. But if she hurts you… she'll have to answer to me!"

Ashley laughed.

"What did your folks say?"

"Shit!" Ashley sprung up. "I forgot to call them!" She gathered her things and leaned over to kiss Rhonda on the cheek. "See you on Tuesday."

"Have fun and be careful!" Rhonda yelled after Ashley. She shook her head and went back to her lunch. "The girl is fish food."

* * *

Ashley looked at her watch, 5:58pm. She stood in the same spot that Dillon dropped her off in. She was nervous and excited. She could hardly wait to be alone with Dillon. Finally! She looked up to see Dillon turning into the lot. Ashley's midnight blue Volvo s80 was shinning.

Dillon put the car in park and jumped out and opened the door for Ashley. She smiled and started to get in. She noticed the single rose sitting on the car seat. She took it and sat down.

Dillon closed the door and smiled as she got in the car.

"This is beautiful. Thank you."

"You're welcome. How was your day, Doc?"

"Long. I couldn't wait for my shift to end."

"Me too." Dillon chuckled and squeezed her hand.

"Did you get the car detailed?" Ashley asked looking around.

"Is that ok?" Dillon looked concerned.

"It's great. Thank you." Ashley smiled.

"Good. Cause I also got your oil changed and had your tires rotated."

Ashley laughed. "Remind me to pay you back."

"Remind me to teach you about cars."

"I know about cars. You put gas in them and they go."

Dillon laughed. She hadn't felt this good in a long time. A real long time.

* * *

The drive up to the cabin was long. They stopped at the truck stop on Weed Patch in Bakersfield. Dillon was delighted that they had her favorite little burritos fried up. Ashley ate three. Dillon marveled at the petite doctor's hearty appetite. Dillon filled the car up and they were off again.

"Oh Spit, I almost forgot. My folks wanted us to stop by on the way back if you don't mind?"

Dillon got a little nervous. She had never met anyone's parents before. That was a big fat hairy deal!

"Ah, sure Doc.... that's great."

Ashley saw the tension in Dillon's face.

"Relax, my parents are cool. They'll love you."

She took Dillon's hand and laced her fingers through hers and squeezed.

Dillon smiled. She knew that everything would be ok.

Although it was very dark out, the ride up the Kern was beautiful. The moon was full and bright. Just before entering the canyon Dillon pulled over and rolled the windows down. She took a deep breath and closed her eyes. The orange blossoms were in bloom and they smelled so sweet.

Ashley watched as Dillon kept breathing in the sweet orange scent. She saw the relaxation come to her face. Dillon was at peace. Ashley remembered coming into Dillon's room late at night after rounds. She looked the same way, very content.

As they drove on, Dillon tried to point out some of natures best.

"It's kind of hard to see in the dark." Dillon pointed out. She was driving for a bit when a Bobcat dashed across the deserted two-lane road.

"What was that?" Ashley asked with excitement.

"A Bobcat." Dillon smiled.

"This is so awesome." Ashley smiled.

Dillon laughed. "Wait till you see it in the daylight."

Dillon hung her arm out the window. It was hard for her to get used to being in a car. She felt closed in.

"Spit, please bring your arm inside. That's dangerous."

"I ride a motorcycle, this is not dangerous." Dillon chuckled. "Unless a bear rips it off as we drive by."

"I'm a doctor, I know about these things."

Dillon was now intrigued. "It's dangerous to drive with my arm out the window?"

"Yes." Ashley said seriously

Dillon laughed.

"Laugh if you want to. A rock could lodge under you skin, an infection could set in."

Dillon's smile was quickly replaced by a frown. She felt it. It was big. It was bad and it was ugly!

"Oh no." Dillon slowed the car down and pulled over.

"Are you ok?" Ashley asked.

"No."

"Spit? What is it?" Ashley was getting a little concerned.

Dillon pulled her hand inside. A bug! A big juicy bug had decided to end its life on Dillon's hand. It was gooey and it was gross.

Ashley couldn't contain her laughter.

"Not funny." Dillon flipped the interior light on and looked for a tissue.

"No, it's not funny." Ashley had tears streaming from her eyes. "It's down right hysterical!"

Dillon had to admit that it was indeed funny. Besides, she'd have a million bugs splatter on her if she could see Ashley laugh like this all the time. Tears were streaming down her face as she continued to laugh. *What a sight.* Dillon thought. *I would never get tired of it.* Dillon started to chuckle.

Ashley reached under the seat and pulled out a container of wipes. She pulled out a couple and handed them to Dillon.

"Thanks." Dillon grinned. She took the wipes and cleaned herself up. She looked at Ashley smile, put the car in gear and continued to drive.

After another hour Dillon pulled over to the side of the road and turned the car off.

"What's wrong?" Ashley asked.

"Get out of the car." Dillon said.

"Why?"

"Just get out!" Dillon demanded.

Ashley was dumbfounded. She opened the door and got out just as Dillon did.

She thought about what Rhonda had said. *Oh my God! Could it be true? Was Dillon going to? No, not Dillon,* Ashley told herself. She remembered the pepper spray just as she heard the doors lock and the alarm set on her car.

Dillon came up behind her and put her hands on her shoulders. *This is it!* Ashley thought. She was paralyzed with fear and couldn't move. Rhonda was right.

Dillon leaned over to Ashley's ear. "Look up." She whispered.

"What?" Ashley asked.

"Look up."

Ashley looked up toward the sky. She was speechless.

"It's the Milky Way." Dillon smiled.

"Spit...................Wow." Ashley said as she looked around.

A layer of thick stars formed a strip across the sky.

"It's magical." Ashley said mesmerized.

"That it is. I said the same thing the first time I saw it."

"Look at all of the stars." Ashley spun around

"Yeah, you can see them all when it's this dark. No city lights to hamper the view."

Dillon reached into her jacket pocket and pulled out the little gold box. "Doc."

"Yeah?" Ashley answered, still looking toward the heavens.

"I...sort of ...kind of...got this for you." She said as she handed the box to Ashley.

"You didn't have to get me anything." She opened the box. The moon was shining bright enough for her to see it. "Oh my...I can't."

"Yes you can. It was made to be worn by you. We both knew that the minute we saw it." Dillon took it from the box and put it around Ashley's neck "It's perfect. Just like you."

"Spit this is so sweet."

"Ya know, I've been waiting for you." Dillon choked out the words as tears formed in her eyes.

"You have?" Ashley looked up.

"Yeah. All my life I've waited for someone like you, and now you're here."

Ashley watched as Dillon fought off the tears that now overtook her. She had such a beautiful soul. "I can't think of any other place I'd rather be."

Dillon took Ashley's face in her hands placing a soft kiss on her lips. Then another. "I've wanted to do that for a long time." Dillon smiled.

"Why didn't you?" Ashley asked.

"I.... I.... guess I just didn't think you wanted me to."

Ashley tiptoed to kiss Dillon. It was soft and gentle, filled with passion. Dillon pulled Ashley close and held her tight. After what seemed like forever Ashley broke off the kiss.

"I think we need to get to the cabin." Ashley smiled.

This time it was Ashley who was blushing, but Dillon couldn't see it.

Dillon opened the car door for Ashley.

"Thank you." She kissed her again. She got into the car and Dillon closed the door.

Dillon walked around the car and stopped. She looked up to the heavens. "Thank you" she whispered and got into the car.

Neither one said a word the rest of the way. They held hands and listened to a CD. Their touch said more than any words could have.

* * *

Dillon unlocked the cabin door and turned the light on.

Ashley was in awe. It was beautiful. It was all wood and river rock. The furniture was made of logs, and there was a huge fireplace.

"Make yourself at home Doc. I need to turn on the water and gas."

Ashley set her bag down and looked around. She went to the kitchen and turned the light on. She reached over and plugged the fridge in. She could live here forever, she thought. It was just as amazing as it's owner.

"You like it?" Dillon asked startling Ashley.

"It's wonderful."

"I'll show you the rest of it before we unload."

Dillon took Ashley's hand and led her down the hall. "This is the bathroom."

"Ooooooh indoor plumbing." Ashley giggled.

"This is the guest room." Dillon opened the door.

It was nice. A bed, a chest of drawers, a closet. It had a painting of a cowboy and Indian riding and some Indian rugs and baskets. Ashley went to get a closer look at the baskets.

"My great-grandmother brought them over with her when she crossed the Oregon trail."

"Wow, really?"

"Yeah. And the rugs too."

"I love them." Ashley smiled.

"C'mon. I'll show you the master bedroom."

They walked down the hall to the back of the cabin. She opened the door and turned on the lights. Ashley had to catch her breath... it was beautiful. A bed frame made out of logs with a matching chair. More rugs and baskets hung on the wall; there were big double doors that led to a deck.

"Check this out." Dillon unlocked one of the doors and took Ashley outside.

It was getting cooler and a breeze was cutting through the trees. The rushing water from the Kern River echoed below.

Ashley looked up to see all of the stars still shining bright. They glowed like little lights dancing over the water and rocks.

"Ah.... so, where would you like to sleep?" Dillon blushed. She knew that she and Ashley professed their love to one another, but she wanted to be sure.

Ashley answered with a kiss. This one was different. A bit more intense and Ashley wanted to explore. She could tell that Dillon was nervous, so she backed off.

"I'll go get the rest of the stuff." Dillon made a quick escape. Her heart was racing, and she felt like running. Things were moving so fast. She needed to tell Ashley why she kept bailing out in the heat of the moment. *How do you tell the woman of your dreams, the woman you've waited for and dreamt of all your life, that you're scared?* She couldn't keep pushing Ashley away. She didn't deserve to be treated like this.

Dillon came back in carrying the last of the supplies. Ashley emerged from the bedroom already showered and in her pj's.

"I'm starving!" She smiled as she grabbed a bag off the table.

"I hope I brought enough food. I forgot about the bottomless pit."

"Cute." Ashley laughed, as she stuck her tongue out at Dillon.

Tell her now! Dillon's inner voice said. She couldn't. She watched as Ashley went through the bags.

"Where's the food?" Ashley turned to Dillon.

"What?" Dillon was surprised.

"The real food?"

"It's right there." Dillon pointed.

"This is all a bunch of fruit and health crap."

"What do you call food then?" Dillon asked.

"Anything from the three food groups." Ashley shot her answer back.

"Oh, I see. And they are?

"Frozen, canned, and packaged."

Dillon playfully shook her head. "And you call yourself a Doctor?"

"Damn straight Skippy I do." Ashley smiled.

Dillon laughed and grabbed a bag off the table. "What about all that tofu crap? Here, try this one."

Ashley took the bag from Dillon. "Just a clever ruse to get you to notice me…mmm…jackpot!" Ashley squealed with delight. The bag was filled with all kinds of junk food. "Now we're talking." She smiled as she pulled out a bag of pinwheels. "How did you know these were my favorite?"

"Just a lucky guess." Dillon smiled.

Ashley opened the bag and took one out. She dangled it seductively in front of Dillon. "You know you want it." She winked at her. She moved in close. "C'mon, be bad for once in your life hot shot firefighter." Ashley teased.

Dillon chuckled and took it. "FYI Doc. I love Pinwheels. She bit into it and licked her lips.

Ashley pulled her down to her and kissed her.

"Better get the stuff in the fridge before it melts." She looked at Ashley.

As they unloaded the rest of the groceries, Dillon told Ashley of her times at the cabin with her grandparents. Dillon could have stayed there talking all night. It was safe for her. Safe from what would come in the morning when Ashley would be gone.

* * *

Dillon finally turned the water off from her long hot shower. She kept putting off what she knew was coming. She needed to talk to Ashley before it was too late.

Ashley sat in the lounge chair out on the deck. The night was cool, so she wrapped herself in a blanket. There was no way she would miss the show in the sky. She looked up at the stars trying to remember some of the constellations from her high school astronomy class. She drifted off in a dream of what it would be like to make love to Dillon out here underneath these glorious stars. She wanted Dillon so bad. She noticed that Dillon kept holding back and Ashley hoped she wasn't being too pushy. Maybe Dillon wanted to date awhile. But she knew that Dillon was the one for her and she wanted to start building their life together.

Dillon came out of the bathroom in her flannel pants and muscle shirt. She noticed the cool breeze from the open door right away. She grabbed a sweatshirt and threw it on and stepped out onto the deck. "There you are."

"Spit, I'm in heaven looking at all of these stars."

"It's pretty amazing." Dillon agreed.

"So are you." Ashley looked at Dillon.

Dillon's stomach started to churn. She knew what Ashley wanted. She wanted it too. She also knew that the outcome would destroy her heart.

Ashley stood up and took Dillon by the hand and led her back into the bedroom.

Dillon stopped and looked into Ashley's eyes. Ashley continued to lead Dillon to the bed. She pulled her down on her as she lay on the bed.

Dillon continued to search Ashley's eyes. She was looking for anything that would put her mind at peace.

Ashley tugged at Dillon's shirt until the firefighter's lips were softly kissing hers.

Dillon kissed her passionately, then moved to her cheek, then down her neck.

Ashley's heart started to race as she arched her back toward Dillon. Heat was quickly taking over her body. Something she never had felt with any of her lovers before.

Dillon continued to slowly explore Ashley with her lips. She made her way back to Ashley's sweet tender lips and kissed her. It was a long, passionate kiss, and Ashley wanted to taste every part of Dillon leaving her tongue just dangling on Dillon's lips and nibbling on them. Dillon fought to catch her breath.

Dillon moaned as Ashley reached under her shirt and touched her breast. Dillon pulled away and stared at her. She slowly lifted Ashley's T-shirt. *Oh she is so beautiful,* Dillon thought. Just how she imagined her body would look. Dillon swung her leg over to straddle Ashley. They never stopped looking into each other's eyes.

Ashley tugged at Dillon to remove her shirt. Dillon obliged. Her biceps and shoulders were perfect. Ashley traced their curves with her hand. She slowly moved to Dillon's collarbone, all the while fixed into each other's stare.

Dillon leaned down and started to kiss Ashley's neck again. They were both very aware that their skin was now touching one another, the internal sparks it was creating. Dillon found her way to Ashley's lips. She sucked and probed, slowly teasing her. Dillon could feel her arching again trying to push up against her.

Ashley broke off the kiss. "Make love to me, Dillon." She whispered.

Dillon froze. Every alarm and bell went off in her head. She wanted to make love to Ashley, but like it had been with Kris, she new it would be all over by morning. Panic overcame Dillon as she jumped from the bed and fumbled for her shirt. "I'm sorry, Doc," was all she said as she left the room and closed the door behind her.

Ashley lay there, very still, part in shock, part in sadness, tears streaming down her cheeks.

* * *

Dillon sat on the front porch, in a sleeping bag. It was one of her favorite things to do. It was special to her to watch the sunrise. This time it didn't feel so special. Tears fell, and her heart ached.

The front door opened, and Ashley stepped out.

"Hey." Dillon choked out. She tried to cover the fact that she had been crying.

"Hey." Ashley's horse voice responded.

"Doc....I...I...I'm so sorry." Dillon said.

"It's not you..............It's me. I shouldn't have pushed myself on you."

"You didn't. Trust me."

There was a long pause as the two looked at each other.

Ashley shivered.

"C'mon, get in here."

Dillon unzipped the bag so Ashley could get in. She sat on her lap.

She leaned into Dillon's warm body. Dillon wrapped her arms around her.

"I need to tell you something."

"I already know."

"You do?" Dillon was surprised.

"Yeah. I know I'm not your type."

"What? Whatever gave you that idea?" Dillon asked.

"Spit, do you really want to re-live what happened?"

"Please, let me explain."

Ashley looked at Dillon.

"For starters, you are very much my type. In fact, I think you are the most beautiful, incredible woman that God has ever put in my path! It's just ...." She took a deep breath.

"Tell me. Please." Ashley looked at Dillon.

"After my folks passed, I lived with this woman. She told me that she loved me. The night we made love for the first time, the earth moved for me. I thought, 'this is it. I found my true love.' The next morning, there was a note on the pillow that told me to move out." Tears started to run down Dillon's face.

"Oh, Spit." Ashley gently wiped them away.

"After that night, I swore I would never let myself get that close to a woman again. Then I met you and wham! My heart didn't know what hit it. I'm just so...............so scared that you'll leave too." Dillon couldn't believe that she poured her soul out to Ashley. She had never cried about Kris until now. She felt the release as the ghosts from her past flew away.

Ashley kissed Dillon's tear-stained cheek. She took her face in her hands and looked into her eyes. "I promise you, I will never leave you." She smiled at her. She kissed Dillon on the lips... the kisses grew longer. Ashley looked at Dillon and smiled. She unzipped the sleeping bag and stood up. She took Dillon's hand and pulled her to her feet. Dillon followed Ashley into the house and back into the bedroom. She laid Dillon on the bed.

Dillon watched as Ashley peeled off her clothes until her beautiful body was in front of her. Dillon felt a stir inside her. Heat was rushing through her body. She pulled Ashley to her and kissed her.

Ashley took Dillon's hand and placed it on her breast. Dillon caressed her until a soft moan came from deep within Ashley. Dillon rolled Ashley onto the bed. She stood up, stopping to look at what lay before her. She took off her shirt and then her pants. She slid into bed next to Ashley, her heart pounding.

Ashley climbed on Dillon, making sure that every inch of their bodies were touching. She could never be too close. Ashley kissed Dillon, starting at her lips and slowly moving downward. Her chin, her neck, her shoulders, her chest, taking in every inch of Dillon by kissing, licking and nibbling. Dillon was about to explode as Ashley traced small circles around Dillon's erect nipples.

No one had ever touched Dillon like this. Then again, there never was one until now. No one from Dillon's past existed. It was all about Ashley now, and the life they would make together.

Ashley continued to descend upon Dillon's body. She kissed and licked the firefighter's tight stomach. She looked at Dillon wanting to go further, but not sure if she should.

"Doc..........." Dillon managed to get out between her heavy breaths. "Make love to me."

Ashley kissed Dillon long and hard. "I love you, Dillon McCabe," were the last words they spoke as the two now became one.

* * *

Dillon sleepily opened one eye. She was sore, exhausted, and exhilarated. She looked at the clock on her nightstand. 3:30! She had slept the entire day. She rolled over to find Ashley sitting in bed reading.

"Hey there." Dillon grinned.

"Hey there, yourself." Ashley smiled "How are you?"

"Kind of sore." Dillon chuckled.

Ashley tossed her book to the floor and slid into Dillon's arms. "You should see a

Doctor." Ashley giggled.

"Oh really?"

"Yes."

"You know a good one?" Dillon grinned.

Both women laughed at their childish behavior.

Dillon looked deep into Ashley's eyes. "Oh Doc, what you're doing to me."

"Dillon I-"

"Shhh." Dillon put her finger to Ashley's lips. She followed it with a kiss. As they made love that afternoon, Dillon felt free. Free of her doubts, free of her past. She had one thing to live for and she was holding her in her arms.

Dillon let the cool water run over her tired sore body. She and Ashley stayed in bed the entire day. She finally dragged herself into the shower. She reminisced on the past twenty-four hours. She felt a little awkward in bed with Ashley. It had been a while since she last made love to a woman, and then it wasn't really love. More like sex after a date. Ashley was different. She was wonderful in bed. A great lover. Very kind and gentle. She only hoped that she couldn't see her inexperience. Dillon smiled as she recalled the way Ashley called her name. She was so wrapped up in her thoughts that she didn't hear Ashley walk in.

Ashley quietly slipped out of her clothes and into the shower behind Dillon. She slowly rubbed Dillon's back.

"Mmmm. You're hired."

Ashley looked up at her lover's back. She once again saw the scar that hovered above her right shoulder blade. She wanted to know about it, but knew not to ask Dillon. She started to finger it.

"You not knowing about that scar is gonna be the death of you isn't it?" Dillon turned around and took Ashley in her arms.

Ashley laid her head on Dillon's chest. "I just want to know everything about you, Dillon McCabe."

"Well darlin' after what we've been doing the last twenty-four hours, I'd say you pretty much do." Dillon chuckled.

Ashley looked into Dillon's eyes.

Dillon kissed her. "All right. I'll tell you. The morning I got that note from Kris, well, I also found out that she had a girlfriend, a very big, very butch girlfriend. I didn't want any trouble, so I packed up my stuff. As I was about to leave, this chick burst into the house. She had a knife."

"Spit, no." Ashley said.

"She tied me up for three hours. She was very methodical about it. She cut my buttons off my shirt. Cut the sleeves off. My bra. She kept asking me if I was fucking her woman. I told her no. I said I was just packing my things and moving on. She backhanded me with such force she broke my nose. But when I came to, I was on the ground, the chair was broken and my hands were free. She was drinking a beer and I knew I had only one shot. I grabbed part of the chair, to strike her with it. She heard me and came at me with the knife. I turned my back in time cause she was aiming for my heart." She squeezed Ashley tighter.

"How did you get away?"

"Kris came in and stopped her. Told her that we hadn't done anything, that I was just a charity case she helped out."

"Oh baby, I'm so sorry." Ashley kissed Dillon's chest.

"I learned a lot. I don't take things for granted anymore."

"Well you're all mine now, so I'll protect you from that mean butch bitch."

Dillon laughed. She leaned over and kissed Ashley again.

Ashley's knees weakened. Dillon had such a way with her kisses. They were long, lingering, and very passionate.The fact that Dillon was unaware that she kissed that way made her even sexier, Ashley thought.

"You finish up and I'll get dinner started, " Dillon said, smiling.

Ashley wouldn't let her grip go. "I have all I need right here." She nuzzled back into Dillon's chest.

"What, no food? Oh, baby, you got it bad." Dillon laughed.

Ashley dropped her arms and looked up. "Oh, food?? I'm starving!" She winked at Dillon.

Dillon laughed. "There are some things we need to talk about too." Dillon kissed Ashley one last time and smiled at her as she left the shower.

Who would have thought that just five weeks ago she would find the key to her happiness lying in a hospital bed?

* * *

Ashley opened the bedroom door expecting to have her senses filled with some delicious meal that Dillon was preparing. She too was a bit sore from the past hour activities. She walked into the kitchen. There was nothing, not even Dillon.

"Hey, what gives?" Ashley called out. There was no answer. She looked around and went to the back porch. "No way!" Ashley smiled. "Where's my camera?" She ran back to the bedroom to retrieve it. She stepped out on to the porch and started snapping pictures.

Dillon was lying on a patch of grass facing a fawn that was doing the same. They were almost nose-to-nose, as Dillon talked to the baby, gently stroking it. The doe was close by, grazing.

"Don't move fast." Dillon instructed in an even tone.

Ashley continued to snap pictures. "Spit, this is incredible."

"Put your camera down slowly."

Ashley did.

"Now step off the porch in even slow steps. The mother will come up to you. She'll check you out. Just let her smell you."

Ashley did as she was instructed. Sure enough, to her delight, the doe walked over to her and smelled her. She stuck out her hand. The doe sniffed it and went back to grazing.

"Oh, Spit." Ashley beamed.

Dillon grinned. "You did it. You passed the test, Doc. Now, slowly walk to my feet."

Ashley did.

"OK, one knee at a time get down to my level so that you're lying next to me."

Ashley now lay beside Dillon. The curious fawn licked Ashley's extended hand.

"She likes you."

"She should. I cried during Bambi."

Dillon shook her head, trying to stifle her laugh.

The doe suddenly heard a noise from the road and took off with the fawn following close behind.

"Oh no." Ashley said.

"They'll be back." Dillon assured her, as she got to her feet.

"How do you do that?"

"I don't know, I just do." She held her hand out to Ashley and helped her up.

"Well, you must be pretty special." Ashley looked at Dillon. "In fact, I know you are." She kissed Dillon. "Now, what about my dinner?"

Dillon laughed as she took Ashley's hand and walked back into the cabin.

* * *

The next day was beautiful. It was sunny, but cool. Dillon wanted to get an early start. She was taking Ashley up to the Giant Sequoias. She woke up early and made lunch. She wanted to talk to Ashley about their next step since they didn't do much talking last night. Dillon grinned. She couldn't believe how each time they made love, it only got better. More intense. More permanent.

Ashley came out dressed and ready. She was glowing. She was in love and she wanted everyone to know it. Rhonda was in for a big surprise when she got back.

Ashley snapped photos as Dillon drove and pointed out some sites. It was stunning, green everywhere. They stopped along the river and Dillon took Ashley down to feel the coolness of the water.

They made it to their destination of the Trail of 100 Giants. It was still cool up that high, with fall coming soon.... and most of the tourists had gone. The girls had the trails to themselves. Dillon loved it. She could walk around with her arm around Ashley's waist.

Ashley was amazed at the size of the Sequoias. There were some that were struck by lighting. They remained living trees with charred middles, while others stretched 300 feet into the sky.

"Some of these bad boys are hundreds and hundreds of years old." Dillon told Ashley.

Dillon took Ashley to one tree that stood tall, almost reaching to the heavens. The trunk was enormous. Ashley climbed into the fork in the trunk and Dillon snapped a photo of her. Ashley had Dillon stand inside too. She pulled Dillon to her and kissed her. "Ever make love in a Giant Sequoia, Spit?" Ashley grinned. She took Dillon's hand and laid it on her breast.

Dillon swallowed hard. She wanted Ashley.

A nearby park ranger stopped and peeked inside.

Dillon quickly pulled her hand back and turned about three shades of red.

"Hello there," he said.

"Hi." Ashley smiled. "How are you?"

"Fine, thank you, ma'am." He grinned.

Ashley asked if he wouldn't mind taking a picture of the two of them. He happily obliged.

Dillon was thrilled to have the first of many photos taken of them together.

"Thanks." Dillon said to the ranger.

"My pleasure. Enjoy yourselves."

He walked away.

"We were trying to, before you came by." Ashley said under her breath.

Dillon snickered. "Come on before you get us thrown in the pokey." Dillon grabbed Ashley's hand.

"The pokey?' Ashley laughed.

"It's a jail."

"Yes, I know that, I just didn't know that anyone ever used that word anymore."

Dillon looked at Ashley. She chuckled. "C'mon."

After a couple of hours of exploring, they went back to the car to get lunch. They found an out-of-the-way picnic table near a stream.

"I'm starving." Ashley proclaimed as she inspected the ice chest.

"I swear, Doc, I now know why your folks wanted you to become a Doctor...to help pay the food bill"

Ashley laughed. She handed Dillon a sandwich. "You have no clue what you're getting yourself into."

"I'll take my chances." Dillon grinned and pulled Ashley to her knee. She kissed her. "I could kiss you forever, Doc."

"Mmmm. And I'll let you kiss me forever." She kissed her again. Dillon's hands started to caress Ashley's breast. It took her breath away. "Hey, now you behave."

" Oh, I'm tryin' real hard." Dillon nibbled on Ashley's neck, sending a rush of chills over her body. She let Ashley go. Pouting at her.

"Got to keep our strength up, babe." She teased.

Dillon arched her eyebrow. "Oh, don't worry about that."

Ashley laughed. "I can see why you love it up here. I wish we could stay forever."

"Well, we can come up anytime you want to."

"I want, I want." Ashley grinned. "What's further up?"

"More trees and a little town. The Ponderosa. I'll take you there for dinner tonight."

"It's a date." Ashley said. She poured some ice tea for them.

"So, Doc.... I kind of wanted to know...what happens next?"

"What do you mean?"

"Well, what about Gia?"

"I told you. She's the past. We're the present, and the future."

Dillon grinned. She loved the sound of that. "I was thinking, since I have the rest of the week off, I thought maybe I could go and pick up your things from the condo."

"You don't have to do that. I can stick it in storage until I find a place."

Dillon rolled her eyes. "Where do you think you're moving to?"

"I'll find something."

"I give up!" Dillon threw her hands in the air. "Doc, I want you to move in with me."

"What?" Ashley asked surprised.

"Well, if you don't want to..."

"No, I do, more than anything. I just didn't want to rush you."

"What rush? I know how I feel about you. I want us to be together."

"I want that too."

Dillon took Ashley's hand and looked deep into her eyes. "I don't need time and I don't want to take it slow. I know in my heart Ashley Wilkerson, that you are the one I want to share the rest of my life with. I want you in my arms, in my house, in my bed, but more importantly, I want you in my life..........forever. Now, if you need some tim-"

Ashley put her finger to Dillon's lips. She kissed her lover. "All I need is you."

Dillon took her in her arms and kissed her. This was one incredible woman.

"Spit. I need to tell you some things. About my past."

"I don't care about that." Dillon looked at her.

"I know, but I need to."

The two finished lunch and found a shade tree to sit under. They spread a blanket out and lay under the tree for hours. Dillon held Ashley, softly caressing her back while she lay against Dillon's chest, telling her of her past. She told Dillon of the baby that she tried to have with Gia, and how she lost it.

Dillon asked her about how she came out. She couldn't believe that Ashley's parents were so supportive. She told Ashley about her parents and how her life choice tore their relationship in two.

They laughed and cried all afternoon, becoming closer, if it were possible. They made love under the tree. It was intense and passionate. As long as they could look into each other's eyes, the world around didn't exist.

* * *

Sunday came and Dillon woke up to find Ashley asleep in her arms. She loved it. She wished she could make time stand still. She watched Ashley as she slept soundly.

Ashley felt the heat of Dillon's stare. She opened one eye to see Dillon 's intense blue eyes looking at her.

"Morning." She grunted at Dillon.

"Good morning, beautiful." Dillon kissed her on the forehead. "How are you?"

"Pretty damn sore thanks to you." She smiled. "It feels great."

Dillon chuckled. "I was thinking, maybe we should head home today. That way we have some time to get you settled in."

"I don't want to leave here. This place is magic for us."

"I know, but I want you to be settled in before you have to go back to work."

"I am settled. Look at me. I'm lying naked in your arms. I'm not going anywhere."

Dillon smiled. "That's not what I meant."

"Spit, I have everything I need. I don't care about the other stuff! It's all material things. It can burn in hell with Gia for all I care."

"But what about your personal things, Doc?"

Ashley sat up. It was obvious that Dillon wasn't going to let this go. "Spit, please! I don't want to talk about Gia, or the condo, or moving! It's about right here and right now. The past is just that, the past. I want to be with you, Dillon McCabe, for at least the next hundred years or so."

Dillon smiled.

"And besides, you promised to take me fishing and to the fish hatchery, and I'm holding you to it!" She fell dramatically back into Dillon's arms.

Dillon stroked Ashley's back softly. "What did I ever do to deserve you and this

much happiness?"

Before Dillon knew what was happening, Ashley's hands were already stroking her nipple. A moan came from the back of Dillon's throat as her eyes started to fog over. Ashley started to suck and trace circles with her tongue expertly over Dillon's now erect nipple. Ashley slid her leg between Dillon's legs. She pushed her thigh up into Dillon. She could already feel the wetness coming from her. As she continued her lip and tongue assault on Dillon, she could feel her own arousal start to stir. Ashley slid her other leg between Dillon's forcing her to spread her legs further apart. She happily obliged. Ashley slowly worked her way down, licking, kissing, and sucking all over Dillon' s body.

Dillon felt the waves start to build deep within from Ashley's touch.

Ashley kissed the inside of Dillon's thigh; she quivered as she knew what was yet to come. Slowly and methodically, she ran her hand up and down Dillon's wetness. Ashley looked at her lover. She knew she wanted more. She slowly started to lick Dillon. Small strokes, up and down. The waves inside Dillon were growing. She couldn't take much more.

Ashley looked up at Dillon as she inserted a finger deep within her.

Dillon gasped and arched her back, as Ashley moved expertly inside of her. Dillon pushed in rhythm with Ashley now moving in and out of her. Ashley inserted another finger, which sent Dillon through the roof. Dillon's rhythms were starting to have an effect on Ashley. She, too, now felt the building of her own passion. Dillon released, strong and hard. Ashley felt the waves as she stayed inside Dillon as her body quaked.

They had made love many times in the past few days. Each time it grew more passionate as they grew together. Dillon was now gasping for air. She pulled Ashley onto her. Feeling Ashley's wetness on her leg, she kissed her long and hard.

"I love you so much, Doc." she managed to get out.

"Show me."

With one quick move Dillon had Ashley underneath her.

"Baby, you just unleashed a wild woman."

* * *

They had been quiet all day. Dillon took Ashley to the fish hatchery when the thunder started to roll in. It was big and booming. It startled Ashley a couple of times. They rushed through the hatchery and got in the car just in time before the sky opened up. Fishing was out of the question now. They came back and Dillon made a fire.

Ashley came out with her bag and set it down. "All packed." She said flatly. She picked a book out, plopped down on the couch and started to read.

Dillon couldn't stand this. What was all of this about? Ashley just completely turned around. Was this weekend simply that? One weekend? The old Dillon would have retreated and left things as they were. The new Dillon couldn't. She slammed her hand down on the coffee table. "Damn it, Doc! Don't do this!"

Ashley jumped. "What?"

"You haven't said but two words to me all morning. Why are you pushing me away?"

"I'm sorry."

"Don't be sorry." She walked to Ashley. "Talk to me."

Dillon took Ashley in her arms. She heard her begin to cry. "What is it?" She took Ashley's face into her strong hands. "Why are you crying?"

"It's just this weekend. It was so...perfect. I just don't want it to end once we get off the mountain."

"It won't." Dillon looked into Ashley's eyes. "I promise you that I'll try to make every day like this weekend for you. We don't have to be here for me to show you how I feel. Just give me a chance." Dillon kissed Ashley until she felt her body relax.

Dillon chuckled inside. She felt like a new woman. She would have expected that this weekend would have been a fling, that once they got home, Ashley would leave, and Dillon would continue being alone. Now she felt strong and sure, capable of loving, caring, and providing. She would cherish every second she had with Ashley.

"Dillon McCabe, do you know how much I love you?" Ashley looked at her.

"I think so, but you have the rest our lives to show me" She kissed her again.

Ashley could feel her knees start to weaken. She broke off the kiss and looked hungrily into Dillon's eyes. She took Dillon's hand and started to kneel in front of the fireplace.

"Hey, what about your folks? I thought we needed to be there for lunch?" Dillon grinned.

"We're gonna be late. Real late," Ashley said as she pulled Dillon to her and kissed her.

5

The rain was still coming down at a steady pitch, sometimes making it hard to see. Dillon took the car expertly down the hill. As soon as they reached the exit of the canyon, the rain let up some. Dillon pulled into the truck stop.

Ashley finally got a signal on her cell phone, and called her parents.

Dillon walked into the restroom. She took a long look in the mirror. She looked different. More at peace. She was nervous meeting Ashley's parents so soon. What if they didn't like her? Here they had made life long plans, and her parents may disapprove.

"NO!" Dillon said out loud. She stopped herself. She wasn't going to let those negative demons back into her head. She loved Ashley and wouldn't let her family's disapproval stop her. She splashed some cool water on her face and dried it with a paper towel.

"You'll be fine." She told herself and walked out.

Ashley was waiting for Dillon, eating a burrito. "Want one?" She offered.

Dillon was still queasy. "No thanks."

"Momma said to bring your appetite." She looked at Dillon who was almost green. "Are you ok?"

"Doc. What if your folks don't approve of me?"

"Are you kidding?"

"No."

"Spit. My parents are going to love you. And even if they don't, they can't tell me who I can and cannot be with."

Dillon looked at Ashley.

"Now, get your ass in the car." Ashley said.

Dillon chuckled. "What was that I heard? Did the good doctor say a naughty word?" She shook her head and jumped in the car.

* * *

They arrived in the valley about 4:00pm. Dillon looked around. It was a nice neighborhood. Very suburban, the houses were all kept very well. It looked like a movie set. They passed a perfectly manicured park. Ashley slowed down.

"I had my first kiss right behind that tree." Ashley smiled as she recalled.

"Yeah? With who?" Dillon asked.

"Oh crap. What was her name?" Ashley tried to think.

"Must have been memorable for you" Dillon teased.

Ashley continued to drive. "Jody! Jody Richards!" she said proudly, having now remembered. "Cute little redhead. Boy what a..........." She stopped herself. "We're here."

Ashley squeezed Dillon's hand for reassurance. "It'll be fine, baby." She smiled at Dillon.

Dillon exhaled... she hoped so.

Ashley turned into the driveway and shut the car down.

Dillon was nervous. She swallowed hard.

"Sweetie, you look like a deer caught in the headlights. Relax."

Ashley's parents came out of the house. Ashley ran and jumped into her Daddy's arms. She hugged and kissed him, then did the same to her mother.

Dillon wiped her sweaty palms on her jeans and stepped out of the car. She smiled as she saw the warm exchange between Ashley and her parents. She missed her family. She would have loved them to have met Ashley.

Ashley came back and took Dillon's hand. "Mom, Daddy. This is Dillon McCabe."

"Hi." Dillon said softly.

"Dillon, nice to meet you," Bill said as he offered his hand to Dillon. "Welcome to our home."

"Thank you, sir." Dillon said as she shook it.

"Welcome Dillon." Mary smiled.

Before Dillon could react Mary was hugging her.

"Thank you, Mrs. Wilkerson." Dillon smiled. She already liked them.

"She smiled at Dillon. "Are you hungry? I hope you're hungry. Mind you it's not much, but I made a little something to snack on before we eat."

"You're late. Did you run into bad weather? Bill asked.

"Just an unavoidable delay," Ashley giggled.

"Come in Dillon, let me show you around."

Ashley laughed as her mother took Dillon by the arm and led her into the house. She hugged her father again.

"You look different sweetheart." He smiled.

"I'm happy, Daddy. For the first time in my life, I am truly happy."

Bill had heard his little girl say this at the start of each new relationship. But he had to admit, this time she did indeed look happy. "You said you met her at the hospital?"

"She came into the hospital one night on a stretcher. I walked into the room to treat her, and bam!"

Bill laughed at his daughter. He knew about the pain Ashley had been through with Gia. It was so nice to see her smiling again. "As long as she makes you happy."

"Oh Daddy, she does. She's kind, sweet, and wonderful!" Ashley beamed.

"Then that makes me happy, pumpkin." He kissed his daughter again. "We better get in there and save Dillon. There won't be much left once your mother gets a hold of her."

They laughed and walked into the house.

They found Dillon and Mary sitting on the couch. Dillon already had an iced tea in one hand and cheese and crackers in the other. Mary was sitting next to her with the family photo album open.

"Aw, Mom! Not the family photos! I don't want to scare her away."

Dillon chuckled. She had a 'help me' look on her face.

"She also plays the guitar and sings like an angel."

"Really?" Dillon looked at Ashley

"She won three talent contests." Bill smiled proudly.

"In high school. I haven't played in years."

"I know, it's sitting in its case under our bed."

"It's a shame."

"Oh, please." Ashley rolled her eyes.

"I hope you like burgers, Dillon?" Bill asked.

"Yes sir. That's great."

"Well, fine, then I'll start the BBQ."

"Can I help you, sir?" Dillon asked.

"Can you fix a starter on a grill?"

"Dillon is a guest, Bill." Mary looked at him.

"I don't mind at all. It would be a pleasure" Dillon looked relieved.

Dillon stood up and smiled at Ashley. She followed her father outside.

Ashley waited until she heard the back porch door close. "Well, mom?"

"She seems very nice dear."

"Oh Mom, she's wonderful!" She plopped down next to her mother and hugged her.

"Does this mean I get a grandchild?"

Ashley laughed. "We haven't talked about it yet, but I think there's a good possibility."

"Then I like her a lot." Mary smiled.

Dillon grabbed the pliers and got the handle to unlock.

"Well, I'll be damned, you are a strong one." He smiled.

"Yes sir, I have to be."

"A firefighter right?" Bill loved to give Ashley's dates the third degree. He remembered the first time Ashley brought Giavanna home. She was rude and disrespectful to him and his wife, and he didn't like the way she treated Ashley. He kept quiet for his daughter's sake, and watched her suffer. He vowed that he would never sit by and let that happen to his little girl again.

"So Dillon, tell me about yourself." Bill looked her in the eye.

"What would you like to know, sir?" Dillon looked back.

Bill slowly smiled, *the interrogation starts now*. "How long have you been a firefighter?"

"Seven years."

"Do you live in a house?"

"Yes sir."

"Do you own it?"

"Paid it off two years ago."

"Do you drink?"

"Wine, occasionally."

"Have you ever driven drunk?"

"Never."

"What do you drive?"

"A motorcycle."

"What kind, a Harley?"

"No sir. A Triumph."

"Have you taken my daughter on it?"

"No sir, I haven't"

"Please see that you don't."

Dillon couldn't believe this. She looked around for Ashley. It was obvious this man loved his daughter, but c'mon. She took a long drink of her ice tea.

"Have you two slept together?"

Dillon started to choke. She started coughing.

Ashley and her mother came to the rescue. Dillon looked liked she had been raked over the coals.

"Is everything ok out here?" Ashley asked.

Bill looked at Dillon, waiting to see what she would do.

"It's great, Doc. Just getting to know your father better." Dillon winked at Bill.

A slow smile came across his face. He liked this one. His little girl was right. She was something special.

Dillon ate two burgers and Ashley three. They were stuffed. They sat in the backyard and chatted with Ashley's folks. She was thrilled. Whenever Ashley brought someone over, her father never talked. He had found that Dillon loved old cars too. They were non-stop talking about them. Bill was amazed at Dillon's knowledge. He could tell she knew her stuff.

"Follow me, young lady." He told Dillon.

Dillon looked at Ashley. She smiled to her. Dillon winked back. She followed Bill into the garage. He turned the light on. There was a car covered neatly.

Dillon grinned. She could tell what was under it.

They pulled back the cover to unveil a 1957 Chevy Bel-Air convertible.

Dillon was drooling. It had a few rough spots but it was in fine condition.

"Wow! Sir, she's a beauty." Dillon grinned.

"I'm still restoring her. I don't get out here as much as I used to."

"Do you drive her much?"

"No, not much. Just to the store and around the block every now and then." He looked at Dillon. "Want to take her for a spin?" He smiled.

"If it's not too much trouble."

"Not at all! Just have Ashley move her car."

Dillon ran back to Ashley and her mother. "Hey Doc. Your father is gonna take me for a ride in the Chevy. Could you please move your car?"

Ashley looked at her mother. *Daddy was taking Dillon for a ride?* He never took the car out for Ashley's dates, not even Gia. "Sure, hon." Ashley smiled. *She's in,* she thought to herself.

Ashley backed the car and parked it on the street.

Bill started up the Chevy and backed it out of the garage. He put it in park and moved to the passenger side. "You drive her, Dillon."

A smile came across Dillon's face. She smiled at Ashley, and jumped into the car.

They drove around the neighborhood. Dillon loved the feel of this car. It was smooth.

"She purrs like a kitten. You've done a great job with her."

"Well, I still have more to do, but thank you. Turn left at the next street and pull over."

Dillon did as instructed. She shut down the car.

They sat there for a few minutes, just looking around.

"Dillon, I think I need to explain my actions earlier." Bill finally said.

"Sir, that's ok. I understand. You just love your daughter."

Bill smiled. "Yes, I do, very much. She's my world, Dillon. It's been very painful to sit by and watch my daughter be mistreated by her girlfriends." He looked Dillon in the eye. "I don't want to see her hurt again."

"Mr. Wilkerson, I may not be the first to say to you that I would never hurt your daughter, but I can promise you that I mean it."

He could tell that Dillon was honest, and that she meant what she said. "I take it you know about Ashley's last girlfriend?"

"Yes sir, I do."

"Well, if you're anything like her, I suggest you keep moving and leave my daughter alone."

"Sir, I'm nothing like Giavanna."

Bill smiled. "I can see that you're not."

Dillon relaxed a little. "Mr. Wilkerson, I respect your daughter a lot. She's a wonderful woman and my best friend." She looked at him. "I... I....'m in love with Ashley, and I want to spend the rest of my life with her."

Bill smiled and shook his head. "She thinks very highly of you."

Dillon smiled.

"I guess I only have one more thing to say." Bill was serious now.

"Yes sir?"

"Ok, two things. First of all, no more sirs, call me Dad."

Tears welled up in Dillon's eyes. What a wonderful thing to hear.

He reached over and gave Dillon a hug.

"Thank you for letting me love your daughter...Dad." Dillon choked out.

Bill looked at Dillon. "And the second thing is a warning. My wife and I are hell bent on having a grandchild." He smiled and winked at Dillon.

Dillon laughed. "I'll see what I can do." She started up the Bel-Air and headed back to the house.

* * *

Ashley looked at her watch, It was already 7:00 and they had a long drive ahead of them. "Well, I think we need to get going." She looked at

Dillon and arched her eyebrow. *It's been way too long since I've had my lips on you,* she thought.

Dillon took the dessert plates and coffee cups into the kitchen. Mary followed closely behind.

"Now Dillon, please don't."

"I don't want to leave you with a mess." Dillon smiled.

"Don't be silly, we've had such a lovely time meeting you."

"Well, thank you. It was nice meeting you. And may I say that was the best Red Velvet Cake I have ever tasted."

"Well thank you, Dillon. Let me wrap the rest of it up for you to take home."

"Oh no, Mrs. Wilkerson, please, you don't have to go to all that trouble."

"It's no trouble Dillon. Besides, Bill doesn't need it."

Dillon smiled as she watched Mary wrap up the rest of the cake.

"It's nice to see Ashley smiling again, Dillon. Thank you."

"She's a wonderful woman, Mrs. Wilkerson."

"She says the same thing about you."

Ashley came into the kitchen. "You ready?"

Dillon smiled. "Yeah, just getting my doggie bag."

Mary came over and handed Dillon the cake. "Dillon, we hope to see you again soon." She took Dillon in her embrace and hugged her hard.

"You too, Mrs. Wilkerson. Thank you for such a nice time."

"Please, call me Mom."

Ashley beamed. This was so great to see her parents accept Dillon so fast. They had never let any of her other girlfriends call them mom & dad.

"Thank you, Mom." Dillon smiled.

Ashley hugged her mother. "Thanks, Mom, I love you."

"I love you too dear. Give us a call when you get home."

"Will do." Ashley smiled. She took Dillon's hand and walked outside.

Bill was watering his roses when they walked outside. His way of protesting his daughter leaving.

"Daddy, it just rained. I love you, you silly man." Ashley hugged her father."

"I love you too princess." Bill said. "You drive safe, you hear." He smiled.

"We will." Ashley said.

"Dillon." He looked at her. "It was a pleasure, meeting you."

"You too sir... er, I mean Dad." Dillon grinned. "And thanks for letting me drive your little baby."

Ashley started to chuckle when Dillon realized what she said. She started to blush. She prayed that Ashley's Mom and Dad didn't catch it.

"Dillon, you don't be a stranger. You're welcome in our home any time." He came up and hugged Dillon.

"Thank you." Dillon whispered in his ear. "That means a lot to me."

Dillon opened the car door for Ashley and walked to the driver's side.

"Thanks again." Dillon said as she got in.

Ashley waved goodbye, as Dillon started the car.

"We want a grandchild!" Mary yelled.

Ashley rolled her eyes and blew them a kiss as they drove off.

6

Dillon awoke to the sound of Ashley in the shower. She sat up. She had a million things to do today. She knew she couldn't move Ashley's things by herself. She planned on calling a mover.

They spent the last twenty-four hours in Dillon's bed, sleeping, talking, making love, and planning. It was a nice way to end a vacation.

Dillon looked around. Her master bedroom wasn't that big. She would have to try to rearrange so Ashley could get her dresser and things in. They would need to buy a bigger place.

Ashley walked out of the bathroom wrapped in a towel. She saw Dillon deep in thought.

"Morning, sweetie." She smiled.

"Huh? Oh, hey beautiful. Good morning."

Ashley sat on the bed and kissed Dillon.

"Penny for your thoughts?" Ashley looked into Dillon's eyes.

"Well, I'm trying to figure out where we can put your things."

"My things?"

"Yeah, your dresser, desk, lamps, TV. I thought I'd call the movers and we could go over at lunch time and-"

"Whoa. Wait a sec."

"What's wrong ? I thought we agreed last night we'd get some of your things."

"Nothing's wrong. It's just that you need to rest. You start back to work in a few days. I know you. You'll want to help and lift stuff. No way!" She kissed Dillon again. "And frankly, I don't care if it gets done today or ever. I told you I have everything I need right here." She hugged Dillon.

" I just want you to feel that this is your home too."

"I already do. That's because of you, not things. I don't want any of it. Just my personal things, I'll stop by after work and pick those up."

"You want me to meet you there?" Dillon looked at Ashley.

They both knew what this was about...Gia. Dillon didn't want Ashley to have to have any more confrontations with her. Ashley wanted to see her and say her peace for once and for all.

"Thanks, sweetie, but I can handle it." She kissed Dillon hard.

Dillon took Ashley and rolled her onto the bed.

Ashley giggled. "You're gonna make me late," she said looking into Dillon's eyes.

"Should I stop?" Dillon asked, as she started to remove Ashley's towel. She bent over and licked Ashley's cleavage slowly. "I'll stop if you want me too."

"No." Ashley said breathless. "Don't ever stop, Spit."

After Ashley left for work, Dillon went into the kitchen. She looked into the fridge. It was pretty well empty. She had a lot to do today. She stopped and smiled. She could have never imagined that she would have met her soul mate, fall in love, and now have her move in. She knew that most would think that they were moving way too fast. Dillon knew in her heart that Ashley was the one. The only one! Things were falling into place and it felt good. There was no turning back now - only going forward! By tonight Ashley would be home, in their home. Dillon looked at the clock. *"Better get your ass in gear McCabe."* She told herself.

* * *

Ashley was thrilled that it was six o clock. She was tired of fielding questions from Rhonda about what happened with Dillon. Although Ashley trusted Rhonda, she always kept her personal life inside the home. Even when she was with Gia. *Ugh!* Ashley thought. She wasn't looking forward to facing Gia. She knew it had to be done. Ashley's cell phone rang, startling her.

"Hello." She said softly.

"Is this that sexy, gorgeous, doctor who works at Mount West L.A.?"

Ashley giggled. "Why, yes it is. How can I help you?"

"Well, you see Doc, I met the most beautiful woman about five weeks ago."

"Oh?" Ashley smiled.

"And now it's like………… I can't even explain it, I just want to be with her. She makes my heart race, and I break out in a sweat. I can't breathe. I think I may even need mouth to mouth."

"I see. Well, you're in luck. I do make house calls."

"You do?"

"Yes. Just make sure all of your clothes are off when I get there……… ya nut!" Ashley laughed.

"How was your day?"

"Long. How was yours?"

"Well, most of it was spent missing you, but I did manage to get some stuff done."

"I missed you too, Spit."

"Are you on your way?" Dillon asked.

"To the condo, yes."

"You sure you don't want me to meet you?"

"No, I need to do this on my own."

"I understand."

"Thank you."

"You can thank me later."

"Trust me, I plan to, and for a very long time to come." Ashley smiled.

"I look forward to it."

"Me too. Oh! I almost forgot. Rhonda wants us to come over for a BBQ on Saturday. And Mom and Dad called. You're in! Daddy loves you!"

"Your folks are great."

"Ok, sweetie, I'm here. Oh, did you want me to pick dinner up?"

"Nope it's waiting for you when you get here." Dillon said.

"I won't be long."

"Call if you need me." Dillon offered

I will. I love you, Dillon McCabe."

"You too, Doc."

Ashley hung up the phone. She took a deep breath and got out of the car. She looked around and didn't see Gia's truck. Maybe she would luck out.

She unlocked the door and walked into the condo. It felt strange. Like it was never her home.

"Hello? Gia?" She looked around. Nothing.

She walked into the kitchen. Everything was hers, but she didn't want it. The past needed to stay right where it was. She took a few of her favorite coffee mugs and the cereal bowl that belonged to her grandmother. She remembered how Gia would always tease her about the bowl and pretend to drop it. She went around grabbing a few knick-knacks here and there. She went to her bedroom and unlocked it. Pity she had to keep it locked now, but she didn't trust Gia or the slime that followed her home.

She found an empty gym bag and started to put her things in it.

She heard the front door open. She knew who it was.

"Hey Ash? Is that you?" Gia's voice came from the front of the condo.

"Yeah, I'm back here." Ashley yelled.

Gia dropped her things and walked back to Ashley's bedroom. "Hey, what's up?" Gia said looking around.

"Sit down. I need to talk to you."

Gia took a seat on the edge of the bed.

"I'm moving," Ashley got out. She looked Gia in the eye.

Gia chuckled. "You're joking, right?"

"No, Gia, I'm not."

Gia searched Ashley's eyes. She could tell she was serious. "Why?"

"Why? Gia come on, our whole relationship was a farce."

"Gee thanks." She looked at her.

"You know what I mean. Sex isn't the foundation of a relationship."

"But I thought you and I could try again, Ash. I can change."

"No. There is no way we could ever go back."

"Where are you moving to? Who with, that Saliva chick?"

"Gia! Her name is Dillon. And yes, I'm moving in with her."

Tears started to well up in Gia's eyes. Ashley was stunned. She had never seen Gia cry before. She didn't know if this was the real thing or just another ploy.

"She's my soul mate and I am very much in love with her."

"From one weekend?" Gia shot back.

"Gia, I knew it from the second our eyes met. We belong together."

"What about the condo?" Gia asked wiping tears from her cheek.

I don't want it. I'll sign it over to you. I'm only taking what I need, the rest is yours."

They looked at one another. Ashley just kept thinking of Dillon, and the fact that she would be waiting for her when she got home.

Gia tried to kiss Ashley one last time. Ashley kissed her on the cheek.

"What can I say?" Gia looked at Ashley.

"Nothing."

Gia looked around. "Well then, good luck, Ashley." Tears were now streaming from her face. "I gotta go." She left Ashley's room and ran into hers. She slammed the door.

Ashley took a deep breath. Tears were now coming down her cheeks as well. She didn't think Gia would have taken it this way. She continued to pack the things she wanted and left the rest of her old life there at 4C.

* * *

Dillon heard Ashley's car pull up. Her heart started to race. This was the day that would officially mark the start of their lives as partners together. There was no turning back now. A smile came across Dillon's face. She grabbed the single rose and a white jewelry box off the table. She ran to the door hiding the rose and box behind her back. She opened the door for Ashley, who stepped inside. Dillon could tell at once that Ashley had been crying.

"Welcome home, Doc." Dillon smiled as she gave the rose to Ashley.

"Thanks, sweetie." Ashley looked at Dillon and fell into her arms. "Just hold me please."

"Forever." She put her strong arms around her.

Ashley devoured Dillon's essence. She focused on her heart beating. They just needed time to be.

Ashley relaxed in her lover's arms. She took a deep breath.

"You ok?" Dillon finally broke the silence.

"I am now." Ashley snuggled closer.

"Dinner's ready if you're hungry."

"No, not really." Ashley looked into Dillon's eyes. "At least not for dinner." She slowly smiled at Dillon. She took her by the hand and led her into the bedroom.

Dillon kissed her as she slowly peeled off Ashley's clothes. She kissed her and slowly moved her to the bed. Ashley watched, her eyes fixed on Dillon's,

Dillon reached down and started to stroke the inside of Ashley's thighs. Ashley shivered with delight as Dillon's strong hand moved over her.

Dillon quickly found Ashley's swollen clit. Ashley arched her back as Dillon teased Ashley, lightly caressing her wetness.

Ashley wanted her lover deep inside her. She wanted to know that Dillon loved no one but her, and that there would never be another.

"Pleaseeee," was all that Ashley could get out. Her breathing was becoming shallow as the volcano deep within her started to reach the boiling point.

Dillon knew what Ashley wanted. She stroked down on Ashley once more and went inside her lover.

Ashley was ready to explode.

Dillon moved deep inside... She could tell Ashley was on the verge of release.

She pulled out a bit, then went in teasing Ashley. "I'm here baby, come to me," she whispered in her ear.

Ashley moaned as Dillon worked her body into a screaming frenzy.

Ashley could no longer hold back the eruption that came from within, her body stuttering as Dillon stayed inside her, their eyes, still fixed on one another.

Dillon lay there holding Ashley.

Ashley turned to her lover and kissed her. "I love you so much."

"You too, Doc."

"I'm so glad to be here in your arms."

"Me too. ....Do you want to talk about it?"

"It was just harder than I thought. " Ashley fingered Dillon's chin.

Ashley told Dillon what happened, finally getting it off her chest and letting it go.

Dillon made sure she listened to Ashley. She wanted to hear every word. This time Ashley spoke of Gia differently... she truly was the past.

When Ashley finished, Dillon presented her with the little white box with red satin ribbon.

"For me?" Ashley smiled.

"Yep." Dillon smiled.

She watched as Ashley fingered the black pearl necklace that Dillon had given her. Since that night under the Milky Way, she never took it off. Ashley untied the ribbon and opened the box. There, inside, was a key. She looked at Dillon.

"It's a key to the house,..........our home."

Ashley smiled and kissed Dillon.

They lay there in each other's arms and drifted off into dreams of their future yet to come.

* * *

Dillon slowly rolled over. Yep, she was still there. She smiled. She softly reached for Ashley's hair and gently stroked it.

"I love it when you do that."

Dillon smiled; she moved up closer to Ashley and spooned her.

"I love it even more when you do that."

Dillon chuckled softly. "Did I wake you?"

"No. I couldn't sleep."

"Why not?"

"I guess I'm too excited. I just can't believe I'm actually here in your bed."

"Our bed. You know, I think we could be the poster children for uhaulin'"

Ashley laughed. "I know. To most people it would seem that way, but it feels different." She turned to face Dillon. "Doesn't it?"

"Way different. I couldn't ever have imagined I would find the one."

"I know. I knew it when I walked into your room."

"When I opened my eyes and saw yours, it was like something inside me just relaxed. It's hard to explain. I just felt like I was at home." She kissed Ashley. "I have a surprise for you too."

"You do?" Ashley sat up and grinned

"Yep." Dillon jumped up and quickly ran into the other room.

"Close your eyes!" She yelled from the hallway."

Ashley chuckled. She loved every minute she spent with Dillon.

"Are they closed?"

"Yes."

Dillon looked around the doorway. "No peeking."

"I'm not."

Dillon quickly jumped back on the bed.

"Can I open them now?"

"Yes."

Ashley opened her eyes and Dillon sat holding a guitar. She strummed it.

"What's this?"

"A guitar."

"I know that silly."

"More importantly, it's your guitar." Dillon grinned.

"It is?"

"I had your folks send it down." She handed it to Ashley. "Play something."

"I don't..."

"Please?"

Ashley strummed a few cords, then started to play a melody. She suddenly stopped.

"What's wrong?"

"That's all there is. I started to write it for..." She sat the guitar down and pulled Dillon to her. "I love you so much for doing this for me."

"I hope you finish that song, Doc."

"Maybe one day. Actually, Spit, there is something I would like to do today."

"Name it."

"Go for a ride."

"What kind of ride? Horseback?"

"No..."

Dillon grinned, "Ohhhh. You mean *that* kind of ride." She raised her eyebrow. "I so didn't know you were like this Doc. I have to say it's a little bit of a turn-on."

Ashley looked at Dillon.

The shade of red Dillon was now turning showed Ashley that she wasn't. Dillon was embarrassed. "I was joking."

"Uh huh."

"Couldn't you tell? Dillon started to become uncomfortable.

Ashley kissed her long and hard. "I can take that ride anytime. Take me on your motorcycle."

"Are you serious?"

"Yes."

"I thought you hated my bike."

"I don't hate it. Just maybe a little jealous of it."

"You? Jealous of my bike?" She laughed, "This I gotta hear! Why?"

"Just how you throw your leg over and settle in to the seat."

Dillon grinned; she kissed Ashley's neck. "Tell me more."

Ashley giggled as Dillon kept nibbling at her ear and down her neck. "The way you grip those handlebars and start it up."

"That makes you jealous?"

"It's just the relationship you have with it."

"You're right. I love my bike. But not half as much as I love you!"

"So you'll take me?"

"I didn't say that."

"Why not?" Ashley sat up and looked at Dillon.

"I don't think you'd like it."

"Stop joking." Ashley lightly pushed Dillon.

"I'm not. It would mess up your hair."

"I'd wear a helmet."

"Oh, helmet hair, even worse."

"Spit!" What is going on here? It sounds like you're trying to avoid taking me out on your bike."

"No, it's not that."

"Then what is it?"

Dillon looked in Ashley's eyes. She remembered the promise she made to her father. She wouldn't take Ashley on the motorcycle. She sighed.

"What? Tell me Dillon, please?"

"Doc, I promised your father that I wouldn't take you on my bike."

"You promised him? When?"

"The day I met your folks. He was grilling me, and he made me promise that I wouldn't take you on my bike."

Ashley looked at Dillon with her mouth open.

"I swear, Doc, he did."

"No, I believe you, I just can't believe he would do that to you."

Dillon kissed Ashley. "I'm sure glad that's settled. So what do you want to do today?"

"Ride your bike."

Dillon rolled her eyes. "Didn't we just go over this?"

"There's something you should know about me."

"Uh oh."

"I don't let anyone, anyone, tell me what to do."

"Yeah, but this is your father."

Ashley stared at Dillon

"And he – "

She continued to stare.

Dillon looked at the fire that was coming to Ashley's eyes. She slowly pulled back the covers and got out of bed. "I'll meet you in the garage."

* * *

"No it's three down and one up." Dillon rolled her eyes.

"OK, OK. Don't get all crazy on me." Ashley looked frustrated as she sat on Dillon's bike.

"Doc, these are the gears. Like a stick shift."

"I know. I got it. One down and three up."

Dillon put her hand over her face. She took a deep breath and exhaled. She looked at Ashley and smiled. "Sweetie, why don't I drive till you get the hang of it?"

"No! I don't want to be on the back of your bike! What's next a t-shirt that says Honk if the Bitch Falls Off?"

Dillon laughed. She smiled at Ashley. She could tell she was in for it with this one! She had a lot of spunk backed with a whole lot of pride. She slid on behind Ashley, and moved up close. She put her hands on Ashley's thighs. "I think I can show you better this way." She said.

Ashley loved having Dillon so close to her. She arched her back and started to rub up against Dillon's chest.

"Umm, ok, now it's three down," she moved her hand to the inside of Ashley's thigh and pushed on it three times, "And one up." She squeezed. "You think you got it?"

"Maybe you should show me one more time." Ashley said, breathing a bit more heavily.

"Three down." She pressed, "And one."

Ashley took Dillon's hand and moved it to her crotch.

Dillon felt the enormous rush of heat come over her.

"Like this?" Ashley started to rhythmically rub up against Dillon's hand.

"Oh yeah, umm, that's good." Dillon took her free hand and started to caress Ashley's breast.

Ashley quickly got off the bike and got back on, now facing Dillon. She grabbed her and kissed her hard. She quickly started to unbutton her jeans.

"We should go back inside." Dillon said, in between kisses.

"Haven't you ever done it on your bike?"

"No, can't say that I have." Dillon leaned Ashley back onto the gas tank. She slowly put her hand into Ashley's jeans,

7

2 YEARS LATER............................

Ashley had taken the day off. She wished Dillon had too. It was a big adjustment for Ashley to be with a firefighter. Their schedules were sporadic. She would be on for three days and off for four. They could be out having dinner and Dillon would have to leave. Ashley hated when Dillon was away. She looked forward to the days when she came home and found Dillon waiting for her. She tried to push that out of her thoughts! Today was their second anniversary. Ashley had planned a wonderful meal, and wanted to talk to Dillon. She went to the doctor's and brought back all of the information. She and Dillon talked last year about starting a family. Ashley now wanted to put that plan into motion. She knew that she and Dillon would be together forever. Now it just seemed like the right thing to do.

Ashley looked at her watch. Dillon had called while she was out and said she would be late. She was at a gas station fire and it was a mess. She sat down in the living room and took out one of the pamphlets on artificial insemination. She knew the deal, pick a donor, go to the clinic, then whip out the turkey baster and..... either you're pregnant or not. The doctor did tell Ashley there were other ways, including doing it in your home. She liked that idea.

She heard the door unlock and Dillon stepped in. She smelled like gas and smoke She was carrying a bouquet of yellow roses.

"Happy Anniversary, Baby." Dillon grinned.

"Happy Anniversary, Dillon." Ashley took the roses. She tried to kiss Dillon but the fumes were intoxicating.

"Pee-ew."

"I showered at the station twice. Let me clean up again and I'll be right out." Dillon smiled, "unless you care to join me?"

Ashley smiled. She was so happy and still very much in love with Dillon. "You go get cleaned up and I'll finish dinner. You must be starving."

"Yeah, I am." Dillon said.

While Dillon showered, Ashley made a carpet picnic in front of the fireplace.

Dillon came out in her sweat pants and t-shirt. "Mmm. Smells good." She smiled. "And the food doesn't look bad either."

They laughed.

Dillon took Ashley in her arms. "Thank you, for two wonderful years."

"Thank you, too." She kissed Dillon. "The food is getting cold."

"Maybe, but other things here are just heating up." Dillon smiled at Ashley.

They kissed again. This time Ashley broke it off. "C'mon, I'm starved."

Dillon took a seat on the floor next to the coffee table. She leaned against the couch. Ashley handed her a plate. Chicken, green beans, garlic mashed potatoes.

Dillon was in heaven. She wolfed down her meal and went back for seconds. She could tell that Ashley was anxious about something.

"How was work today?" Dillon asked.

"I decided not to go in."

"You ok?" Dillon asked.

"Yes, I'm perfect."

"Just needed the day off?"

"Yeah, something like that." Ashley grinned. She grabbed her guitar from the side of the couch.

Dillon grinned. "You?"

Ashley nodded. "You're the reason I could finish it. So that's what it's called. 'You're the Reason'."

Dillon watched, mesmerized as Ashley played and sang the beautiful words. Tears filled her eyes.

Ashley finished. They stared at one another.

"Doc…" Dillon dried her eyes. She kissed Ashley. "I…I..don't know what to say…you're amazing."

"I love you." Ashley smiled. "Time for presents."

"There's more?"

Ashley reached behind the pillows on the couch and pulled out a gift-wrapped box. She sat it in front of Dillon.

Dillon grinned. She loved presents. She sat on the couch next to Ashley.

Ashley loved to watch Dillon open presents. She ripped through the wrapping like a little kid on Christmas morning.

Dillon tore through the wrapping. It was the watch she had been eyeing for months. "Oh, Doc." She smiled at Ashley. " I can't believe you found a Lucky Dog. It's awesome!" She kissed Ashley. "And so are you." She opened the box and put it on.

"It almost took an act of God, but I got hold of the artist, and she had one left." Ashley said.

"Hey it fits!" Dillon held her arm up proudly. She kissed Ashley again. She reached into her pocket and pulled out a box. She looked at Ashley. "I didn't know what to get you. What do you get the woman that has given you one hundred percent happiness for two years now? Doc, I never thought I could love anyone to the capacity I love you, every day. When I look into those beautiful blue eyes, you make me fall deeper." She got down on one knee. "Doc, I want to be with you, forever." She opened the box.

Ashley gasped. To her surprise, it was a ring set. She had wanted rings for the longest time, but Dillon kept putting it off.

"Will you marry me?" Dillon picked up the ring for Ashley and placed it on her ring finger.

Tears started to fall from Ashley's eyes as she looked at the beautiful platinum and diamond wedding band.

"I love you." Dillon choked out.

Ashley grabbed Dillon and kissed her. "I'm so lucky to have you, Dillon." She picked up the matching band and took Dillon's hand. "Dillon McCabe, it is an honor to be loved by you. You are my heart, and you complete me. I never thought it was possible to be loved like you love me. I cherish you and our love every day, and when I look into those big brown eyes of yours, it reminds me of our commitment and that we'll be together forever." Ashley slid the ring on Dillon's finger. "It would be an honor to be your wife." She kissed Dillon long and hard. She remembered her other surprise. "Oh, I forgot. There's something else."

"Boy, I'll say." Dillon took Ashley into her arms and nuzzled her neck.

Ashley giggled as she freed herself from Dillon's tight embrace.

She pulled some papers from the couch.

Dillon laughed. "What else you got hiding in there?" She leaned back against the couch and put her legs up. Ashley crawled onto her lap.

"I went to the doctor's today."

"Babe, are you sure you're ok?" Dillon asked.

"Yes, I'm fine. In fact, better than fine." Ashley smiled.

"Then, what's up?" Dillon looked confused.

"Spit........... let's have a baby!"

Dillon froze. *A baby?* Dillon's mind raced. They had talked about kids in the future when they first met, but she never thought it would ever come to be. "A baby?" Dillon looked at Ashley.

"Spit. I got checked out at the doctor's and she said I'm healthy. Look. I got all the information on artificial insemination. We just have to pick the donor, we bring the sperm back here, we make love and-"

"Hold it, hold it, Doc!" Dillon interrupted. "A baby? Are you sure?" She looked at Ashley.

"Yes, a baby. I'm positive.......... you don't....."

"No, it's not that. I just...." Dillon looked around.

"What sweetie?" Ashley caressed Dillon's cheek.

"I.......... just don't know...if I would make a...good parent."

"Oh Spit, you'll make a wonderful parent. I knew it when you wanted to adopt Ben. You're warm, and kind, and a big kid yourself. Our baby will be raised in a house of love by two mothers that have so much to give."

Dillon smiled. *Ashley was right. Still, there were other things.* "Doc, there's a lot to consider. You have to quit working, we would need a bigger place,......"

Ashley put her finger to Dillon's lips. "I can work while I'm pregnant, and after the baby's born. I'll have a few weeks off."

"A few weeks? I don't want to leave my child with some total nut case while we're at work. One of us needs to be here."

"I'll quit." Ashley said.

"Just like that?" Dillon looked at her.

"Yes." Ashley looked back.

Dillon took Ashley back into her embrace. There was no way she was going to start a fight.

"Doc, I'm all for a baby. A little scared, but all for it. I know you love what you do. We'll work something out. Together."

Ashley kissed her firefighter. "We'll have nine months to figure it out."

"OK, when do we start?" Dillon grinned.

"Well, I have this for us to read." She reached back behind the couch and pulled out a notebook and more paperwork.

Dillon laughed. "Are you going to pull the baby out of there next?"

Ashley laughed and climbed back onto Dillon's lap. For hours they read all the information Ashley brought home. They looked through the book of donors. Ashley said she wanted the baby to look like Dillon.

"Well?" Ashley asked. "I like number 161."

"Yeah, he's ok." Dillon flipped the pages. "What about 211?" She read: "Firefighter, 6'3" 240, BA, into sports, the outdoors, and music. No family history of disease, no mental illnes in his family tree. What do you think?"

Ashley took the book and tossed it to the ground. "I think we have a winner." She kissed Dillon passionately.

Dillon scooped Ashley into her arms and stood up. "Let's go practice."

Ashley giggled as Dillon carried her to the bedroom.

8

The timer was ticking as Ashley and Dillon waited for the results of the in-home pregnancy test. Dillon was a wreck. They had been trying for four months to get pregnant, but it just didn't happen. Dillon looked for a new home to keep her mind off things.

Ashley was beginning to give up hope. Maybe having the miscarriage when she was with Gia screwed up her insides? The doctor assured her that she was in perfect health. She wanted to have this baby for Dillon in the worst way. She could tell how discouraged Dillon became every time they didn't conceive.

Both sat on the edge of the bed, waiting. Dillon took Ashley's hand as tears began to fall.

"Aww c'mon, Doc, don't cry." Dillon put her arm around Ashley.

"I have to be pregnant. I just have to be!" She started to cry harder.

Dillon embraced her. "Hey, now, easy. It's alright." She held Ashley tight.

"Spit, we've been trying for months now! I don't know what's wrong with me."

"There's nothing wrong with you. Remember, the doctor said it was hit and miss with this."

"I just don't want you to hate me." Ashley blurted out.

"Hate you? I could never hate you."

"But what if I can't get pregnant?"

"Then we'll buy a dog."

Ashley laughed a little.

"We can always adopt. Don't you see? It's all about us. We're a team. I would love for us to have a baby, but you're the most important part of my life." She wiped the tears from Ashley's face.

The timer went off. They stared at each other.

"Spit.........I can't..........." Ashley whispered.

Dillon kissed her again and stood up. She walked into the bathroom. She prayed that the test was positive. She couldn't handle Ashley going through this anymore. She slowly removed the stick and looked at it.

Ashley held her breath as she waited for Dillon.

"Oh, hell yeah!" Dillon screamed as she came out of the bathroom waving the stick. "Hot damn, Doc, you did it!" She pulled Ashley to her and kissed her.

"Are you sure?" Ashley was stunned.

"Take a look at the stick! Positivo!"

Ashley smiled as she took the stick from Dillon. "You think it's right?"

"Honey, yes, I think it's right. You got my baby in there!" Dillon leaned down and kissed Ashley's stomach. "Hi baby, it's me, Spit!"

Ashley laughed.

"Hey we need to call your folks." Dillon smiled as she picked up the phone.

"No, wait, Spit. Don't."

"What?"

"I just want to make sure, cause of what happened before." She looked at Dillon. "I'll go see Doctor Brannagan tomorrow."

"We'll both go." Dillon said with a reassuring smile. She took Ashley in her arms. "I love you so much."

"I love you too." She settled into her lover's embrace. "Will you hold me for awhile?"

"Forever, Doc. Forever."

* * *

Dillon's leg bounced rapidly as she and Ashley waited in the reception area. It was crowded and Dr. Brannagan squeezed them in for a test. She knew what a toll this was taking on both Dillon and Ashley.

Ashley kept putting her hand on Dillon's knee. "You're making me sick. Please stop doing that." She whispered.

"Sick? See you must be pregnant, Doc. You're having sickness."

"Ms. Wilkerson? The doctor will see you now," the nurse called out.

Dillon jumped up, and Ashley grabbed her hand.

"Come on babe, it'll be ok." Dillon smiled.

They walked into the doctor's office. Ashley sat while Dillon paced. Her heart was racing. She kept thinking of all the things they still needed to do. She wanted a big home with a yard, a swingset, and a dog. Dillon also thought about selling her bike and buying a car. She had yet to see a child car seat on the back of a bike.

"Dillon, will you sit down please. You're making me nervous."

Dillon took a seat next to Ashley. "What's taking so long?" She looked at her watch.

"I know it seems like forever. Are you scared?"

"Excited." She winked at Ashley. "We're having a baby. I can feel it. You?"

"Just scared it will be another false positive."

They both looked at each other as Doctor Branagan came in. She was carrying Ashley's chart.

"Well hello ladies." She nodded to Ashley and Dillon.

She was so business like, Ashley was starting to feel uneasy. She took Dillon's hand.

"Your pregnancy test came back." She opened the file and read. "Congratulations. You're pregnant." She smiled.

Alright!" Dillon yelled. She kissed Ashley on the cheek.

"How far along?" Ashley asked.

"About eight weeks."

Ashley looked at Dillon. "How can that be?"

"It happens sometimes. False positive readings, and all the while, you are."

"Is it a boy or a girl?" Dillon asked.

The doctor laughed. "I'm good Dillon, but I'm not that good. We will have an ultra sound in a few weeks." She looked in the chart. "This should put your due date around early January."

Dillon's face went blank.

"Dillon?"

"We're having a baby, Doc." She smiled at Ashley. "Thank you, Dr. B, you're a miracle worker" Dillon shook the doctor's hand.

"It's my pleasure, but I can't take all the credit." The doctor smiled. "You both had a little something to do with it. If you'll excuse me."

"Thank you." Dillon and Ashley said in unison.

The doctor smiled and walked out.

"Wow." Dillon smiled.

"We did it! We're going to have a baby!"

The two screamed with delight. Ashley kissed Dillon.

* * *

Dillon unlocked the door and opened it for Ashley. She stepped in and waited for Dillon to lock up. She fell into Dillon's strong arms.

"I am sooo happy sweetie." She smiled.

"Me too, Doc. This will be awesome. Our own family."

"Can we talk about something?" Ashley asked.

"Of course."

Ashley was about to tell Dillon what was on her mind when the phone rang.

"Better get that." Ashley said.

"No, the machine will pick it up. Talk to me."

"It's ok, it can wait." Ashley ran to the phone and picked it up. "Hello. Hi mom, how are you?"

"Hi dear," the happy familiar voice said on the other end.

"Mom, where's Daddy?"

"He's right here." Mary said.

"Tell him to get on the other phone. We're gonna get on speaker phone." Dillon pushed the button.

"Hello?" Bill said.

"Hi, Daddy. Dillon and I are on speakerphone."

"Hey Spit, how are you?" Bill asked.

"Fabulous, Dad, and you?"

"Doing good, thanks."

"Hello, Dillon dear." Mary chimed in.

"Hi, Mom." Dillon smiled. She loved talking with Ashley's parents.

"Guess what?" Ashley asked excitedly.

"What Sweetie?" Bill asked.

"We're having a baby!" Dillon and Ashley screamed into the phone.

"What? Are you sure?" Bill asked.

"Oh my heavens. For real?" Mary said.

"Yes! Yes!" Ashley said. "We're eight weeks."

"Oh my Lord. I'm gonna be a grandmother."

"Yes you are!" Dillon chuckled.

"Is it a boy or a girl?" Bill asked.

"We don't know yet. We have to get an ultrasound in a few weeks."

"I bet it's a girl." Mary said.

"Could be a boy too. Chip off the ol' block." Bill grinned.

Dillon's pager went off. She looked down and saw the 911."Sorry Mom and Dad. I have to run. Love to you both."

She ran into the other room and grabbed her helmet. She walked back into the living room as Ashley was just hanging up.

"I have to go. It's a 911 call." She kissed Ashley long and tenderly. "I love you, Doc." She smiled and leaned down to Ashley's stomach. "I love you too, baby." She kissed Ashley stomach.

Ashley looked into Dillon's eyes. She didn't want her to go. "Be safe Dillon." She tried to hold back the tears. "I love you."

"I'll be home soon. Tomorrow we'll start looking for a new home, and we'll go buy a bunch of baby things." She kissed Ashley again.

Ashley watched as Dillon mounted her bike and drove off. Tears came easy to her. She hated this! She hated Dillon's job. It scared her. It was too hard to sit around and wait to see if this would be the day she didn't come home. Ashley couldn't bare the thought of raising this child by herself. She had decided that when they got pregnant she would ask Dillon to retire from the department and find another job. It was a hard decision, but Ashley knew she had to ask Dillon to make it. Ashley lay down on the couch and picked up the phone. She dialed the hospital's number. She needed to talk to Rhonda.

* * *

A massive barricade was in place when the engine rolled on the scene. From the information they received, they knew it was a meth lab. A woman from inside the house called 911 when she noticed her boyfriend's violent behavior getting worse. There were two other men inside, a woman and two children. There were also enough chemicals throughout the house to blow up the neighborhood. Now the crazy man was running around with a lighter in one hand and a machete in the other.

Dillon and Jack suited up and stood by. Unless there was a fire or a rescue, it was all in the police department's hands. They had the SWAT unit placed around the house.

"It's a waiting game now." Jack looked at Dillon.

"I hate these calls when there are kids inside." Dillon shook her head.

"This is gonna be a long one." Jack said.

Dillon looked at her watch. "I need to get back to Ashley." She said.

"She ok?' Jack asked

"Crap! Man, I didn't tell you. We're gonna have a baby." She grinned.

"Oh man, that's great news, Spit! Congrats to you both." Jack smiled.

"Thanks," was all Dillon could get out when the explosion happened. The force knocked Dillon and Jack to the ground.

Dillon turned on her air pack, and grabbed her pike pole. She and Jack ran to the back of the house. Two women came running out of the house screaming,

"My babies! Save my babies!" She saw Dillon and ran to her. "Please, somebody, save my babies!"

Dillon moved quickly into the house, not waiting to see if Jack followed her in. The smoke was becoming thick and black. More chemicals were starting smaller explosions throughout the house. She saw two bodies lying in the room. She moved around quickly, dodging flying debris, not sticking with the procedures she had been taught.

She heard a scream from the other room and ran to it. There in front of her were the two children, coughing and crying. A man was standing in a pair of boxer shorts between the children, holding a machete.

"I ain't going to prison!" he yelled at Dillon.

"I ain't a cop!" she yelled back. "Let the kids go!"

"I told you, I ain't going to prison!"

"Look pal, this place is ready to come down on your head. I don't care if you want to stay here or not! Let the kids go!"

He stood, staring at Dillon. "Take em' and get the fuck out!" He yelled.

Another explosion went off as part of the wall collapsed. The children screamed louder, panic overcoming them.

Dillon took a step forward and took one of the kids safely in her arms. She felt the burn, then the pain. It was a sharp deliberate pain. She looked down to see that the machete had sliced through her jacket and blood was streaming out of the cut on her forearm. She scooped the other child up and headed out. As she turned the corner to head for the door, part of the roof collapsed behind her. She fell to the ground.

"C'mon kids." Dillon yelled as she regained her footing and made it to the door. She passed the kids off to waiting EMTs and fell to the ground.

Jack and Eric came rushing to her and dragged her back, away from the house.

"Anyone else in there?" Jack asked.

"Not anyone who's alive." Dillon coughed. Jack gave the all clear as the fire department started their assault on the home.

Eric helped Dillon out of her jacket and promptly cut her sleeve away. "Hey, that's a nice one, Spit."

"You know me Eric, I'm your job security." Dillon tried to make light of her injury.

"Well my friend, it looks like you get to go for a ride. You need to be sewn up."

Jack came back over and looked at Dillon's arm.

"I'll live." Dillon smirked. "How are the kids?"

"A lot of smoke and they're scared, but they'll be fine."

"Let's get you to the hospital."

"I'm OK, Eric." Dillon argued.

Jack looked at Dillon. "Spit, shut up and get your ass in the ambulance."

Dillon knew that when Jack gave her the look, it was no use.Besides, it was department policy.

Eric and his partner got her on a stretcher and sat her upright. She was angry. She needed to get back to Ashley.

"I'll come by and pick you up," Jack yelled to her as they wheeled her around the side of the house. The crew had the fire under containment. As they wheeled Dillon to the ambulance, camera crews and news media tried to get past the police barricades to get to Dillon. She wasn't thrilled to see photographers snapping photos of her as she lay on the stretcher.

Dillon's captain led the Police Chief over. "McCabe, that was some fine work you did in there, saving those kids." Her Captain shook her hand.

If he only knew that she didn't follow procedure, she would be getting suspended, not commended. "Thank you, sir." Dillon grinned.

"Ms. McCabe. Did you see any of these men inside?" The Police Chief held up three photos.

Dillon took one of them. "Yeah, that's the guy who cut me."

"Cut you?" The Police Chief asked.

"Yeah, I went in and found the kids in the back room with this guy. He had a machete in his hand."

"Did he say anything to you?"

"I told him to let the kids go. All he kept saying was that he wasn't going back to prison. He said it a couple of times. He finally said to take the kids. When I reached for one of them, he took a swipe at me. He wasn't coming out, sir, so I left with the kids. I couldn't go back in there. The place was disintegrating. There were two other dead bodies in there, both male. It was probably them."

"Thank you for your time Ms. McCabe," the Police Chief said, and walked away. Dillon's Captain stayed behind. "McCabe, when you're felling better, I want you to see me. We need to talk."

Dillon wasn't sure, but she thought she saw a smile crack the face of her Captain.

Eric and his partner lifted the gurney into the ambulance and they drove off.

* * *

Ashley turned the T.V. off. She saw the breaking news story and knew that Spit's crew must have been the one called to the scene. She started having bad cramping feelings. She knew the feeling. She had had it when she miscarried.

"There's no way I'm losing this baby," she said out loud. She lay on the couch and did some deep breathing exercises. The cramping subsided.

The door unlocked and Dillon entered. She saw Ashley on the couch.

"Doc. You should be in bed."

Ashley looked at Dillon, her arm in a sling, blood on her shirt.

"Oh my God, Spit, you're hurt." Ashley got up from the couch.

Dillon put her arm around Ashley. "I'm fine babe, but it looks like I get a few days off."

"What happened?"

"Just a little nick. I'll be OK if you just stay close to me." She hugged Ashley tighter.

Ashley thought it best not to worry Dillon about her cramping.

"I love you so much Doc. And our baby." Dillon kissed Ashley.

"I love you too. Come on, lets get you out of theoe clothes and into the shower."

They worked slowly together as Dillon told Ashley what happened.

They lay in bed together. Dillon on her back, Ashley tucked in safely into Dillon's chest. Neither could sleep. Ashley thought about what Dillon had told her earlier. What if that crazy man stabbed her in the heart? Dillon wouldn't be here, and she wouldn't be in her arms.

Dillon felt Ashley shake. "Are you cold?" Dillon asked.

"No" was all Ashley could say before she started to cry.

Dillon held her tighter. "Hey now, why the tears?'

"Spit, I can't do this anymore." Ashley said through the tears.

Dillon froze. *Couldn't do what?* She thought. *Was Ashley falling out of love with her?* "Can't do what?" Dillon choked out.

"I've been wanting to tell you for some time now, but I just couldn't."

"Doc.... you can tell me anything. You know that."

"I'm scared. We're going to have a baby and all I can think about is what if you don't come home? What if there's a backdraft? What if that freak tonight killed you? I just can't take it anymore."

Dillon tried to calm Ashley down. "I'm a good firefighter. I know what I'm doing. I'll be OK."

"How can you say that? You don't know what will happen."

"What do you want me to say?" Dillon said. "Yes, I could have gotten killed tonight. But I didn't. I could just as easily have stepped off the curb and got hit by a bus. It's my job, Doc. What do you want me to do?"

"Quit. I want you to quit your job. I want our child to be raised by both its parents."

"I'm not going anywhere. I'm too ornery to die. Besides, I still have a whole lot of love left to give you and our kid." Dillon kissed Ashley.

"Promise me you'll think about it? "

"Doc...." Dillon couldn't talk. The most important person in her life wanted her to give up the one thing that meant the most to her.

* * *

Dillon heard Ashley get up. She lay there, still not wanting to face her. She was awake all night thinking about Ashley's request. She loved Ashley so much and now with a baby on the way, she could understand Ashley's fear. She felt Ashley slide back into bed and come up close.

"Are you awake, sleepy head?" She kissed Dillon's back.

"Morning," Dillon said flatly.

"How's your arm?"

"You know me, no big deal."

"OK. So tell me then, why won't you face me?"

Dillon sighed and rolled onto her back.

Ashley looked at Dillon. She was never one to hide her emotions very well.

"This is about last night isn't it?" Ashley asked.

"Doc, I know my job makes you nervous, but I can't just up and leave it. It would be like me asking you to quit being a doctor cause you might catch some strange disease or get stuck by a needle."

"I know how much it means to you."

"It's my life." Dillon looked at her.

Ashley was silent. Dillon just put her job before her family. It was hard for Ashley to take. She grabbed Dillon's sweatshirt and threw it on. She got out of bed.

"I thought we were." She walked out.

Dillon knew she hurt Ashley's feelings. "Damn you!" Dillon said to herself out loud. "What the hell were you thinking, McCabe?" She got out of bed and went after Ashley.

She saw Ashley sitting in the back yard on their swing. It was Ashley's favorite thinking spot, although now her thoughts turned to tears.

Dillon walked over to her and sat down. Ashley fell into Dillon's lap, crying uncontrollably.

"Doc....I'm sorry...I'm a jerk...please don't cry."

Dillon brought Ashley up to her and wiped the tears from her face. She sweetly kissed her. "You and the baby are my life." She kissed her again. "I'll look for another job."

Ashley looked at Dillon. "You will?"

"If it means that much to you, of course I will."

"Oh Spit!" She kissed Dillon. "I love you so much."

"You too." Dillon smiled. She was glad that her decision made Ashley happy. Too bad it was breaking her heart.

Dillon knew that she, Ashley, and the baby were a team and that, within the team, compromises would have to be made. It was a fifty-fifty partnership and Dillon and Ashley had made a vow to one another. Dillon took that vow very seriously.

The rest of the morning Dillon was online looking for new homes, while Ashley was on the couch going through baby books.

"Hey, how about down by the beach?" Dillon looked at Ashley.

"Honey, that's way too expensive."

"We could afford Santa Monica."

"Eww." Ashley made a face. "I don't like it down there."

"There's always Malibu." Dillon offered.

"Did you win the lottery and forget to tell me?" Ashley looked at her.

Dillon shook her head and chuckled. "Hey, what about a real move?" Dillon smiled.

"A what?"

"A real move. Like to Laguna or San Diego."

"Dillon, you're crazy. Remember, we work in L.A."

"So, there are other hospitals and there are other............places for whatever it is that I'll be doing." She looked at Ashley. "How about by your folks?"

"The valley? You want to move to the valley by my parents?"

"Sure it would be great for the baby to know his or her grandparents."

"For the baby yes, for me, I'd go crazy."

Dillon came over and sat next to Ashley. She put her arm around her and brought Ashley to her chest. Dillon softly stroked her hair.

"Wow. This is all so much, Spit."

"I know, pretty overwhelming."

"We're doing the right thing, aren't we?" She looked at Dillon.

"I know we are. When our son or daughter gets here, you'll see all of your doubts will be erased."

Ashley smiled. "How come you always know the right thing to say?"

"I don't know, it just feels right". Dillon shrugged. "OK, let's get back to house hunting."

Ashley held Dillon. "Nooo... can't we just stay here?"

"Doc, there's no room in here as it is for two."

"Let's add up. Or on." Ashley looked at Dillon.

"Let's start a new life, the three of us, in a new home. We can find a home with some land, maybe get some horses. You know we both love them."

Ashley stopped to think about it. They both did love horses and how great would it be to have them in the backyard. It would be wonderful for the baby to get into horses.

"Alright, horses it is."

"Are you sure? I mean this isn't some hormone enraged decision now is it?"

"No." Ashley rolled her eyes.

"Cool...horses it is."

9

For the next three months Dillon and Ashley spent all of their free time looking at houses. If Dillon liked one, Ashley hated it. If Ashley liked it, Dillon didn't.

They wanted to stay in the area. Ashley was being courted by a general practitioner to partner with. She could finally have a normal schedule, be home every night, and have the weekends off. He was so impressed with Ashley's credits, he was willing to wait until she had the baby. It was a dream come true.

Dillon looked for other jobs, but nothing could come close to the rush of being a firefighter. She would talk to Jack about it for hours. He understood Dillon's decision, but wasn't pleased with it. She had promised Ashley that she would retire from the force after taking the year off for personal leave. She had accrued enough time that she would still be paid.

"How about arson investigator?" Jack suggested.

Dillon thought about it. "Something to think about." Dillon smiled.

Johnson came up and sat next to Jack at the table.

Dillon frowned. She knew that when he was around all he wanted to do was start trouble.

"Damn McCabe, you trying to make us look bad?" Johnson looked at her.

Dillon looked at Johnson. She knew what was next. He always had to attack her sexuality. No matter how subtle it was, Johnson knew how to push Dillon's buttons.

"Don't go there, Johnson." Jack warned.

"Come on, Jackson. If my wife knew that McCabe was planning to retire after her little gal pal gave birth, she would want me to do the same."

"Here's a thought. Don't tell her." Jack said.

Johnson ignored him.

"So, on behalf of all us non-dyke's in the department, I just want to thank you."

"Maybe, if you knew how to show some respect to a woman, you wouldn't have that problem." Dillon looked at him.

"You saying I don't know how to treat a woman?"

Dillon stood up. "Just let me know if you need me to show you."

Jack snickered as Dillon winked at him.

She turned to leave as Johnson stood up. He thought about going after her, but remembered the last time he cornered Dillon McCabe. He couldn't sit for a week. She was physically strong, but he knew how to get into her mind. "Let me know if your woman wants to be with a real man.Mine doesn't strap on!"

Dillon froze. Anger came to her fast. She could care less if the little prick tried shit with her. But when he started in on Ashley, it was the last straw.

Jack stood up and stepped between them. They had both been warned before. "C'mon you two." Jack raised his voice. "We're a team damn it! Act like it!"

Johnson just smiled at Dillon. He wanted her to throw a punch. He wanted her ousted from the department.

Dillon looked at Jack. "He's not worth it," Jack said under his breath.

She knew he was right. She backed off just as her Captain came into the room.

He cleared his throat. "Did I interrupt something?" the Captain looked at Dillon.

"No sir. Nothing." Jack smiled and went back to his seat.

The Captain looked at Johnson. "Just congratulating the new daddy on the baby." He raised his eyebrow to Dillon and grinned. He walked away.

"McCabe, can I see you in my office?" The Captain said. He turned and walked away with Dillon following behind him.

The Captain's office was always cold. No matter what time of year it was, or how the weather was outside, it was the frozen tundra in there.

Dillon was always amazed at how clean the Captain kept his office. He was always the "show by example" kind of guy. Dillon liked him. He was always fair.

"McCabe, I wanted to make sure you were OK."

"You mean Johnson? Sir, he's just an ass with a big mouth."

The Captain chuckled. He liked Dillon. She was a great firefighter and a wonderful role model.

"No, I mean you. You seem sort of pre-occupied these last few months. Nervous about the baby?"

Dillon looked surprised. She never talked about her personal life. It must have been Johnson flapping his trap. "Yeah, a little, among other things."

"You need to talk?" The Captain gave Dillon a warm inviting smile.

"Well, sir… I kind of promised my…um………wife that I would retire before the baby comes."

"And you don't want to?"

"No, sir, I don't. It's like having to choose between the two, and soon to be, three things I live for." Dillon looked at her Captain. "I love what I do."

The Captain grabbed Dillon's file from his desk. "You're good at it. McCabe. I've been going over your file. Seven years you've been here. It's quite impressive."

"Thank you, sir. I think." Dillon wasn't sure what the Captain was up too.

"Let me get to the point. You could retire, and you're entitled to do so. However, I think that it would be a waste of talent. Although, I would regret losing someone like you on my team, I think I may have the answer you've been looking for."

"Really?" Dillon looked up.

"There'll be an opening at the Fire Academy in March. I think you would be a great teacher, Spit."

Dillon smiled.

"Of course, you'd have to take some classes. It's paid for by the department. I just think if one Dillon McCabe can make such a difference.... then the hundreds who would be taught by you could only be better."

"Wow. Sir...I don't know what to say? Thank you."

"The pay is about the same, but the hours are better. You take some time and think about it, and of course, you'd have my highest recommendation."

"Thank you, sir." Dillon stood and shook the Captain's hand.

"You're welcome, McCabe. Please let me know your decision by week's end."

"I will, sir. Thanks again." Dillon left the office.

Dillon found Jack and told him the news. He seemed happy. She would still be close by and could see her friend, but more importantly, she could be home every night with Ashley and the baby.

After her shift ended, Dillon stopped at the store. She bought some flowers for Ashley and some sparkling apple cider. This was a time for celebration.

She thought about a lot of things on the way home, mostly about their baby. She wondered what it would be. Was there a slim chance that he or she would look like her? They both chose at the ultrasound not to know. Dillon secretly wanted a little girl. Someone she could share things with, like Ashley. Dillon smiled. A little Ashley! That would be incredible. With those beautiful green eyes. Oh yeah, this kid already had Dillon wrapped around its finger.

As Dillon came to a stop at the signal, her pager went off. She looked down and saw the 911 call with the hospital's number on it. "Doc!" She said as she put her bike in gear and headed for the hospital.

Ashley was already in a room, when Dillon arrived.

She was lying in bed, hooked up to all kinds of machines. Rhonda was taking her vitals when Dillon walked in.

"Doc?"

"Oh Spit. I'm glad you're here." She took Dillon's hand.

"Are you ok? Is the baby?" Dillon looked at Rhonda.

"Everyone seems to be fine. Little miss 'over-do-it fainted'."

"I'm OK. I just got a little queasy."

"She's been running around like a chicken with her head cut off! Taking Dr.Cannon's load. She needs to rest."

"Is the baby...."

"The baby is fine. Ashley started having labor pains and cramping. The doctor is on her way."

"Honey, we're fine, really. Just a little tired." Ashley smiled.

"I'll be back. You keep an eye on her." Rhonda said.

Dillon half smiled. She was so grateful to Rhonda and her family. She was such a good friend to Ashley. Dillon loved her husband Daniel, and the boys would always go crazy when Ashley and Dillon would come over for a BBQ. She would play basketball or football with them.

Dillon leaned over and kissed Ashley.

"Mmm. That's more like it. I'm glad you're here." Ashley smiled.

"Where else would I be?" Dillon smiled back.

"I think we're gonna have a soccer player." Ashley giggled.

"We are?" Dillon chuckled.

Dillon took Ashley's hand and placed it on her stomach. The baby was kicking like crazy. Dillon could see the discomfort in Ashley's face.

"Talk to your child, will you?" Ashley gave Dillon a look.

Dillon leaned over to the spot where the baby was kicking. She put her lips to Ashley's stomach. "Hey, Little Bit, it's me, Spit. Go easy on mom, ok? She's had a rough day."

In an instant the baby stopped kicking. Dillon beamed. She was already bonding with her child. She would talk to the baby every morning, when she came home, and before they went to bed. When she was on duty, she would have Ashley hold the phone to her stomach so she could talk to them.

Ashley was amazed at the baby's response to Dillon. "I think the baby missed you." Ashley let out a sigh. It was the first time the pain subsided all day.

"Doc, I have some news." Dillon was excited. "I got called into the Captain's office today."

"Were you fighting with Johnson again?"

"I always fight with him, he's a homophobic asshole."

Ashley shook her head and laughed.

"Anyway, the Captain heard about our situation and wants to recommend me for an academy teacher."

"What?" Ashley smiled.

"He said he's very impressed with me and thinks I'd be a great academy teacher."

"Really? Oh baby, that's wonderful."

"Yeah, and he said the pay was about the same and I'd be home every night and on the weekends."

"What more could you ask for? Spit, I love you."

"You too." Dillon looked into Ashley's eyes.

Ashley started to drift off. Dillon sat with her and stroked her hair. She was thrilled that Ashley was happy with the news. Too bad she wasn't. The more Dillon thought about it, the more she tried to adjust to her feelings. This was the best thing for them. Still, Dillon knew that she could never not have that desire every time she heard a siren.

* * *

Ashley was bored. She had been placed on limited activities and was going out of her mind.

Spit was still working at the department, and Ashley missed her when she was gone. She made time to chat with her college friends. She couldn't believe that she let them talk her into a baby shower. To make matters worse, they were having it at their house.

Ashley and Dillon loved their new home. It had three acres and was in between Malibu and the Valley. It was a four bedroom, single story ranch house. It had a huge kitchen for Ashley and a four-car garage. Dillon bought a truck. Not the typical mom mobile Ashley thought, but it was a start.

They had decided to wait until after the baby was born to buy horses. Plus Dillon wanted to fix up the backyard.

* * *

Dillon insisted on going with Ashley and Rhonda to register for baby gifts. Ashley spent over an hour trying to talk Dillon out of going. She hated shopping with her. Dillon was always indecisive, three hours to pick out a pair of jeans; a whole day spent at the outlet stores in the dessert, only to have her buy one pair of shoes and a watch.

Ashley sighed. She tried to relax and just see the good in this. At least Dillon was interested and wanted to be a part of everything. *Gia would have never had done the things Dillon did! Good Lord!* Ashley stopped herself. *Where did that come from?*

"You getting excited Doc?" Dillon took Ashley's hand and kissed it.

"Sweetie, it's just a baby store. You didn't even need to bother coming. Rhonda and I could have handled it."

"That's the third time you've said that. I'm starting to think you didn't want me to come."

"Don't be silly! I just know how much you hate shopping."

"True, but this is shopping for *our* baby! And, we're not just shopping at some slacker discount store.No ma'am, this is the mega baby-o-rama store! She grinned at Ashley.

Rhonda looked at her watch.

"We're on time!" She heard behind her. Rhonda looked up.

"Oh Lord, she brought Spitfire. Heaven help us all."

"Hey Auntie Ro-Ro!" Dillon said and gave her a hug. "Ready for the baby-o-rama shop-a-thon?"

Rhonda chuckled. "Good question. Are you?"

"Yes ma'am, ready and waiting."

"Baby, grab a cart and we'll meet you inside."

"One mega shopping cart coming up." Dillon ran to the carts.

"I thought you weren't bringing her with you?"

"She insisted."

Rhonda gave Ashley a look.

"It's her baby too…It'll be fine, you'll see." Ashley smiled.

"Famous last words."

After Ashley and Dillon registered, the clerk handed Dillon a bar-code scanner. They were instructed to scan any items they wanted to appear on the baby registry. Before the clerk could finish, Dillon was on her way down aisles scanning almost anything she saw.

"Dillon, please slow down." Ashley pleaded.

Dillon stopped and turned to Ashley. "Do you know how cool this thing is? If you want a pacifier, boom, you got one." She scanned the item. "You want two, bam, ya got two!"

Ashley shook her head and laughed.

Rhonda smiled, "Looks like you have two kids."

"Honestly, I've never seen anyone so excited over a baby store."

"It's not just a baby store, it's a mega baby-o-rama!" Rhonda reminded her.

Ashley laughed. "Dillon wait!" She wheeled the cart over to Dillon, with Rhonda in hot pursuit.

"Four car seats? Dillon, we don't need four."

"Yes we do."

Ashley looked at Rhonda.

Rhonda quickly threw her arms up. "Hey, don't put me in the middle of this one."

"Thanks a lot Rhonda!" Both Dillon and Ashley said in unison.

"Sweetie, hold on a sec." Ashley composed herself. "Why do we need four car seats? We aren't having quadruplets. One baby, one car seat."

"Doc, one for you, one for me, one for your folks, and one for auntie Ro-Ro. Four." Dillon smiled proudly.

"We'll always be in the same car Dillon, and if we're not, only one of us can have the baby at a time. If Rhonda is sitting, we can leave the car seat with her." She could tell Dillon was a bit deflated.

"But I do think it's a great idea to get one for Mom and Daddy."

Dillon smiled. She kissed Ashley on the cheek. She held up the bar-code gun.

"Even better!" Dillon took off toward the car seats.

"Have I thanked you again for coming?" Ashley hugged Rhonda.

"Hey, you can't pin this one on me *Doctor Wilkerson*. I warned you not to get involved with her."

Ashley looked at Dillon, then back at Rhonda. "I'm so stinkin' glad I didn't listen to you."

Rhonda laughed. "Me too...besides, it's nice to see how much her heart is totally into this. Could you just imagine if you were having this baby with Gia?"

"Oh My God. I can't believe you just said that."

"Chill Ash, I was just making a point."

"No, on the way over, I was thinking the same thing."

"Girl? What on earth are you thinking of Gia for when you have that?"

They watched as Dillon tried to juggle three car seat boxes.

"I wasn't thinking about Gia, I was comparing. I have no clue why; Gia couldn't even wipe Dillon's shoes.

"Amen!" Rhonda confirmed.

They walked over to Dillon.

"So which one did you decide on Spit?" Rhonda asked.

"Well, I've narrowed it down to three - the duckies, the fishies, or the horsies."

Ashley laughed.

"What?" Dillon looked puzzled.

"Nothing. I just think it's so cute the way big tough Spitfire is saying, 'duckies', 'fishies', and 'horsies'."

"I'm going to ignore the fact that you said that. OK, so, which one do you like?"

"The ducks." Ashley said.

"Definitely the fish." Rhonda commented.

"Great, and I like the horses. So in the event of a tie, the baby gets the final vote."

"Say what?" Rhonda looked at them.

"Yeah wait till you get a load of this one. I've seen it and I still don't believe it myself!"

"OK hands on." Dillon instructed.

Rhonda followed as both Dillon and Ashley put their hands on Ashley's tummy. Dillon bent down. "OK baby, it's me, Spit. I'm here at the baby store with Mommy and Auntie Ro-Ro."

"You're kidding right?"

"Sssh!" Ashley shot Rhonda a look.

"OK, we have three cars seats here. You tell o' Spit which one you want kiddo? First we have mommy's favorite, duckies."

Nothing happened.

"Ok, next is Auntie Ro-Ro's fishies."

Still nothing.

"Finally, we have Spit's favorite, horsies!"

The baby started to kick wildly.

"Ouch!" Ashley grabbed Dillon for support.

Rhonda stood there looking in amazement and bewilderment. "I don't believe it."

"I know. There's no explanation for it. I guess it's the tone of Dillon's voice."

Dillon beamed as she put the car seat in the shopping cart, and went on.

"Ok that was just..."

"Magical?" Ashley offered.

"Freaky was more of what I had in mind, but call it what you want."

"Told you she was somethin' special."

"Uh huh. Well look at Ms. Special."

Ashley turned to see Dillon trying to figure out a machine. "I never said she was perfect, just special."

"You tend to Ms. Special, and I'm gonna find the bathroom. Excuse me."

Ashley walked over to Dillon, who now had the box open and spare parts scattered on shelves.

"Hi."

"I don't need any help thanks." Dillon said quickly. She looked up and saw Ashley. "Oh hey, Doc." Dillon's cheeks flushed.

"Whatcha' got there?"

"Doc, this kind of blows me away." Dillon whispered.

"It does?"

"Ssssh, keep it down. Where's Rhonda?"

"Bathroom." Ashley whispered back, "Why are we whispering?"

"I can't believe that they would have these things here."

"What are you talking about?"

"You know, look. They have toys here."

Ashley started at her lover. "Sweetie, it's a baby store, of course they have toys."

"Nooo... adult toys." Dillon held up the item in her hand.

Ashley burst out laughing.

"Doc, it's not funny. There are kids who come into this store."

Ashley continued to laugh. She kissed Dillon softly on the cheek. "Baby, that's a breast pump, not a sex toy."

Dillon quickly turned five shades of red. "I'm such a dork, huh?"

"You're not a dork. You're adorable."

"So you use this to…"

"Express milk, in case we're out or something. Dillon you didn't know about a breast pump?"

"Do I look like I would know? This is the first time I've been in a baby store."

"Do you know how cute I think you are right now?" Ashley smiled.

"It's cause I'm holding a breast pump, isn't it?"

Ashley giggled and kissed Dillon softly on the lips.

"So tell me you're not going to put that on the registry?"

"Well, we do need one."

"Then we'll buy this one." Dillon quickly put the pump back into the box, and in their cart.

Rhonda walked up, holding a bottle of water. "Here, thought you may need this."

"Oh, thank you." Ashley quickly took a drink.

"You have to see the wall borders on aisle six. They have some adorable ones."

"Lead the way." Ashley felt a strong kick. "Whoa!" She stopped.

"You OK Doc?" Dillon moved to Ashley.

"Yeah, just a good kick." She took a deep breath. "OK, I'm good. Lead the way to the adorable borders. I want to see them."

Rhonda took the cart. She looked down at the box, then back at Dillon.

"It's not a sex toy, it's a breast pump. Haven't you ever seen one before?" Dillon looked at Rhonda, her defense up.

"I have…. have you?" She raised her eyebrow at Dillon.

Dillon cleared her throat. "Of course. Don't be silly… OK, where did you say those border's were?"

"Spitfire, you're blushing. I don't know why, but by the shade you're turning, I'd say it was a good one."

Dillon grabbed Ashley's hand and walked over to aisle six. Rhonda followed, chuckling to herself.

* * *

Dillon helped Ashley to the couch.

"Oh yeah, that feels good."

"You overdid it, you need to slow down."

"I'm OK." Ashley gave Dillon a reassuring smile.

"Well, you rest, and I'll bring in our loot from the baby store."

Ashley closed her eyes. The baby was taking a lot out of her. She never thought to say anything to Dillon. She would be fine. Dillon had read every nutritional book known to man, and put both she and Ashley on a nutritious eating plan. For the most part, Ashley would adhere to the plan, but at work, she would sneak a candy bar in every now and then. She chuckled when she remembered Dillon finding the Payday wrapper in her pocket. She got an hour-long lecture about the dangers of high fructose corn syrup, and peanut induced allergies. She would just have to be more careful next time not to get caught!

Dillon laid out everything to show Ashley.

"We bought that much stuff?" Ashley looked at the living room.

"We needed it."

"What's that? Ashley pointed.

"What?"

"That, over there."

"The car seat babe, don't you remember?"

"I know what it is Dillon, but where is the one with the horses?"

"Oh… well I was thinking, sometimes the other mommy does know what's best, and you did like those cute little ducks, so…."

"Come here you." Ashley pulled Dillon to her and kissed her.

"All this for ducks?" Dillon grinned, she kissed Ashley again.

"I love you so much."

"You too, Doc."

Ashley played with Dillon's hair.

"Sorry I was such a dork today."

"You weren't. I'm real glad you came, Dillon. I had a lot of fun."

"Yeah, it was fun. Guess I lost my head though." She looked around.

"Our friends will have a tough time getting us something, but, oh well."

"Who knows, maybe someone will buy us a horsey car seat." Dillon smiled.

Ashley giggled. She kissed Dillon again. "You make me so happy."

"That's all I ever want to do." Dillon could tell Ashley was tired. "You close your eyes and rest. I'll put this stuff away." She kissed Ashley's forehead.

Dillon watched Ashley for a moment. She could fall asleep so fast. She looked upward. "I know I've thanked you before, but I'll thank you again for bringing her to me. I don't know what I ever did to deserve her love, but I treasure every second I spend with that woman, and with our new baby on the way."

Her eyes started to well up. She started to pick up some of the items. "Oh." She looked up again, "It's a breast pump… but I guess you knew that." Dillon picked up the rest of the things and put them away.

* * *

Ashley looked at her watch. Her parents were due to arrive any time. Her mom and Rhonda agreed to help out and Daddy would hopefully keep Spit busy. Ashley felt uncomfortable and Dillon could feel it.

Dillon had the party catered so Ashley could just relax. She decorated the place and really went all out. Ashley knew that there would come a time she would have to come out to her friends. She figured that by now, most would have drifted off and started their own families. Now she was having fifteen of them in her house and they would all be asking questions.

Dillon walked in and saw Ashley standing at the closet. "Tough choice, Doc?" Dillon came up behind Ashley and started to rub her stomach. It always relaxed her.

She laid her head back on Dillon's chest and took a deep breath. "Spit, I really don't want to do this."

"Aww, how come?" She kissed Ashley's neck. "Ya don't want to see all your friends?"

"It's not that. I just don't want all the questions that are gonna come from today."

"Oh. That explains why all the photos of us are missing."

Ashley could tell that Dillon was hurt. "Spit, don't take it that way."

"You're embarrassed. It's OK. I understand."

"I could never be embarrassed of you! I just know how they are."

"They're just jealous, Doc. You have a great job, you've moved into a totally cool home, we have probably the most beautiful baby in the world on the way, and I might add, out of pure modesty of course, you have an incredibly cute and sexy wife, who loves you very much.

Ashley chuckled. She turned and kissed Dillon. "I am so lucky to have you." She smiled.

"We're both lucky." Dillon said. "But, I can see what this is doing to you, so I'll get lost while they're here."

"Spit, are you sure?"

"Yeah, I can go to the movies or something."

"Daddy will be here, just hangin' out in the garage. That way I can have you close."

"I can do that." Dillon kissed Ashley.

The doorbell rang. "You get dressed, I'll get the door." Dillon turned to the door.

"You know you look mighty cute in those coverall's and bandana!" Ashley called after Dillon.

Mary and Bill hugged and kissed Dillon as they came in.

"Oh Dillon dear, the place looks great." Mary said.

"Thanks. I had to hide the last of the moving boxes, but I think it's pretty good. Ashley is getting dressed. Make yourselves at home. The eggs are cooked and in the fridge ready to be deviled. I'll take your bags to the room."

"That's silly. Let Bill take the bags so you can get dressed for the shower."

"Ah, well, I'm not going to the shower." Dillon looked at Ashley's parents.

"Why not?" Bill looked at Dillon.

"Well Dad, Ashley is a little uneasy about what her friends may think, so I thought it best to hide out with you for the duration of the party."

Ashley's parents exchanged glances.

Ashley came out of the bedroom.

"Hi Mom, hi Daddy." She smiled.

"Well look at you!" Bill smiled.

"Please, I look like a beached whale."

"How are you feeling?" Mary asked.

"OK. I'm just wishing that this party was over."

"Excuse me." Dillon half smiled and took the bags to the guest room.

"Sweetie, Dillon just said she wasn't coming to the shower, is that true?"

"Mom, please. I'm just not in the mood to field all the questions from my friends, that's all. Besides, Spit understands."

"If these so-called friends are that petty, I don't think I would be wanting them as my friends."

"Daddy, that's not fair," Ashley whined.

"And what you're doing to Dillon is? Excuse me. I'm going to join my daughter- in-law." Bill kissed Ashley, then walked away.

"Mom, please don't look at me like that! She understands."

"Of course she does, she loves you. She would do anything for you."

"I know."

"Well, I know that I didn't raise a daughter that would put her partner through such a thing. This is her child too. She's entitled to be at this shower just as much as you."

Ashley watched as her mother stormed off. The baby kicked her hard. She rubbed her stomach. "Don't you start on me too."

Dillon ran the sand paper over the handmade crib she had made for the baby. She had planned on surprising Ashley with it for Christmas.

Bill opened the door balancing a plate of food and two bottles of water.

"Did ya get the boot too?"

"Yeah, it's just a bunch of squealing, giggling, silly girls in there. Who needs 'em right?

Dillon looked at Bill.

"Oops. Sorry Spit, sometimes I just forget, you know?"

Dillon smiled. "Apology accepted. It's OK. Really. I've never been accused of being a squealing, giggling, silly girl." She went back to sanding the crib.

Bill watched for a moment. "Can I ask you something?"

"Of course, Dad. What's on your mind?"

"Well, I'd like to think of myself as kind of hip, and up with the times and all, and both Mary and myself understand about Ashley's choices and being with you, but… I was just kind of curious about the girl with the girl thing, you know, how the whole thing works…you know?"

Dillon blushed as she tried to contain her laughter. "Umm, well… it's just like you and mom. There's friendship, communication, love, partnership…it's the same really…just minus a few parts." Dillon smiled awkwardly.

"And you love my crazy daughter after all she's put you through?"

"Oh yeah, more than anything in this life."

Bill searched Dillon's eyes. There was nothing there but love for his daughter. "You can honestly tell me that loving Ashley is easier that any three alarm fire you've fought?"

Dillon chuckled. "I wouldn't say easier, but defiantly worth it!"

Bill reached for the plate. "Deviled egg?"

"Thanks." Dillon popped one into her mouth. "Mmm. Wow, these are fantastic!"

"Yep, Mary still has the knack."

"I'll say."

"Speaking of knacks Spit, this crib is amazing. Look at the craftsmanship! Who taught you how to do this?"

"My grandfather."

"He must have been a master. He taught you well. Look at that dovetailing."

"Thanks." Dillon smiled proudly.

Bill continued to watch Dillon work, the sounds from the party inside echoed into the garage. Dillon stopped. Her heart sank. She wanted so much to be in there with Ashley, celebrating their child with her friends. *Maybe one day,* she kept telling herself.

Bill put his hand lightly on Dillon's shoulder. She sighed.

"I thought so." Bill said, "This is eating you up, isn't it?"

Dillon put down the sandpaper. She hesitated for a moment, then turned to Bill.

"I don't care if Doc doesn't want to be out at work. It's fine with me and all, but I thought she would at least be comfortable enough in her own skin, and with who she is, to be honest with her friends."

Bill scratched his head. Maybe it was time for his daughter to have a serious wake-up call. "Say Spit, would you do an old man a favor?"

"Sure."

"How about you go in there and try to get Mary to give up some more of those eggs? I'm sure she'll run me off if I go back in."

Dillon laughed. Not giving it a second thought, she walked into the house. She stopped when she heard Ashley and the other's talking about baby names, and cute men.

"You know Ash, I know this real cute tennis player at the country club. He would be so right for you."

Rhonda looked at Ashley. "Am I missing something here?" She whispered to her.

Dillon frowned. She quietly walked through the hall and into the kitchen. Mary was busy slicing the cake.

"Pssst, is the coast clear?" Dillon asked, peaking around from the side of the fridge.

Mary jumped. "Oh Dillon, honey, you startled me."

"Sorry, Mom. I just came in to get some more of those deviled eggs for Dad, but that cake sure looks good."

Mary cut two slices and put them on plates.

"How's it going in there?"

"It's a nice party…would be nicer if *both* my daughters were there.

Dillon smiled and kissed Mary on the cheek.

"Where do you keep the extra paper towels?"

"I'll get them for you."

Dillon squatted next to the sink to retrieve a roll of paper towels, when Terri walked in.

"Mrs. Wilkerson, Ashley said to bring the camera, she's gonna start opening…and who is this?" She smiled as she spotted Dillon's backside.

Dillon froze, not sure of what she should do.

"Oh,. that's…that's the…plumber," Mary tried to cover.

Terri walked over to Dillon and looked down. "Nice…assets."

Dillon rolled her eyes.

Mary quickly took Terri's arm. "Let's not keep Ashley waiting dear."

"OK." Terri got out before Mary pulled her away.

Ashley opened her gifts while Rhonda wrote down what everyone gave her. As she was getting close to the end, she looked up and saw Dillon in the kitchen. She felt her heart sink. She couldn't think of anything else except what her father had told her. She was so proud to be loved by Dillon. Why should she care what any of them thought?

She grabbed a box that had no card. "Who is this from?" She looked at her friends. No one answered. She opened the box to find a cute stuffed Pony. Ashley giggled at the fuzzy toy. She looked in the box and saw the card. She opened it. Tears came to her eyes as she read the card. *"You have given me many things in the two plus years we've been together, two stand out. First, your love. I treasure it every second of every day. Second our child. This is a gift from God for us coming through you. I will look in and our child's eyes every day and see you in them. What more could I ever ask for? I love you. Spit."*

"Ashley, are you OK?" Rachel asked.

"No. No, I'm not." She wiped her tears away.

Dillon watched.

"I have something I need to say. First off, thanks for coming to my shower. But more importantly, I want you to meet someone." She walked to the kitchen.

"Doc....no, what are you doing?." Dillon whispered.

"Something I should have done three years ago."

"It's OK. You don't have to do this."

"Yes, I do. And I also need to apologize to you for being an incredible ass! I don't know what I was thinking, putting my so-called friends lame prejudices in front of someone I love so very much. I'm so sorry, Spit." She kissed Dillon softly. "I love you so much."

"I love you too…thanks, Doc."

"What could you possibly thank me for?"

"For finally being you."

Ashley smiled. "It feels good. C'mon, there's some people I want you to meet,"

Ashley said with a smile.

She took Dillon's hand and came back into the living room. "Ladies, I'd like you to meet Dillon Spitfire McCabe."

Various women nodded and said hello. Dillon shyly nodded back mumbling hello.

"OK, here it is, plain and simple." Ashley looked around. She saw the smile on her mother's face.

"Dillon and I are...partners. We're having this baby."

A few gasps were heard. Most were in shock.

"Well, it's about damn time." Rhonda smiled.

"You and the plumber? No way!" Terri said.

"No, Dillon isn't a plumber." She pulled the bandana off Dillon's head. *She* is a firefighter. My firefighter.

"You mean, you two are……." Rachel looked up.

"In love? Yes, we are." Ashley smiled, and looked at her mother.

Mary gave her daughter the thumbs up.

"We've been together for almost three years and plan on being together for a long time to come. Right, Spit?"

Dillon looked at Ashley and smiled.

10

The next month was hectic. The baby was almost here, and Christmas was only five days away.

Ashley's parents were coming to visit. Doctor. Brannagan pushed up Ashley's due date to the first week of January. Ashley's folks decided to stay and help out for a while.

Dillon was still at the station. Her job had been put on hold. She decided to take a year's leave when the baby came, then decide what she wanted to do. Ashley reluctantly told her to stay on at the department until the academy position became available. Dillon was guaranteed a job, but it could take up to three years.

They had fully moved into their new home and loved it.

Dillon brought home a 10-foot Christmas tree. Their vaulted ceiling in the family room was perfect for it. She also came home with a carload of ornaments, for the tree and the house.

Ashley laid on the couch, reading cards while Dillon decorated the tree.

"Look hon, a card from Ben."

"Really?" Dillon smiled.

"He says Merry Christmas and he hopes that everything goes well with the baby."

"He's a special little guy."

"Ten is hardly little, Spit."

"He's ten already? We're getting old."

"Speak for yourself." Ashley looked at Dillon.

Dillon smiled. "You're still beautiful." She leaned over Ashley and kissed her.

"You better say that." Ashley chuckled. "Hey maybe we could go see Ben and his family after the baby is born."

"That would be great. I miss seeing him."

"Me too. Now shut up and kiss me again." Ashley pulled Dillon to her and started to kiss her when the doorbell rang.

"Must be Mom and Dad." Dillon smiled. She went to the door to let them in.

Ashley was glad they were coming down. She had a hard time with Dillon leaving her side when she wasn't working. For the past two weeks she was with her twenty-four-seven. It was driving Ashley crazy. She couldn't buy Dillon any presents except online when Dillon was in the shower, or went to work.

Mary and Bill came in and hugged their daughter.

"That tree is a beauty!" Bill grinned.

"Dillon picked that out. Four hours and eight tree lots later! She wanted the baby to have the best."

They chuckled.

"You should have seen her. She took each ornament out of the box and sat down and explained what each one looked like to my stomach" She smiled.

"I think Dillon's excited." Mary said.

"Oh yeah. She's going to be a great mom. Sometimes I have to pinch myself to make sure this is all real. It's too good to be true."

"Well, it is real." Bill grinned. "And soon we're going to have us a grandson!"

"Or daughter." Mary added.

"And we'd know that if someone would have wanted to find out the results of the ultrasound."

Ashley felt it. She wasn't sure if it was just the baby moving around or what. She took a deep breath.

"Pumpkin?" Bill looked concerned.

"I'm fine. I swear all this kid does is kick, kick, kick." She smiled at her father to ease his concern. Ashley knew that the baby wouldn't wait until after Christmas to make its debut.

That night, Dillon and Bill fired up the BBQ. Though it was cool outside, it was still nice enough to heat the grill up.

Dillon and Mary did the dishes while Ashley and her father wrapped some gifts.

"Dillon, the house is just so beautiful and festive. It's coming along nicely." Mary smiled.

"Well, thanks, Mom, but your daughter is the one with the eye for design."

"Oh come now, take a little bit of the credit."

Dillon chuckled. "Well, we try to make it a joint decision."

Mary grabbed Dillon's arm. "Dillon, I want to thank you."

"Thank me for what?" Dillon looked at her.

"For making our daughter so very happy." She hugged Dillon.

"It's easy with the kind of woman like Ashley. You have a wonderful daughter'."

"Thank you, dear." Mary smiled.

"Well, thank you and Dad for letting me love her. May I add that I have never seen two parents who love their daughter and are so very understanding."

"Dillon, we didn't understand at first. It did take some time, but in the end, it came down to love and Ashley's happiness...that's what counted. For awhile, Dad and I didn't think Ashley would ever be happy, but with you, we truly believe she is."

Dillon smiled. What amazing people to have in her life. So warm and caring.

Mary hugged Dillon again. She remembered telling her folks that she was gay, and the yelling and accusations that came with it. She could see the fear in her parent's eyes. The unknown was a scary place. It was scary for Dillon as well. Too bad they never got to meet Ashley.

Ashley waddled into the kitchen.

"Doc, what are you doing up?"

"I need to move around. This baby is kicking the stuffing out of me."

Dillon walked over to Ashley and put her lips to her belly. "Hey now little bit, settle down. Spit's here."

Just like that, the baby settled down.

"See." Ashley said looking at her mom. "This baby will do anything for her."

Mary smiled. "If I recall correctly, I think you gave me a couple good ones when I carried you."

"Mom, I don't know how you did it." Ashley looked at Dillon. "The next one comes out of you."

Dillon froze. Mother tried to cover her laugh with a dishtowel. Ashley started to chuckle too. Soon all three women were sharing a good laugh.

* * *

Christmas Eve was very peaceful.

Ashley and her mom made cinnamon logs out of leftover pie dough. Dillon loved them! Last year she made herself sick on them. But she still waited for the fresh cinnamon treats to come out of the oven.

Dillon and Bill were watching T.V. when Mary and Ashley came in carrying a tray of cinnamon logs and glasses of milk.

A grin came over Dillon's face. "Oh yeah," she said as she took the tray from Ashley and sat it in front of her. She took a warm cinnamon log and bit into it, slowly letting the pie dough, cinnamon, and sugar, swirl around in her mouth. "Great as ever, ladies." Dillon smiled.

Ashley handed Dillon a glass of milk, then froze. The sharp pain was intense. She looked at her watch. This was the third one about twenty minutes apart. She knew the baby was on its way.

"You ok, Doc?" Dillon asked.

"Fine, sweetie. The baby is just sitting on my bladder. Excuse me." Ashley walked down the hall. She made it into the bathroom, when another contraction hit. She cringed as she tried to shake it off. *Who's idea was it to have natural child birth?* She felt the wetness as her water broke... she went to the door.

"Spit! Spit!" Ashley yelled.

Dillon jumped to her feet and raced to the bathroom. "Doc?"

"Honey, its time." Ashley looked at her.

"Time for what?" Dillon looked blankly. "Oh shit!" Dillon blurted out.

She went into overdrive. This was it. She ran back out to Ashley's folks. "It's time! This is it!" Dillon yelled. "Mom can you? While I?"

"Go get changed Dillon. I'll get Ashley."

"I'll get the car." Bill said.

"Thanks, Dad. The keys are by the door." Dillon ran off to the bedroom. She slipped on her jeans and a t-shirt. She grabbed her leather jacket and hunted for Ashley's bag.

"Doc? Doc?" She ran back to the bathroom. Ashley's mother was helping her clean up. "Where's the bag?" Dillon looked at Ashley.

"By the door Spit, where you put it."

Dillon ran off.

"Well, she's calm under pressure." Ashley giggled

"I can see that," Mother smiled.

Ashley was so glad her parents were here.

Dillon drove like a maniac to the hospital. She'd called Doctor Brannagan on her cell phone. The doctor told Dillon that she was on her way in and to stay calm and get Ashley there in one piece.

They took Ashley straight in while Dillon tried to fill out the paperwork. All she wanted was to be with Ashley.

"Dillon let us fill that out." Mary said. "She needs you to be with her." Mary's warm smile seemed to calm Dillon down a bit.

"Thank you. Thank you, both." She hugged and kissed them. "The next time I see you, you'll be grandparents." Dillon grinned. She ran to the elevator.

By the time Dillon scrubbed up and changed, Ashley was in a room, hooked up to monitors.

"Where have you been?" Ashley asked, trying to breathe through a contraction.

"I'm sorry, baby. I couldn't get past the wicked witch of the west. Good thing I saw Rhonda."

"I saw her too. She went to find you." Ashley breathed.

"This nurse kept questioning me, wasn't gonna let me in." Dillon leaned over and kissed Ashley." But I'm here now." She whispered in her ear.

"I'm glad." Ashley kissed Dillon again.

"Does it hurt?" Dillon questioned?

"Yeah, pretty much." Ashley was trying to be a good sport about it. It really hurt like hell.

"I was thinkin', maybe we should have a few more after this. What do you think?"

Ashley looked at Dillon. "You better be kidding," Ashley got out when a big contraction hit. She tried to breathe through it.

"You want me to have them give you something?" Dillon hated seeing Ashley in this much pain.

"No, I'm OK," she panted. "If I ever mention natural child birth again, you have permission to slap me." Ashley grunted.

Dillon rubbed Ashley's back. It always calmed her down. "Doc, I want you to know how much I love you, and how much our baby and your family mean to me." She kissed Ashley tenderly.

The wicked witch of the west came in armed with a disapproving scowl on her face. *Two women having a baby,* she thought. *What was the world coming to?* She took Ashley's vitals and checked her dilation. "Not too much longer." She looked at Dillon. "Are you two related?"

Dillon was just about to say something when the doctor came in.

"Well, I guess this is the moment we've all been waiting for." She smiled.

Dillon started to get a little nervous. This was all happening so fast. She was going to be a parent. A lifetime of responsibility, joy, pain, laughter and heartache. A true miracle. And it was all Dillon's and Ashley's.

Another contraction hit Ashley hard, making the monitor alarm go off.

"Looks like we're going to have us a Christmas baby." Doctor Brannnagan smiled.

Dillon got Ashley to breathe.

"Ok, Ashley, last chance for an epidural?" Doctor. Brannagan said.

"C'mon Doc.... take it." Dillon whispered.

"No," Ashley panted. "I said I was going to do this natural and I will."

Dillon looked at Doctor Brannagan and shrugged her shoulders. She knew that Ashley had a stubborn streak and when she set her mind to do something, it was best just to step aside and let her do it.

The nurse placed Ashley's legs in the stirrups, all the while with a frown on her face, glaring at Dillon.

"OK kids, it's time." Doctor Brannnagan got into position. "Ashley, I need you to focus on something and keep breathing. When I say push, lean forward and push for an eight count. Dillon, I want you to breathe with her and when she's pushing, support her back. OK?"

Dillon nodded.

"Ashley, on the count of three, lets push. One...two...three...push."

Ashley leaned forward and pushed. Dillon supported her. She took Dillon's hand.

"Spit, I'm scared. I don't know if I can do this."

"Doc..... this is the easy part. We still have to raise it!"

Ashley tried to laugh. The pain was increasing.

"You're doing good, sweetheart." Dillon encouraged.

"OK, Ashley, we need another push on three...one...two....three... push."

Ashley pushed again as Dillon watched wide-eyed.

Two hours later, it was 12:30 am, and Ashley was exhausted. So was Dillon.

She felt sorry for Ashley. She was having *their* baby and there was nothing she could do to help her.

"Ashley, are you ready to push again?" the Doctor asked.

"I can't." Ashley started to cry. "It doesn't want to come out."

Dillon chuckled and kissed the top of Ashley's head. "The baby just needs a little push and it'll be right on out." Dillon tried to comfort her.

"Why won't the baby come out doctor?" Ashley snapped.

"That's why we call it labor, I'm afraid. Come on, Ashley I need you to push again."

"Come on, Doc, we're almost there." Dillon said.

"No, I can't".... Ashley cried. "I just want to sleep."

Dillon bent down to Ashley's belly and put her lips to it. "Hey baby, it's Spit. It's Christmas and we're all waiting for ya."

Ashley smiled. She knew she had to do it. She took a few deep breaths. "I'm ready."

"Alright, Ashley.... one.... two...three. Big push..........."

Ashley leaned forward and pushed with all her might.

"Great job, Ashley. We have the baby's head."

Dillon smiled.

"Now, just a couple more. Ready, and, push," the Doctor ordered.

"I can't, it hurts." Ashley cried.

Dillon leaned over. "I know you can do this. Just one more big one and our baby is here."

Ashley took a deep breath and pushed hard. Her body ached. The baby came out.

"That's it. You did it." Doctor Brannagan said, as she held the crying infant.

The nurse handed Dillon a pair of scissors. She looked at the doctor.

"Don't you want to cut your daughter's umbilical cord?"

"Daughter?" Dillon looked at Ashley. She was crying. "Doc, we have a daughter." Dillon leaned over and carefully cut the cord. She handed the scissors back to the nurse. She watched as the nurse started to clean the baby up.

"Spit." Ashley called to her.

Dillon walked up to Ashley and took her hand. "You don't mind a girl do you?"

"Are you kidding?" Dillon kissed Ashley. "Do you know how beautiful you look?"

"Please, I'm a disaster."

"No, you're not." Dillon smiled and kissed her again.

"Congratulations," the doctor said as she brought over their daughter and laid her on Ashley's chest.

Dillon couldn't take her eyes off of her. "Doc, she's perfect." Her eyes started to fill with tears.

"Do you have a name for her?" The nurse asked.

"A name? Oh shoot, we forgot about a name."

"Spit, if it's alright with you. I was thinking we could name her Zoë."

"After my...." She looked at Ashley.

Ashley nodded.

"Oh, Doc," Dillon choked on her words. She was so touched that Ashley would want to name their baby after her mother, a woman she had never met. "Zoë it is." Dillon smiled.

"Middle name?" The nurse asked.

"You pick this one." Ashley said as she caressed their new baby girl.

Dillon looked at the clock. It was Christmas Day. That was it! "Noel. Zoë Noel." She looked at Ashley for approval.

"Perfect." Ashley said in a slight daze. Zoë Noel McCabe Wilkerson."

Dillon leaned over to little Zoë, now snuggled close to Ashley. "Hey little bit, it's me, Spit."

Zoë smiled and wiggled. Dillon beamed.

"She knows you." Ashley giggled.

Dillon kissed Ashley softly on the lips. "Thank you, Ashley. I love you."

Tears came to Ashley's eyes. It was the first time that Dillon had ever called her Ashley. "I love you too, Dillon. Very much."

The nurse came and took the baby. "If you want to gather the family, I'll take her to the nursery window."

"Guess I have to go tell your folks, huh?' Dillon winked.

"Send them my love." Ashley smiled. Dillon watched Ashley as she drifted off to sleep. She went to find her parents.

* * *

Bill and Mary waited patiently.

Dillon finally came out. "Hey Grandma and Grandpa!" She hugged them both.

"Well?" Bill asked.

"Come on." Dillon smiled as she led them to the nursery window. "Ashley sends her love."

"How is she?"

"Exhausted, but fine." Dillon assured them. "She was falling asleep just as I left. She did it all natural."

"Oh my." Mary shook her head.

"They offered her an epidural, but you know your daughter."

As they reached the window, Dillon came behind them. "Mom, Dad, may I introduce your granddaughter, Zoë Noel."

"Granddaughter?" Bill asked.

"Yep, all seven pounds, fourteen ounces of her."

The nurse brought her up to the window.

"Dillon, she's beautiful." Mary smiled.

"My thoughts exactly." Dillon grinned.

"I think she looks like me." Bill said proudly.

"Oh, Bill." Mary shook her head.

"I can see that, Dad." Dillon agreed. "I know it's late. Why don't you go home and get some sleep? I'm gonna check in on Doc."

"OK dear. Do you need anything?" Mary asked.

"No, I have everything I'll ever need." Dillon grinned. She hugged Ashley's parents and went to find her.

Dillon stopped to talk to Rhonda in the hall. Rhonda was so happy for them. She told Dillon that Ashley was already in a room and that her blood pressure was a little low.

Dillon found the room and walked in. Ashley was asleep. She carefully walked over to her and gently kissed her forehead.

"Spit?" Ashley groggily opened her eyes.

"I'm here." Dillon kissed her again. "You get some sleep."

"Did Mom and Dad......." was all she could get out.

"Yes, they met Zoë. And they said to tell you that they love you."

Ashley tried to smile. "Zoë looks like you."

"Naw. She's beautiful....like you." She kissed Ashley again. "Merry Christmas."

She watched as Ashley drifted off to sleep.

Dillon walked back down to the nursery and watched Zoë. She too was fast asleep. Dillon couldn't sleep. Her mind was racing. She had so much she wanted to tell her little daughter.

Dillon went downstairs to wish Rhonda and Ashley's co-workers a Merry Christmas. She was already bragging about her new daughter.

She went to the cafeteria and grabbed a bite to eat, then went outside to watch the sunrise.

Ashley was sitting up nursing Zoë when Dillon came in.

"Merry Christmas to the two most beautiful women in the world." Dillon smiled.

"Merry Christmas, Spit. Mom and Dad called. They should be here soon."

"Great." Dillon smiled.

"Have you had any sleep?"

"I'm fine." Dillon looked at Zoë who was now falling asleep. "Hey there little bit." She softly touched the baby's cheek.

"Want to hold your daughter?" Ashley smiled.

"I sure would," Dillon had a goofy grin on her face as she slowly and awkwardly took Zoë from Ashley. The baby wiggled and cooed at Dillon. "Hey little bit. It's me...Spit." As on cue the baby giggled. Dillon looked at Ashley and beamed.

There was a knock on the door.

"Come in." Ashley said

Mary and Bill walked in holding a teddy bear and some flowers.

"Merry Christmas." Ashley smiled.

Mary smiled. "Is that my......"

"Yep, this is Zoë." Dillon walked over. "Zoë, this is your Grandma and Grandpa."

"She's a cutie." Bill smiled.

"I know this is impossible, but the baby looks like Dillon." Mary kept comparing the two.

"That's what I said," Ashley giggled.

"How's my other little girl doing?" Bill asked, as he kissed Ashley.

"I'm fine. Just tired. The Doctor said my blood pressure is a little low."

"After what I saw you doing in there Doc, my blood pressure would be low too!" Dillon walked over to Mary. "Here Grandma, get a load of this." Dillon slowly handed Zoë over to her. Dillon smiled as she watched Zoë interact with her grandparents.

She sat on the bed next to Ashley and took her hand.

Ashley leaned on Dillon. It felt so good to be close to her. Like her own safety zone. She could hardly wait for Zoë to grow up and be able to discover the magic of this woman.

Dillon remembered she had the camera and snapped some photos. Bill took Zoë in his arms. He couldn't take his eyes off of her. "Hi there little Zoë. This is your Grandpa."

Zoë cooed. She knew who these people were and she could feel their love.

Daddy handed Zoë back to Ashley. "There now. We should let you rest."

"You don't have to leave so soon do you?" Dillon asked.

"We have a million things to do before you come home." Mary smiled.

"Don't you be going to any trouble." Ashley looked at them.

"Hogwash!" Bill looked at his daughter. "Anything for our three gals." He winked at her.

Dillon hugged Ashley's parents and sat back down with Ashley. She looked at Ashley holding their child. "I love you so much, Doc."

Ashley smiled at Dillon.

"I know I keep saying it, but I never thought I could find someone like you and get all of this."

"I know. Me either." Ashley said.

Dillon leaned over and kissed her softly on the lips.

Doctor Brannagan walked in. "Am I interrupting something?" She smiled.

"Yes. But you can come in anyway Dr. B," Dillon joked.

Doctor Brannagan chuckled. "How are you feeling, Ashley?"

"Better."

"Good. Good. You had quite a time in there. It took a lot out of you. Your blood pressure is still a little low."

"When can we go home?" Ashley asked.

"I'd like to say tomorrow, but I think we may keep you to see if we can't get that pressure back up."

"Is she OK?" Dillon asked.

"Yes, she's fine. It just might take a day or two to bounce back. If it comes back up in the next twenty-four hours, we'll send you home." The Doctor reached into her pocket. "Oh, before I forget," she handed the envelope to Ashley. "I'll check back on you later. Again, congratulations."

"Thank you, Doctor." Dillon smiled as the Doctor left.

Ashley looked into the envelope and smiled. She looked at Dillon. "Merry Christmas, Spit." She handed it to Dillon.

"Is this the Dr. bill?" she joked as she slid the papers out of the envelope and carefully unfolded them. She looked at Ashley. Tears started to fall as she read the paper. "Doc..."

"Sign them and Zoë is ours legally." Ashley started to cry.

Dillon took the pen out of the envelope and signed the papers. She looked at Zoë.

"OK Little Bit, it's official. I'm your mommy too." She looked at Ashley. "I know I say this a lot, but I love you so much, Doc."

"I love you too, and I'll never get tired of hearing it! Merry Christmas."

* * *

Ashley finished feeding Zoë. She looked at the clock. 8:30. The doctor came in early to check her pressure. She said she was normal again and they were free to leave. She called Dillon, who said she'd be on her way. There was a knock at the door.

"Come in." Ashley said.

The door opened and Giavonna came in. She was carrying five red roses and a pink bunny. "Hey there." She smiled.

"Gia...what are you doing here?"

"I was visiting a friend of mine in here yesterday, and I thought I saw your folks... so I asked the nurses and here I am." She handed Ashley the roses.

"Thanks." Ashley said.

"Wow. That's her?" she smiled. "What's her name?"

"Zoë."

"Cool." Gia looked at Zoë. She was sound asleep. "So Ash, how are things going for ya?"

"Real good. I 'm very happy." Ashley was starting to feel uncomfortable.

"That's good."

"And you?"

"Can't complain. You still with what's her name...ah"

"Dillon. Yes. Together, and very much in love."

"Good to hear." Gia's tone was any thing less than excited.

Ashley looked at the clock. Dillon was due anytime now. She would flip if she came in and saw Gia. "Why are you here?"

"I told you-"

"I know what you told me Gia. Now tell me the truth."

"You know, baby, I still care about you. I think about you a lot."

"Really?" Ashley chuckled. "So that's why I haven't heard from you in over two years?"

"Ash, I'm not here to fight with you." She looked at Zoë then at Ashley. "She could have been our little girl."

Ashley couldn't believe what she was hearing. *Now Gia wanted to play mommy?* "Gia, please stop. Things work out the way they do for a reason. We weren't meant to be."

"You know, Ash, I've grown up a lot since you left. I wanted to tell you that I was sorry for how I treated you in the past. I was a real shit to you."

"I don't know quite what to say. I accept your apology. I'm glad you grew up. It takes a lot to admit when you're wrong."

"Yeah, well, hey, you know me." Gia fought back the tears. She knew that she had lost Ashley for good. "Well, I gotta go. I'm happy for you and Dillon." She looked at Zoë one last time and walked out.

Ashley sat on the edge of the bed, stunned. Gia had grown up. Too bad it took her this long to do it. She put all thoughts of her out of her head and picked Zoë up.

"Spit will be here soon to pick us up and we'll live happily ever after. Yes, we will."

Zoë gurgled and cooed.

There was another knock on the door. This time Ashley knew who it was.

"Come in Rhonda." Ashley called.

Rhonda came in and made a beeline for Zoë. "Let me hold that baby before you leave." She took Zoë in her arms.

"Rhonda, you're meeting us at the house." Ashley giggled.

"I know, but I need a little sugar before she goes. "How are you feeling, girl?"

"Much better. Just waiting on my gal to come and pick us up."

"Oh, she's here. She's busy passing out cigars to the staff." Rhonda laughed.

"Figures." Ashley joined in. "Guess I'm officially out of the closet too."

"Yep, it's all the buzz in ER." Rhonda kissed Zoë.

"Great." Ashley snickered.

"They'll get over it. They always do."

"You know I'm so happy right now, I just don't care what anyone thinks." Ashley smiled.

"Wow, there's a surprise." Rhonda smiled.

"Want another one? Gia was here."

"What? When?..........Why?" Rhonda was never fond of Gia.

"Just a few minutes ago. She said she was visiting a friend and heard about the baby. She wanted to see if I was OK."

"When will it end with her? I suppose she wants you back now too?"

"She apologized for everything." Ashley looked at her friend.

"Yeah, uh huh. Read my lips Ashley. Forget about her. Leave it where it should be. All I've heard was how that was the past and Spit is your future. Look at what I am holding in my arms.... she and the woman coming upstairs to take you home, is all you'll ever need to know."

"I know Rhonda. I love Dillon."

As on cue, Dillon walked in and looked around. She was armed with the video camera.

"Ok Zoë, this is it. You and mommy get to come home today. This is Auntie Ro-Ro holding you. And these are all the nice cards and flowers and balloons that our friends have sent you." She looked up over the camera and turned it off. She spotted the pink bunny. She picked it up and looked at it. "Where did this come from?" She asked.

Rhonda and Ashley exchanged a glance.

Rhonda handed Zoë back to Ashley. "Let me go hurry up that wheelchair. I'll see ya'll at the house in a little bit." She smiled at Dillon.

"Thanks, Auntie Ro-Ro." Dillon smiled back. She waited until Rhonda left. "So, what was the look for?" Dillon looked at Ashley.

Ashley wasn't about to start lying to Dillon now. "Gia was here."

"That was her I saw downstairs. I wasn't sure at first."

"You're not angry?" Ashley looked at her.

"Did she upset you or the baby?" Dillon asked.

"No."

"Then who cares? I know who you're going home with." She smiled at Ashley.

Ashley smiled. "I do love you, Dillon McCabe."

Dillon grabbed the video camera and turned it on. "Tell Zoë how much you love me."

Ashley laughed. "Zoë honey, mommy loves Spit and you more than anything else in this world!"

Dillon zoomed in on Zoë. "OK, Little Bit, you heard Mom. You're my witness."

Dr. Brannagan came in followed by a nurse with a wheelchair. "Well, you're now a free woman." Dr. Brannagan smiled.

"Hey thanks, Dr. B, for everything." Dillon turned the camera on. "Little bit, this is the doctor that helped bring you into the world."

The doctor smiled and waved.

"Excuse her Dr. Brannagan." Ashley shook her head.

"Not a problem. And may I say it's an extreme pleasure to see a family like yours, with so much passion for their child, and for one another."

Dillon smiled.

"Thank you, doctor. You were very supportive of us. That's rare now adays." Ashley smiled.

"I need to get back to rounds. If you need anything, don't hesitate to call."

Thanks again, Dr. B." Dillon shook her hand.

The nurse stayed and helped Ashley get into the chair with Zoë.

Dillon grabbed the bags and gifts. She turned the camera on. "OK Little Bit, here we go."

Dillon ran ahead with the video camera and taped Ashley and Zoë getting into the elevator and down to the main lobby.

"Spit, honey?" Ashley looked up.

"Yes?" Dillon smiled behind the camera.

"The car." Ashley giggled.

"Oh!" Dillon stopped filming. "The car. That would be a good thing." Dillon kissed Ashley, then Zoe. "The car. Be right back." She ran to the parking complex to get the car, while the nurse waited with Ashley just inside the doors.

The drive home was wonderful. Dillon gave Zoë a full tour of the town. She was unaware that she had fallen asleep along the way. Ashley turned the camera on and filmed Dillon.

Ashley was so happy to be going home...finally.

"Everyone alright back there??" Dillon looked in her rearview mirror?

"Perfect, sweetie. Just happy to be going home." Ashley smiled.

"Me too, I've missed having you in my arms for the last three days."

"I've missed being there."

As Dillon turned down the street, she stopped the car. "Oh Man! Doc, hand me the camera." She took the camera from Ashley and pointed it to the house. "Zoë look at this."

Their front yard was transformed into a pink palace of balloons, signs, and banners. There was a huge wooden stork on their lawn that read, *"It's a Girl!"*

"Spit, did you do this?"

"No, not me."

Dillon pulled the car into the drive. She narrated to the camera for Zoë as she walked around and opened the car door for Ashley.

Mary, Bill and Rhonda came rushing out. "Welcome home!" they all yelled in unison.

"This is so wonderful. Thank you, everyone." Ashley said

"OK, now bring my granddaughter in the house before she catches cold." Mary said.

"Spit, will you bring my things in?" Ashley smiled at Dillon.

"I'll take care of that." Rhonda winked at Dillon. "You take your little girl inside and show her around."

Dillon grinned. "You're a doll, Auntie Ro."

"Yes, I know." She looked at Dillon."But don't let that get around."

Dillon chuckled. "Your secret is safe with me." She squeezed Rhonda's arm and went inside with Ashley and Zoë.

* * *

The next few weeks were hard on Ashley and Dillon. The baby kept them awake. Ashley was having trouble breast-feeding, Dillon started to go to academy class. In her spare time she would play with Zoë. Ashley was tired, sore, and confused. All Zoë did was cry around her. The doctor told them no physical contact for three weeks, Dillon all but slept in another room. Ashley missed having Dillon's arms around her all night.. Ashley was beginning to feel neglected. Ever since Gia had come to the hospital, Dillon seemed different. Ashley waited until her parents left before she talked to Dillon.

"The baby is finally asleep." Ashley announced.

"Mmm that's nice." Dillon mumbled from her book.

Ashley walked over to Dillon and plucked the book out of her hand. "Enough!" She looked at Dillon.

Dillon could tell by the look in her eyes that Ashley meant business.

"We're not going to do this anymore."

"Do what?"

"This little dance we've been doing."

"What?" Dillon looked confused.

Ashley sat on the couch and started to cry.

Dillon hated to see her in this state. Rhonda told her that this might happen. She moved to Ashley and sat next to her. "Come here." She took Ashley in her arms. She held her until Ashley stopped crying. "You're exhausted, Doc."

"I know, and I'm fat and ugly and you don't want to be with me, and the baby hates me. All she does is cry."

"Hey, now, wait a sec." Dillon looked into Ashley's eyes. "The baby doesn't hate you. And you're not fat. I happen to think you're still the most beautiful woman in the world. As far as not wanting you...well that can't be further from the truth. I want you Doc, but we have to wait. I want to hold you. But every time I do, you seem distant. I want to help you through whatever you're going through, I just don't know how."

"Are you mad that Gia came to the hospital?" Ashley looked up.

"Well, it wasn't my favorite thing to have happen, but as long as you're OK?"

"When she walked into the room, it felt like a stranger came in."

"OK. Now, can it be over? No more mention of her?" Dillon looked at Ashley.

"Promise." Ashley smiled.

Dillon kissed Ashley. "Whatta' ya say to a little walk on the wild side?"

Ashley giggled, "What did you have in mind?

"How about a little snuggle nap?

"Now you're talkin'."

Dillon led Ashley to their room. She kissed her again. Ashley lay in Dillon's arms. She listened to Dillon's heartbeat and quickly fell asleep.

Dillon heard the baby making noises. She listened until Zoë fell back asleep. Her family was all that ever mattered to her and she would do anything to show Ashley just how much.

* * *

They walked through the pier, over to the midway games.

"C'mon, let's play some games. You can win me a prize. Spit, stop! Look!" Ashley pointed to the stuffed monkey sitting on the shelf. "He looks like you when you pout."

"I don't pout."

"Yes you do. C'mon."

"Should we call Rhonda again?" Dillon asked, as she pulled out her cell phone.

"We've been calling her every hour since we left. This is our first date since the baby. Can you just try and relax?"

"What if something happens and Rhonda doesn't hear it?"

"Baby, she'll be fine. Rhonda is a registered nurse and a good friend. She won't let anything happen to Zoe."

Dillon smiled, "Sorry Doc."

"It's OK. Tto be honest, I did call Rhonda myself twice when we were at dinner."

"Ah ha! I knew it!"

They laughed.

"Guess we're just two suckers when it comes to that little girl."

"She definitely has us wrapped around her finger." Ashley agreed.

"Step right up little ladies!" The game barker yelled to them. "Simply shoot the star out of the center of the target and win a prize! It's so easy even a child could do it."

"Let's play, Spit." Ashley smiled.

Dillon looked over to the game. "Five bucks! Are you serious?"

"It's just a game." Ashley shook her head. Dillon could be so damn stubborn sometimes.

Dillon reached into her pocket and pulled out a five. She reluctantly gave it to the man.

"Here ya go. Aim well and let her rip."

She picked up the rifle and took aim. She squeezed the trigger and shot.

Ashley looked on, trying not to laugh.

The barked pulled the target up and examined it. "Aw, better luck next time." The man took the rifle from Dillon.

"This is fixed!"

"Lady, it's a game of skill, of which it seems you do not possess."

"What the fu-."

"No need for obscenities. Tell ya what I'm gonna do."

"Oh, brother." Dillon rolled her eyes.

"I have a big heart. In fact, they call me Big Hearted Wayne."

"I know what I'd like to call you." Dillon said under her breath.

Ashley giggled.

"For three bucks, I'll let the little lady take a shot."

Dillon and Ashley exchanged a glance.

He took the rifle and handed it to Ashley, then stuck out his hand to Dillon. He grinned, "Three more please."

Dillon took out three more bills and slapped the money into his hand. She bent over and whispered into Ashley's ear. "Aim left and shoot him in the nuts."

Ashley laughed. She quickly hit Dillon on the arm. "You're awful."

Ashley got herself into position. She held the gun up and aimed.

"Now, take your time. Breathe."

Ashley looked at Dillon.

"What?" Dillon shrugged her shoulders.

Ashley took aim again.

"The gun has a little bit of a kick, so make sure you compensate for it."

Ashley looked at Dillon wide-eyed.

"Do you put up with that every night?" The barked asked.

Dillon shot the barker a look. "OK go for it."

Ashley took aim once again. She sighed and took a couple of breaths, just in case Dillon decided to talk again. She squeezed the trigger.

Dillon was amazed how well Ashley shot. "Hey you did it. Nice shooting, Doc."

"Sorry, but she didn't."

"What? You said the star had to be shot off, and if we're looking at the same target, then we both see that the star is gone."

Wayne took the target down and held it up. "See the corner? There's red right there."

"You're joking?" Dillon's eyes narrowed.

"Sorry lady, just the rules."

Dillon's blood started to boil.

"Its OK Spit, let's just go." Ashley tugged at her sleeve.

"He's a cheat!" Dillon yelled.

"Look, you played, and you lost!"

"What happened to Big Hearted Wayne? It's more liked Wayne's full of big shit!"

"C'mon sweetie." Ashley started to walk away.

"Or how about 'No Teeth Wayne'?" Dillon kept on him.

Dillon noticed Ashley had left. She gave Wayne another dirty look and followed Ashley. "Wait a sec, Doc. I'm sorry."

"It's OK."

"These games just get me crazy. "

Ashley giggled. "I can only imagine. You're very competitive."

"Too much at times."

"Well, I guess we'll have to warn the socceer parents when Zoë starts to play.

They laughed. Dillon looked at her. "If you want it that badly, I'll go back."

Ashley smiled. "Its only a stuffed animal. Besides, I have the real thing." She kissed Dillon's cheek.

Dillon looked into Ashley's eyes.

"What?"

"I want to make love to you so damn bad. Right now"

Ashley squeezed Dillon's arm. "I know. Me too."

"Well hell! We're blowing this taco stand." Dillon said.

Dillon took Ashley's face in her hands and softly kissed her.

"Will you two get a room!" Ashley's friend Terri and her friend walked up.

"Hey, Terri." Ashley blushed. She hugged her.

"How are you two? Ashley you look amazing. How's the baby?"

"She's wonderful. In fact this is our first date since we had her."

"Uh oh - calling every five minuets?"

"Actually, she's been pretty good, I on the other hand….." Dillon laughed.

"Hi, I'm Ashley and this is Dillon." She held her hand out to Terri's friend.

"Oh, this is Steve." Terri smiled.

"Nice to meet you." Dillon shook his hand.

"So what are you two up to?" Ashley asked.

"Nothing, just winning a bunch of games. Isn't this monkey adorable?" Terri asked holding up the stuffed toy Ashley had wanted.

"Stunning." Dillon said flatly.

"Steve got it on the first try."

"Way to go, Steve."

Ashley could tell Dillon was upset. "It's nice."

"Would you excuse me for a moment?" Dillon said.

"You OK?" Ashley looked at her.

"Yeah, I just want to make sure the baby's OK. Keep talking, I'll be right back."

Dillon ran back over to the shooting game. "OK pal, how much to buy the monkey?"

"Oh, sorry, we can't sell em."

"Ten bucks." Dillon pulled the bill out of her pocket.

"Sorry. No can do."

"C'mon Wayne, I know we all have our price. Fifteen?"

"Look, lady, if you want the monkey, you shoot for it. Plain and simple."

Dillon was getting frustrated. "Twenty bucks!"

He looked at her.

"Thirty?"

"Nope."

"Forty, and I won't tell anyone what a rip off and a cheat you really are?"

"And we have another winner." He took the monkey off the wall and handed it to Dillon. She handed him the money.

"She must be some gal." He winked at her.

"She is." Dillon smiled.

"Spit?" Ashley walked up, "I thought I'd find you here."

Dillon smiled and proudly handed Ashley the monkey.

"You won?"

Dillon smiled.

Ashley hugged her. "My hero. I knew you could do it." She kissed her, "wait till we get home. I'll thank you properly."

"Let's go home Doc."

Wayne watched as they walked off arm in arm. He shook his head and smiled.

11

The next two years were ones of change.

Ashley loved her new office. It was great to be in one place and not running all over the hospital. Her partner, Kent Cohen, was great too. She joined him in the medical plaza across the lot from Mount West. They worked great together. They had a solid reputation and a six-month waiting list for new patients.

Dillon was out of school and back at the department waiting for a teaching job to open. Though Ashley didn't like the idea much, it was nice to always have someone with Zoë. Their relationship suffered from it. Rhonda would take the baby on her day off, and Ashley's parents would come out once a month to stay so Dillon and Ashley could go out, or go away for the weekend.

Ashley felt blessed. Everything in her life was going perfectly. Zoë was becoming quite the little character. Dillon bought her a pony on her first birthday. They would ride almost every day. She taught Zoë responsibility, and even now, at only two, Dillon thought she was ready for the Olympics.

Ashley looked at her watch. *Mom and dad should have Zoë down for her afternoon nap,* she thought. *Dillon would be off at 4:00.* Ashley had a romantic evening all planned. Dinner, dancing, a moonlit walk on the beach, and a night at the Hotel Laguna. She had a few more things to take care of.

Dillon looked at her watch. One more hour. She could hardly wait. She opened her locker and smiled at the photo of Ashley and Zoë. The alarm went off. *Damn!* Dillon thought. She grabbed her gear and ran to the truck.

They arrived quickly to the intersection, where the three cars were entangled. Broken glass, car parts and twisted metal covered the street. As the truck pulled up, Dillon froze. She recognized Ashley's car. Zoë's car seat was lying in the middle of the street.

Dillon's heart skipped a beat as the realization of what was in front of her sank in.

"No!" Dillon yelled as she jumped off the truck. "Doc!" She screamed. She raced to the driver's side of the smashed car. Ashley lay there, her blonde hair now red, soaked, with blood. "Doc!" Dillon called to her. She tried to open the door but it was too damaged. Jack came running up to her. "It's Doc!" Dillon yelled at Jack. She started to pull the broken glass out of the window to the car. "Doc." Dillon kept calling to her. She saw that Ashley was still breathing. "Doc, hold on." She looked at Jack. "She's alive!" She yelled to him.

Jack called the crew over with the Jaws of Life.

"Zoë!" Dillon looked around for the baby. "Zoë! Where are you?"

"Spit, you need to step out of this one!" Jack told her. He could see his friend was now on the brink of losing it.

"Your ass I will!" She looked him in the eye. "That's my whole fucking life in that car!"

"I know Spit. But you won't do her any good if you lose it now! Back out!"

She knew Jack was right. She had to keep it together.

"There's no one else in this car." Nelson told Jack. "Total loss in the pick up truck, and a drunk dude with a couple of scratches on him."

"Dillon ran to the other side of the car. She reached in and pulled out Ashley's phone. "Come on, Doc. Hold on." She dialed the house number frantically.

"Hello." Mary's voice was on the other end.

"Mom, do you have Zoë?" Dillon said.

"What? Dillon is this you? I can barley hear you."

"Do you have Zoë?" Dillon raised her voice.

"Well, yes she's here. She's napping"

"Thank God. I can't talk now; there's has been an accident. It's Doc. Just meet us at the hospital!"

Dillon put the phone in her pocket. She was relieved to know that the baby was safe. She could now fully concentrate all her efforts on Ashley.

Dillon crawled on the hood of the car while Eric and his partner tried to stabilize her. They put on the neck brace and hooked her up. Dillon stuck her head into the car. "Doc? Doc?" Can you hear me?" Ashley could hear her. But words wouldn't come out.

The fire crew went to work. They used the Jaws of Life to peel back the roof of the car.

"Doc, don't you leave me!" Dillon's voice cracked. She looked around and saw that Ashley's legs were pinned under the steering wheel. "Hey, we need to get her legs out!" Dillon yelled.

The crew carefully removed the steering wheel to free Ashley's legs.

After forty minutes they had Ashley on a stretcher. She was badly cut and her leg looked broken. Dillon was worried about the impact of the crash, and her back. She leaned over to Ashley. "Hang in there sweetie, I'm here."

Jack came behind Dillon. "You go with her. We have this under control."

"Thanks, man." Dillon looked at Jack.

"She's strong, Spit! She'll make it." He gave Dillon a reassuring smile.

"She has to Jack." Dillon choked on her words. She followed the stretcher into the ambulance. Eric did a vitals check and called in his report.

Dillon fought back the tears. Her life lay before her, cut up and lifeless. "Come on, Doc. Please...I need you. Zoë and I both need you."

A slight audible moan came from Ashley.

Dillon took her fingers and slightly brushed past Ashley's cheek.

"Spit?" Ashley said faintly.

"I'm here, I'm here."

"Where...baby."

"She's with your folks. She's safe."

The ambulance pulled into the ER parking lot. Rhonda was outside to meet them.

They carefully lowered Ashley out of the ambulance.

Dillon followed her out. She looked at Rhonda.

"Let's get her inside stat, "was all that Rhonda could say. She cleared a path as they rolled her into ER. Dillon followed them into the room. She watched as they hooked Ashley up to the countless number of machines.

"Give it to me!" Rhonda looked at Eric.

"Drunk driver took out two cars. One dead and her."

"Scratches and bruises?"

"Yeah, that's him." Eric said.

"He's in the next room." Rhonda realized what she had just said.

It was too late to stop Dillon as she was already on her way. She blew through the door and saw the guy sitting with his arm in a sling. She walked to him, her adrenaline pumping. She grabbed the guy by his shirt and picked him up off his chair.

"Hey man what the fuc-"was all the kid could get out. He was now face to face with Dillon.

"I outta tear you apart piece by piece, starting with your heart, you mindless pile of pig shit!"

"Who are you?"

"I'm your worst fucking nightmare if the lady in the next room doesn't make it."

Rhonda entered the room followed by a cop. "Spit, don't" she yelled. "It won't solve anything."

Dillon knew that Rhonda was right, but she still wanted a piece of this guy.

"Let him go." The officer said sternly.

Dillon searched the guy's eyes for some sign of remorse. He stared blankly at her, reeking of alcohol.

"I said, let him go." The officer's tone was now louder.

"Think of Zoë, she needs you now." Rhonda said.

Dillon froze. Oh God. Zoë. Their sweet little girl. Dillon released her grip and pushed the guy back into the chair. She leaned over to him and whispered in his ear. "If she doesn't recover...I'll come looking for ya." She stepped back and continued to stare at him.

"Come on." Rhonda took her arm. "Let the police take care of him."

Dillon watched as the officer took the guy away. "How is she?"

"She's alive, that's all we know now. They need to get her stable and get some x-rays done."

"I can't lose her." Dillon's voice cracked.

"I know, sweetie. Ashley is strong though. She fought for you, didn't she?"

Bill and Mary came in. Zoë was with them. Dillon saw them and walked to the lounge.

Zoë saw Dillon. "Spit! Spit." She yelled and ran to her.

Dillon swooped her up in her arms. "How's my girl?"

Zoë wrapped her arms around Dillon's neck. "Love my Spit." Zoë kissed Dillon on the lips and then giggled.

"Love my Zoë." Dillon held her tight.

They were more than just mother and daughter. They were best friends. Ashley would sit for hours and watch them play. Zoë's first word was Spit. When she first said it, Dillon walked around for days, just proud as a peacock. Now, more than ever, Dillon needed this little girl. She had to be her focus so she wouldn't fall apart.

"What happened?" Bill asked.

"DUI ran a red." Dillon said flatly.

Tears started to roll down Mary's cheek. Bill put his arm around her to comfort her.

Rhonda came out.

Dillon looked up.

"The doctor gave me authorization to tell you. They're getting ready to prep for surgery."

"Surgury?" Mary's eyes filed with tears.

"Here's what we know. She broke her back, left ankle and her collarbone. There's some internal bleeding, and she has a concussion. They're just about to take her in."

Dillon fought to hold the tears back. "Can I see her?"

"Spit, you know the rules." She looked hard at Dillon. "Give me the baby and hurry." Rhonda took Zoe from Dillon.

"Dillon." Mary called out. "Tell her we love her."

Dillon slightly smiled. "I will."

She walked into the room. Ashley lay there. Dillon wanted to take her in her arms.

A tech came in and saw her. "Excuse me, but we have to take her to the OR."

"Please, just give me a second." Dillon pleaded with the tech.

The tech smiled and left the room.

"Hey, Doc," Dillon whispered. "Your folks send their love, and Zoë too. We're all here waiting for you." She slowly put her hand on Ashley's. "I know you're strong, you'd have to be to love someone like me." She chuckled through the tears that were now streaming from her eyes. "I know you'll be OK." She kissed Ashley tenderly on the lips. "Ashley Wilkerson, I love you, and I'm gonna be here waiting for you." She looked at Ashley. "I need you so much ....don't you leave me."

Two techs came in. "Sorry, but we have to get her in there."

"Yeah." Dillon said as she watched them wheel Ashley out the door.

Rhonda walked in. She put her arm around Dillon. "C'mon, Spit. She's in good hands. She'll be OK."

"She has to be, Rhonda.... she just has to be." Dillon turned to Rhonda. She embraced her as Dillon cried openly. Rhonda could see just what Ashley meant to her.

* * *

All they could do for the next six hours was wait. Rhonda brought in some toys for Zoë. Mary read, and Bill watched golf on TV. Dillon paced the floor, praying that Ashley would make it through.

"Spit, play." Zoë tugged on Dillon's pant leg.

Dillon looked down at the smiling face. It was Ashley's beautiful blue eyes looking back at her.

"Spit play wif me." Zoë asked again.

Dillon smiled and sat on the floor. "What ya playing little bit?"

"Play horsey, Spit." Zoë giggled.

"Horsey huh?" Dillon smiled at her daughter.

They played with the little toy figures. Zoë stopped and jumped into Dillon's lap.

"Where's mommy?" Zoë asked Dillon.

"Well, little bit, mommy has a boo boo and the doctor's are trying to make it all better."

"I want to see mommy." Zoë said.

"Me too baby, me too."

Two more hours passed when a doctor finally came in.

"Ms. McCabe, Mr. and Mrs. Wilkerson?" he asked, "I'm Doctor Woods."

Dillon jumped up. "How is she?"

"Please have a seat." The doctor pulled up a nearby chair. He had some blood on him and had been sweating. "Ashley is stable. She's lucky to be alive, but she has a very long road ahead of her."

"What happened?" Mary asked.

"She broke her back cleanly. We did a bone graft from her hip and inserted two steel rods to shore up her vertebrae. Her central nervous system short circuited from the impact of the crash."

"She'll be OK right, doctor?" Bill asked.

"Right now, that's hard to say, sir."

"What does that mean?" Dillon looked at the doctor.

"She has nerve and muscle damage. Not to mention the internal bleeding, and her other fractures." He looked at Dillon. "Right now, Ashley is paralyzed from the waist down."

"What? Are you saying Doc won't ever walk again?" Dillon's voice cracked.

"She was in good shape when this happened. It'll help her heal. Personally, I think she'll walk again, but right now, it's way too early to tell. She has a lot of healing to do."

"When can she come home?" Mary asked.

"Well, Mrs. Wilkerson, she'll be here for at least the next three weeks or so. It depends on how she heals."

"Can we see her?" Dillon asked.

"She's heavily sedated. She won't know you're here, but I know you want to see her. When she gets out of recovery and into a room, I'll have Rhonda come and get you."

"Thank you, Doctor Woods." Dillon shook his hand.

"If you'll excuse me...." The doctor smiled and left.

Dillon looked at Ashley's parents. "Could you stay for a while and help with Zoë?"

"Of course, Dillon. We aren't going anywhere." Bill smiled.

Two hours later Rhonda took Ashley's folks up to see her. Dillon thought it best not to let Zoë see Ashley like this. When they came back, Dillon could tell that they had been crying.

"Dillon, we'll take Zoë home and put her to bed." Bill took her from Dillon.

"Thank you so much." Dillon hugged Mary.

"Dillon, if you need anything, you call us, ok?" She said.

"Thank you both. I'll be ok." She hugged Zoe. "You be good for Grandma and Grandpa."

"I wanna stay wif you, Spit." Zoe threw her arms around Spit's neck.

"Spit's gotta work baby. Go with your grandparents, I'll be home soon."

"I wuv you." Zoe kissed Dillon.

"Oh you too, kiddo." She handed Zoe to Mary. She half smiled at them and headed to the elevator.

Rhonda was getting off as Dillon was getting on. Rhonda decided to stay on with Dillon.

"How you doing?" She asked.

"Hanging on." Dillon said flatly.

"Spit, why don't you go home and rest? I'm on duty all night, and you know I won't let anything happen to her."

"Thanks Rhonda, but I can't. I have to be with her."

"Well, at least let me get you some scrubs to wear."

Dillon looked down and realized she was still in her turn out gear. "Thanks."

They stepped off the elevator and Rhonda led Dillon to Ashley's room.

Dillon stepped in. The room was dark and still. Dillon had chills, seeing Ashley lying there. "She looks so helpless."

"She needs our prayers right now." Rhonda said. "It's gonna take a long time."

Dillon moved to Ashley. She took her hand. It was cold and clammy. She kissed Ashley on the cheek and whispered to her. "I'm here, Doc."

For the next week Dillon never left Ashley's side, even though Ashley was awake. Dillon took a personal leave from the department and moved

Ashley's parents in to help with Zoë. She had to concentrate on getting Ashley better and walking again.

Dillon had a team of professionals install an in-home gym and made the house more user friendly for Ashley. Ashley's father built ramps and installed rails in the bathroom.

Anything that Dillon could think of, she bought and had it put in. She wanted Ashley back, up and walking again as soon as possible.

12

It had been almost a month since the accident and Ashley was going to be able to go home. She was healing well with the exception of the paralysis. She was refusing to do her exercises and she was agitated most of the time. She had sent two therapists packing already. Ashley said both were too rough with her.

The doctor examined her. "This is nice, Ashley. You're doing great." He reassured her.

"Really? Then how come I can't walk?" Ashley snapped.

Dillon put her hand on Ashley's shoulder. "Easy there, Doc."

"Don't easy me, you're not the cripple in the wheelchair!"

Dillon looked at the doctor. "Excuse me." She left the room.

The last two weeks were starting to grate on Dillon. Ashley was in a lot of pain still and she took it out on everyone. Dillon tried hard to understand what Ashley was going through, but Ashley was making things difficult for everyone. She snapped at Zoë twice and made her cry. Dillon thought it was best if she didn't bring Zoë around. She would call and let her talk to Ashley over the phone. It was becoming a problem, and Dillon knew she had to talk to Ashley.

The doctor came out of the room.

"Sorry, Doctor Woods. It seems to be her norm of late."

"Dillon, let me explain this to you. Ashley can walk again. Her nerve patterns are close to normal. The shocks she gets are her nerves waking up again. She needs her PT to get stronger."

"But she says she can't walk."

"It's partly in her mind. She's so negative about the prospect of never walking again, she's refusing to try."

"What can I do?" Dillon asked.

"For starters, don't fuss over her too much. Treat her like you normally would. Make her do things. Swimming is good. Just keep her involved in her day-to-day routine, so she can see that she can still do things."

"Tough love then." Dillon smiled.

"Yes." The doctor smiled. "I'm going to have the therapist come to the house now. That might make things a bit easier."

"Thank you, Doctor."

"I think I know just the right person for her too. I'll see if she's around and I'll send her up."

"Great." Dillon smiled as she watched the doctor. leave. She walked back into Ashley's room.

"I think you're going to get to leave, Doc." Dillon smiled.

"Yippee." Ashley said sarcastically.

"You need to start changing your attitude."

"Really? And how would your attitude be Dillon, if you were in my shoes? You have no clue how I feel." She looked at her.

"Maybe I don't know exactly how you feel, but I would know that my family is here to support me and that they love me. You're acting like a child, and we already have one! She's at home, asking and waiting for her mommy." Dillon looked at Ashley, waiting for a response. She finally threw her arms up in disgust. "Sorry, but I can't stay around for this. I'm outta here."

Dillon stormed out of the room. She would have loved to have just jumped on her bike and taken off. Just get lost so that no one could find her. Free from her commitments and her responsibilities. She stopped as she was about to get on the elevator.

As much as she wanted to run, she wanted that much more to stay. She loved her life. Ashley and Zoë were her world. She walked back to Ashley's room and looked inside. Ashley was in tears. Dillon walked in and took Ashley in her arms.

"I'm sorry, Spit. It just hurts so bad, I can't take it anymore."

"I know, but the doctor said it's a good sign. Things are waking up and starting to heal."

"It sure doesn't feel like it." Ashley wiped tears off her cheek.

"It's only been about a month." Dillon stroked her hair to try to get her to relax.

"Please don't remind me." Ashley sobbed. "I just want to go home."

"We want you home, Doc. I miss you not being in our bed. And Zoë asks about you constantly."

"Well, the doctor went to check my tests. He said I might be able to leave today."

"See! That's the spirit. You know the doctor felt that you will be walking again real soon."

Ashley looked blankly at Dillon. "When are you going to face it? You now have a wife who's a cripple in a wheelchair."

"Doc, don't say that." Dillon's eyebrow's narrowed.

"Well, it's the truth." Ashley said.

Before Dillon could answer, Dr. Woods came back in. "Well Ashley your tests are great! I can't see any reason you can't go home today."

"That's awesome!" Dillon smiled.

"What about my legs?" Ashley asked.

"Ashley. You've had a severe trauma to your system. Your muscles are weak. Through physical therapy and exercise you'll build them back up and be walking in no time."

Ashley rolled her eyes.

"I understand you have a gym at home and a pool?" The doctor asked.

"Yes, we do." Dillon answered.

"Great! We're going to let you do all of your physical therapy at home Ashley."

"You trust me, Dr. Woods?" Ashley smirked.

"I'm not totally crazy. Your physical therapist will be in shortly to talk to you. I have a feeling you'll really like her. She reminds me a lot of you, Ashley."

"Thank you for everything Dr. Woods." Dillon shook his hand.

"My pleasure. I'll see you in a week. We'll check your progress and take a few x-rays."

He smiled at Dillon. He walked out. *Boy, Dillon had her hands full with her,* he thought.

"Wooohoo Doc, did you hear that? The new therapist is a she."

"Probably some psycho enforcer type." Ashley looked out the window.

Dillon sighed as she tried to regain her patience. Ashley was getting harder to live with by the second. *Where was the woman I first fell in love with?* She thought. "I'd better call your folks and let them know we're coming home.

There was a knock at the door.

"Come in." Ashley said.

The door opened and in walked a beautiful redhead. She was built like Ashley, very toned. She had on jeans and a t-shirt rolled up at the sleeves. She had very nice biceps, and wasn't afraid to show them off. She too, like Ashley, had beautiful blue eyes. *Wow, what a knock out,* Dillon thought. She quickly got off the phone.

"Hi. I'm Jan." She smiled and stuck out her hand to Ashley.

Dillon had seen her somewhere before, but couldn't remember where. "Hi. This is Ashley and I'm Dillon. Please to meet you, Jan." She shook her hand.

Ashley looked at Dillon who was almost drooling.

"Dillon? Dillon McCabe?" The pretty therapist asked.

"Yeah, that's me." Dillon looked at Ashley and shrugged her shoulders.

"It's me, Jan. Jan McKinley. I used to sit behind you in third grade and all the way through high school!"

"Oh - no way! Jan? I remember you!" Dillon smiled.

Jan hugged Dillon in a tight embrace. "This is a small world." Jan laughed.

"Yes, it is." Dillon blushed.

Ashley was getting upset. Was this visit for her to get better or a stroll down memory lane with Dillon?

"Did you hear that Doc? Jan and I went to school together."

"Yeah, great." Ashley said sarcastically.

Jan could see she would have her work cut out for her. "Well Ashley, I read through your reports, and I think we can get your strength back and you up on your feet again."

"Sounds great." Dillon smiled at Ashley.

"The doctor said that we'd be doing in-home PT. You have a gym?"

"Yep. State of the Art." Dillon smiled. "And a pool"

"I'm sure it's fine. I'll need to check it out before we start anything. We may need to add a few things."

"That's not a problem." Dillon said.

She couldn't get over it. Jan McKinley was standing in front of her. *Jan always sat behind Dillon in school. Jan was very smart. She would help Dillon with math and Dillon would always protect her from the playground bullies. No one would mess with Dillon McCabe. And if you were her friend, they wouldn't mess with you.*

"I heard you're going home today, so I'll let you get settled in and I'll come by tomorrow."

"Oh, goodie." Ashley smirked.

"OK then. Ashley, it was nice meeting you and I look forward to working with you. Dillon, it was great to see you again." She hugged Dillon again.

"Nice seeing you too, Jan. See you tomorrow." Dillon grinned.

Dillon watched as Jan left. She turned to Ashley. "You ready to blow this taco stand?"

"Was she one of your girlfriends?" Ashley looked at Dillon.

Dillon chuckled. "Jan? Please! We were friends in school. Kids used to pick on her. I protected her. That's all it was."

"And you never had the hots for her?" Ashley continued to question.

"Of course I had the hots for her and anything else with boobs! Please don't make this something it isn't." She kissed Ashley. "Besides, she doesn't have the boobs you do." Dillon winked, and kissed her again.

Dillon picked Ashley up out of the bed with ease and set her in the wheelchair. "You happy to be going home?

"Yes, I can't stand it here anymore."

"I know a cute little girl who's going to be thrilled."

Ashley smiled at the mention of Zoë. She could hardly wait to get home and be a family again.

* * *

Dillon and Ashley pulled up to the house. Rhonda was watching Zoë. Mary and Bill thought it best to give Ashley time to adjust. They had both done so much to help out, they were beat and needed some time to rest also.

There was a banner out front that read: "Welcome Home, Mommy!" with colorful squiggles on it.

Ashley chuckled. "Let me guess - Zoë's handy coloring?"

"Nope, the squiggles are mine." Dillon winked and turned off the car.

Dillon got out and walked to the back to unload the wheelchair.

Zoë came running out of the house over to Dillon. "Spit! Spit! You bring mommy home." She jumped into Dillon's arms.

"I sure did Little Bit. Hey, lay one on me." She made a fish face as Zoë kissed her.

Dillon set Zoë down and opened the car door for Ashley.

"Mommy!" Zoë squealed with delight.

"Hi, baby." Ashley smiled.

Zoë crawled onto Ashley's lap. Ashley held her tight. "I missed you so much Zoë." Ashley's voice cracked.

"Did doctor fix your owie, mommy?" Zoë asked.

"Almost baby. We have to help him get me better."

"I'll help you. Promise." Zoë looked at Ashley. "Lay one on me," she said just like Dillon.

Ashley laughed and kissed Zoë.

"Welcome home." Rhonda smiled.

"Thanks. It's nice to be out of that hospital."

"I feel the same way every day about five." Rhonda smiled.

"Thank you for helping out with Zoë."

"Girl, you know it's a pleasure. Just not sure of that woolly mammoth thing you got out back."

"It's a pony, Rhonda." Dillon shook her head.

"All I know is that it eats a ton and poops two tons and has big teeth." Rhonda said.

Dillon and Ashley chuckled.

"Lets get you inside." Dillon looked at Ashley.

Zoë came up and pulled on Dillon's pant leg. Dillon grabbed her and raised her up over her head. "Monster, monster, monster!" She snarled and growled, tickling Zoë's tummy.

Zoë giggled and laughed wildly "Spit! Spit! Spit!" She got out.

They shared something so close that Ashley couldn't even be included. Ashley smiled. It was nice to see a mother that close to her daughter, especially since Dillon never had the chance with hers.

Dillon set Zoë down and took the chair over to Ashley. She leaned in and lifted Ashley out of the car. She stood for a second holding Ashley.

"What's wrong?" Ashley looked at Dillon.

"Come to think of it, I never did get to carry you over the threshold."

"Oh Spit, please." Ashley blushed.

"Do it! Do it!" Zoë yelled.

"Ah, you heard our daughter." Dillon grinned at Ashley and started to walk in.

"You're crazy." Ashley giggled.

"For you, yes. Welcome home."

"Thank you. It feels nice to be home," she kissed Dillon as she was carried inside. "I think I need to rest for a while."

"Sure." Dillon carried Ashley to their bedroom and sat her down on the bed.

Rhonda came in pushing Zoë in the wheelchair.

"More Auntie Ro-Ro." Zoë giggled.

"Can I get you anything?" Dillon asked Ashley.

"Some water would be good."

"You two get settled in and I'll get the water. "Come on, Zoë, you can help me."

Dillon waited for them to leave and sat down next to Ashley. "Doc, I've missed you so much. Missed having you in my arms. And in our bed."

Ashley half smiled at Dillon.

Dillon leaned in to kiss Ashley and was surprised by the cold peck on the cheek she got in return.

The first night back was hell. Ashley would scream, waking up in a cold sweat.

The doctor had said this was normal. Dillon felt sorry for her.

The only thing Ashley could do was to medicate herself in hopes that she'd pass out. But anything she took, the pain would just blow right past it. She was so skin sensitive at times, that Dillon couldn't touch her. The bed sheets even hurt.

Dillon couldn't sleep. She was aware of every little sound or move that Ashley made. "Sorry, you hurt Doc." Dillon whispered. "I wish I could take the pain away."

"I know, thanks." She squeezed Dillon's hand.

"Just remember, it's healing." She tried to kiss Ashley's shoulder.

Ashley moved away. "Please." Tears started to run down Ashley's face.

Dillon sat up and turned the light on. "Should I call the doctor?"

"No, it's not that."

"Do you need another pain pill?" Dillon wanted so badly to hold Ashley.

"I just don't want to become a burden to you."

"You're not." Dillon looked at her.

"What if I never walk? How could we ever have a normal life again?"

"You will walk again." Dillon tried to smile. "This is crazy talk."

"And if I don't? You won't want to stay with a cripple, who can't make love to you!"

Dillon had heard enough. She got out of bed and grabbed her pillow. "You must really think that I take our commitment lightly. I'm not that shallow. But I'll tell you one thing, your negative attitude is really starting to drag you down and I won't hang around here and have you drag me there with you. Have your pity party and get over it" She walked out of the bedroom.

Dillon checked on Zoë who was still sound asleep.

She stopped at the door of the bedroom. She remembered the first time Ashley slept in her bedroom. She waited by the door for Ashley to fall asleep. And now four years later, they were still together and had a daughter. *Why was Ashley being so stubborn?* Dillon thought. The doctor said she was fine. She just didn't want to try. Dillon hoped that maybe Jan could turn things around. She settled herself on the couch and tried to get some sleep.

Dillon was awakened the next morning with Zoë sitting on her back.

"Gihe up! Gihe up!" She was shouting.

"Hey, easy you." Dillon snarled sleepily. She pulled Zoë off her back and hugged her. "Good morning, Little Bit." Dillon puckered her lips.

"Morning, Spit." Zoë kissed her. "Mommy crying." Zoë looked at Dillon.

"She is?" Dillon sat up. She put Zoë on the couch and ran to the bedroom. "Doc?" she yelled as she opened the bedroom door. She saw the wheelchair tipped over in the doorway of the bathroom. The water was running. "Doc?" She called out again. Again there was no answer.

She ran to the bathroom and found Ashley on the floor crying. She knelt next to her.

"Spit." Ashley said sobbing.

Dillon stood and turned the water off. She set the wheelchair upright. She picked Ashley up and took her to the bed.

Zoë walked in. "Mommy, why you cry?"

"Mommy's just tired baby." Ashley tried to smile.

"Are you OK?" Dillon looked her over.

"Yeah, I am." Ashley looked at Dillon. "Spit, about last night-"

"Sssh...." Dillon whispered. "I know." She leaned in and kissed Ashley.

Their kiss was passionate. Dillon missed the closeness she once had with Ashley. This kiss was sparking a fire in Dillon. One that she thought was starting to fade away.

Dillon looked at her watch. Jan wasn't due for a while. "Give me a sec." She grinned as she bounced off the bed.

She turned the TV on and put in a DVD for Zoë.

"Not that one." Zoe pouted.

Dillon clumsily looked for another DVD. "Umm OK, here." She put the new one in.

"Not that one."

"What? You love Baby Zoo Buddies."

"That's for babies!"

"Well, hello?" Dillon shook her head. Sometimes Zoe was more a pint-sized adult than a child. "OK, what do you want to watch?"

Zoe walked over to her shelf of DVD's. "Ummm." She grabbed a disc. "Dis one."

"OK, fine. Sit down and watch your DVD, I'm gonna go check on mommy." She ran to the kitchen and poured two glasses of orange juice into champagne glasses and came back to the bedroom.

"What are you doing?" Ashley giggled.

"Can't you tell?" Dillon kissed Ashley. She closed the door then got into bed next to her.

Dillon wanted to make love to Ashley. She wanted to let her know that she still found her desirable. She pulled Ashley's shirt up and started to lick and kiss her stomach.

Ashley felt it. A stirring, lower this time. She felt the shiver. It scared and excited her.

"Spit, I feel something." She said.

"Yeah, me too, baby Big time." Dillon said as she continued to kiss Ashley's body. She slid her hand up Ashley's shirt and started to slowly caress Ashley's breast.

The more Ashley became aroused the more her nerves were going into overdrive. Dillon touched her nipple with her tongue. Ashley let out a scream.

Dillon jumped. "Did I hurt you?"

"Man, that was a good one." Ashley was trying to breathe it off as she broke into a cold sweat.

There was a knock at the door. Dillon knew that their playtime was now over. She rolled off the bed and opened the door. Zoë stood there.

"Spit, some at door." Zoë smiled.

Dillon scooped up Zoë. She looked at Ashley "We'll finish this later." She smiled at her.

The doorbell rang again as Dillon and Zoë reached it. Dillon opened it.

Jan was standing at the door, smiling. She was in a tight workout outfit and looked good. Dillon remembered the geeky awkwardness of Jan growing up.

"Good morning." She smiled.

"Hey there, Jan." Dillon smiled back.

"Am I early?" Jan asked as she looked at her watch and then how Dillon was dressed.

"Ah, no, it's cool. We just had a delay. Come on in."

"Mommy fall down and cry." Zoë giggled.

Jan looked at Dillon.

"She's OK. This is our daughter, Zoë."

"Hi Zoë." Jan smiled. "I'm Jan."

"Jan. Jan." Zoë smiled proud of her newly learned word.

Dillon put her down and closed the door.

"Can I get you some coffee or juice?" Dillon offered.

"Sure, juice would be great."

Jan followed Dillon to the kitchen. She was impressed. It was a very nice place. She loved the western theme. "Dillon, your house is great. Real cozy."

"Thanks." Dillon smiled. "What kind of juice would you like? We have orange, apple-cranberry, or pine-orange-banana."

"Cranberry's great, thanks." Jan smiled. She couldn't believe how much Dillon had changed. She was muscular and toned, lean and tall. Jan was very turned on by her old school friend.

Dillon handed Jan her glass of juice. "Help yourself to anything and I'll go see if Doc is ready."

Dillon ran to the bedroom and opened the door. She couldn't believe it. "You're dressed." She smiled.

"Yep.... amazing huh?" Ashley grinned. "I think it was your tongue and ah, you know."

Dillon walked over to Ashley. "Yeah?" She kissed Ashley. "I could send Jan home and we can do a little more tongue therapy?" She chuckled.

"Hmm. Tempting." Ashley kissed Dillon. "I'll be right out."

Dillon smiled. It was the first time she had seen Ashley smile since the accident. She put on her sweats and a sports bra and grabbed her favorite muscle shirt and tossed it on as she walked out of the bedroom and back into the kitchen.

Zoë was now chatting with Jan.

"Spit!" Zoë giggled and smiled.

"Are you keeping Jan company, Little Bit?" Dillon took Zoë and sat her on her lap.

"She's adorable, Dillon."

"Yeah, like her mommy." Dillon grinned.

"How old is she?" Jan asked.

"I almost tree." Zoë said proudly.

Jan and Dillon laughed.

"Gee, Dillon look at you - a daughter, an awesome house. Wow."

"Yeah, well. We have some more work to do out back, but it kind of got put on hold cause of Doc."

"Pony ride, Spit!" Zoë looked at Dillon.

"Later, little bit. Mommy has to exercise with Jan."

"No, now peeeze, Spit." Zoë pleaded with Dillon.

"Why don't you go see if mommy is ready." Dillon looked at Zoë.

"OK." Zoë smiled as she climbed off of Dillon's lap and ran to the bedroom.

"Wow, Dillon McCabe, a mother. Who would have thought?" Jan smiled at Dillon.

Dillon chuckled. "Yeah, can't believe it myself sometimes."

"So, tell me Dillon, what happened in your life to get you here?"

"Well, let's see, I came out to my family. On graduation, when I came home, my house had burnt down, and my family was lost."

"Oh, Dillon. I remember that. I wanted to call you but..."

It's OK. You couldn't of found me. Besides, we didn't say much to one another once we got to high school."

"Dillon, it wasn't OK.........I need to tell you, I purposely tried to stay away from you."

"You did? Why?" Dillon looked confused.

Jan looked down. "Dillon.... do you remember Billy Ford?"

"Yeah, captain of the football team."

"I married him right after we got out of school."

"No way! Really?"

"It only lasted two years."

"I'm sorry to hear that."

"Don't be, Dillon. I wasn't being honest with myself." She put her hand on Dillon's arm.

It sent chills through both. Dillon looked at Jan. They froze, locked into each other's stare.

"Dillon, can I tell you a secret?" Jan asked breaking their stare. "I had the biggest crush on you in junior high."

Dillon felt the heat rush to her face. Ashley came in with Zoë on her lap.

"Doc, hey." Dillon got up and walked to Ashley.

"Mommy wheel more peeze." Zoë said.

"Later baby, mommy has company."

"That Jan wiff Spit." Zoë giggled

"Yes, I can see that." Ashley said, looking at Dillon who was still flushed with color. Ashley wondered what had been said.

"Good morning, Ashley." Jan smiled. "How are you today?"

"Still in this stupid chair."

"Stupid chair! Stupid chair!" Zoë repeated like a parrot.

Dillon plucked Zoë off of Ashley's lap. "Come on, squirt. There's a Goofy DVD with your name on it. Excuse us." She took Zoë to the other room.

"Well Ashley, I'm here to help you lose that stupid chair." Jan smiled.

"That's the only thing I intend to lose." Ashley looked at Jan. Message received - loud and clear.

"Well, should we get started?" Jan smiled like nothing was said. She thought to herself that she really had no intention to steal Dillon away from Ashley. She had dreamt of what it would be like to sleep with Dillon. Was she wild and kinky, or gentle and romantic? She had such a knack of seducing women, this would be a piece of cake. And, if in the process, Dillon were to leave Ashley, she would be there to pick up the pieces of Dillon's broken heart. She smiled to herself. Starting today, she would put her plan in motion.

Dillon wheeled Ashley to the gym followed by Jan. Jan was impressed with the state-of-the-art equipment. Dillon had the room completed when Ashley was in the hospital.

"I should get lost and let you two get to work." Dillon smiled.

Ashley grabbed Dillon's hand. "Please stay." She squeezed her hand.

"Sure." Dillon smiled at Ashley.

For the next twenty minuets, Ashley worked on her upper body. She was sore, but determined. Jan and Dillon pushed her through her workout.

"OK, stop you two.... I need a break."

Dillon grabbed a towel and a bottle of water and handed it to Ashley. "You're doing great, Doc."

"Yes, Ashley, nice job." Jan smiled.

Zoë walked into the gym and went over to Dillon. "Down ups, Spit. Down ups." She squealed.

"Well, I guess you've been a good girl today, so OK, c'mon."

Dillon lay on the floor ready to do push ups. Zoë climbed on her back. Dillon proceeded to do push ups effortlessly.

Jan watched with excitement as the firefighter's muscles flexed.

Ashley could see the grin on Jan's face.

"OK, Little Bit." Dillon stopped.

The phone rang and Dillon jumped up to answer it.

"Was that fun, Zoë?" Jan asked.

"Yes. Me love Spit." Zoë told Jan.

"I can see that." Jan said.

Dillon came back. "That was Stan at the fire academy. He wants me to come in." She walked over to Zoë and kissed her. "You behave." She looked at Ashley. "You behave more." She smiled and kissed her. "You did great, baby." She whispered in her ear. "Jan, I'll see you later." Dillon ran from the gym.

Jan watched her as she left.

"So what's next?" Ashley broke Jan's stare.

"Ah, let's work on those legs." Jan smiled at Ashley.

For the next hour Ashley worked her legs. It was painful, but she had to admit that Jan was a great therapist.

"So Ashley, how did you meet Dillon?"

"She was injured in a fire and I was her doctor at the hospital."

"Oh cool. It must be hard though."

"What?" Ashley asked.

"You know, keeping a relationship going with the countless women you see everyday at the hospital."

"Well Jan, it makes me love Dillon that much more. She's one of a kind."

"Yes, she is." Jan cooed.

Childhood friend my ass! Ashley thought. She was after Dillon. "So, you went to school with Dillon?"

"Yes, third grade through high school. She was very kind to me." Jan smiled.

"Dillon's a very kind person." Ashley grunted in between reps.

"She helped me understand a lot of things I was going through. You know, I had the biggest crush on her in junior high."

"Is that so? And you never told her?"

"Nope. Not until today." She smiled at Ashley. "People change or try to change. It's a pity though. Just when you think you're doing the right thing, you realize it was for somebody else and not for yourself. You think you have it all figured out and then bang, you don't. I had big time feelings for her, but where I come from, it just wasn't accepted. So, I just kept my distance from Dillon in high school. She probably thought

I hated her or that she wasn't good enough for my circle of friends. I hid my feelings and married right out of high school. I finally realized who I was and divorced after two years. I came out to my family and my friends, finished my degree, met a gal and had a wonderful relationship. I wanted more. She didn't. So I left."

Ashley looked at Jan. *What was she driving at?* Ashley thought. *So you married a man? Half the lesbians in the free world do. But, if she thinks she's moving in on Dillon, she has another thing coming to her.*

"You're very lucky to have each other." Jan smiled.

"Yes, we are." Ashley said.

"Don't let her go."

"I don't intend to." Ashley looked at Jan. She knew her type. She finds out about the struggles they've been having and then she moves in. It was like Gia. Look for the smallest of openings and step right on through it.

* * *

Dillon looked at her watch as she came in through the door. It was 11:30pm. She had a great meeting with the Dean, and had a tour of the academy. She ran into some of her crewmembers and went to play poker at Jack's house. It was the first time she had been out in months. It felt good to let off some steam. Ashley had told her that it was fine and that Rhonda was coming over to help with Zoe.

She walked into the bedroom and found Ashley asleep in bed with Zoë cuddled next to her. She smiled as she took her jacket off. She took a quick shower and then took Zoë back to her room. The kid slept like a rock. Dillon stood in the doorway for a moment and watched Zoë sleep. How she loved that little girl.

Dillon came back to the bedroom and slowly crawled into bed. She came up close to Ashley and kissed her on the back of her neck.

"Hey Doc, I'm home."

Ashley halfway opened her eyes. "Wha? What time is it?"

"Almost midnight."

"Oh, where's the baby?"

"I put her back in her room."

"Mmmm. Good." Ashley started to fall back asleep.

Dillon wanted to pick up where they left off this morning, but it was obvious that she was fighting a losing battle. Although the doctor said that Ashley could try anything within her pain threshold, sex was one thing she didn't want to try. Dillon was amazed that they had gotten as far as they did earlier.

Dillon kissed Ashley again. She felt the goose bumps overcome Ashley's arms.

"You behave." Ashley said sleepily.

"Don't want to. Do you?"

Dillon slowly started to caress Ashley's body.

"Spit, please stop." Ashley snapped.

Dillon knew it was hopeless. She rolled over and tried to sleep. She tossed and turned. She finally got up and went into the guest room. She turned on the TV and finally fell asleep.

* * *

For the next two weeks Ashley worked her tail off in therapy. She was getting stronger. But her relationship with Dillon was weakening. She noticed how Jan would show up early and spend an hour talking and laughing with Dillon. *Was this it? Was she finally losing Dillon? She never thought that she would ever ask herself that, but what could she do?* She knew Dillon wanted to make love to her, but she felt like she couldn't. Like she was only half a woman. It was easier to just not be intimate.

Dillon had moved into the guest room. She had started her new job as an academy teacher and loved it. She was home by five and made sure she took Zoë riding and made dinner. After Zoë's bath, Dillon was either planning her lessons or on the computer. She would stop by and say good night to Ashley.

Ashley would spend the rest of the night crying herself to sleep.

* * *

They were out in the backyard. Ashley was sitting out on the patio watching Zoë and Dillon play in the pool. The phone rang. Ashley picked it up.

"Hello."

"Hi Ashley, it's Jan."

"Oh, hello." Ashley said flatly.

"Is Dillon there by any chance?"

"Yeah, hang on. Spit, phone for you."

"Come on, squirt, out of the pool." Dillon took Zoë and climbed out. She walked over to the phone and looked at Ashley.

"McCabe here."

"Do you always answer the phone like that?" Jan giggled on the other end.

"Hey." Dillon smiled. "What's up?"

"A bunch of us are going to play pool tonight. You guys want to come?"

"Sounds like fun. Let me ask Doc." Dillon put her hand over the phone. "Jan and her friends are going to play pool tonight and they wanted us to join them."

"I can't play." Ashley looked at Dillon.

"So, we could sit around and chat, maybe make some new friends."

"No thanks."

"Doc, come on... it'll be fun." Dillon asked hopefully.

"I'm tired. You go if you want to."

Dillon looked at Ashley before she put the phone to her ear. "Where are you meeting at?" Dillon wrote the address down. "If we can make it, we'll be there."

Ashley shot Dillon a look as she hung up the phone. "Why did you tell her that?

"Cause, I thought it might be fun to possibly go out on a date with my wife! Damn it, you never leave the house except to go to the doctors."

"You think it's easy for me?" Ashley raised her voice.

"No, I don't think it's easy for you. But guess what? It's not easy for me, or Zoë, or your folks, but we're all trying to work with it! All of us except you." She got up and went inside.

Dillon was already showered and dressed when Ashley came in.

"So, you're going?" Ashley asked.

"Yeah, you wanna join me?" Dillon asked.

"There's no one to watch Zoë."

"I'll call Rhonda." Dillon offered.

"She hasn't eaten dinner and she needs a bath."

Dillon looked at Ashley. "I think Rhonda is totally capable of sitting with Zoë. She's only done it a million times. Stop making excuses. Do you want to go or not?"

"I'm kind of tired." Ashley said. "It's been a long day."

Dillon shook her head. "Do you not want me to go?"

"No, don't be silly. You go on and have fun."

Dillon grabbed her leather jacket. "I'll call you." Dillon leaned over and kissed Ashley on the cheek.

Zoë walked in and saw Dillon dressed. She hated it when she left. "Spit stay!" Zoë pouted.

Dillon scooped her up. "I'll be back soon, little bit." She kissed Zoë and tossed her on the bed, much to her daughter's delight. "Love you both," Dillon said as she left.

Ashley just stared at Zoë on the bed.

* * *

The bar was packed. It was Saturday night and all the single women were on the prowl. Dillon was a top catch from the second she walked in. She had a look about her that would turn women on. She never noticed it. She spotted Jan and her friends at the pool tables. Dillon had to admit that Jan had really blossomed into a beautiful woman.

"Dillon, you made it," Jan smiled. She jumped into Dillon making sure she squeezed extra hard so Dillon could feel her. "Kim and Val..... This is Dillon. Dillon, Kim and Val."

"Nice to meet you both." Dillon politely shook their hands.

"Dillon, what can I get you from the bar?" Kim smiled at her. She could see why Jan was talking about her non-stop.

"A club soda, thanks."

"You got it." Kim smiled as she walked to the bar.

"Hey Dillon, take your jacket off and stay awhile." Val said.

Dillon smiled and slid out of her jacket, her arms now exposed from her muscle shirt she was wearing.

Val looked at Jan and mouthed WOW. Jan winked back and nodded.

Dillon searched for a pool cue, as Kim came back with their drinks.

"Ashley couldn't make it?" Jan asked.

"Naw, she was tired and it was too late to find a sitter." Dillon said

"Oh, you have kids?" Val asked.

"A daughter. Zoë."

"She is just a doll too." Jan smiled.

"Thanks." Dillon smiled.

"So Dillon, Jan says you two met in school?" Kim asked.

"Yeah, we did way back in grade school." She looked at her watch. It was 8:30pm. She'd stay until 10:00pm and make it home in time to see Ashley before she fell asleep.

"So what are we playing?" Jan asked.

"Eight ball?" Kim looked around.

"Sounds good to me." Dillon smiled. She had always had a competitive side to her. And being in a station house with a bunch of men, Dillon had always pushed herself harder. Tonight was no different. She wanted to win. She paired up with Jan and they ran the table three straight games.

It was a nice time. Dillon wished Ashley would come out and do the things they used to do. She looked at her watch.

"Got a date?" Val chuckled.

"No, I just have to get going soon." Dillon smiled.

"Ah yes...home to the little woman." Jan said. She was on her fifth rum and coke and she was starting to show it.

Dillon looked at the couples dancing on the floor. *Yeah gotta get home to the guest room* she thought. *What the hell was happening?* She and Ashley were best friends and so much in love. Dillon went over it in her mind a thousand times. She had done everything for their relationship. Now there was Zoë. Dillon's other passion. *How could she look into those beautiful blue eyes and tell her that mommy and Spit no longer loved each other.*

"It's your turn Dillon." Val broke her train of thought.

"Oh." Dillon looked at the table. "Eight ball side pocket," she called as she lined up her shot. She cracked the cue ball and sent it spinning wickedly into the eight ball. It hit the back of the side pocket and dropped in.

Jan shouted wildly. The booze was finally taking over. She jumped on Dillon's back and started to shout. "We're number one!!! Wooohoooooooo!"

Dillon chuckled.

Jan jumped off her back.

"Well that's it for me," Kim said as she laid her cue down. "Come on, good looking, let's continue this party at home." She smiled at Val.

"Dillon, it was a pleasure meeting you. Let's do this again soon."

"It was nice meeting you both. Drive safe now." Dillon smiled.

Jan watched them leave. "They're great huh?"

"Yeah, very nice." Dillon said as she looked down at her watch. "I need to get going too."

"What's the rush? Come on, Dillon let's dance."

"Ah, Jan I don't think -"Dillon started to say.

"Dill...It's for old times' sake. Remember, I taught you how to dance in junior. high."

She pulled Dillon to the dance floor as Wynonna's "Who am I Suppose To Love?" started to play.

Jan pulled Dillon close, wrapping her arms around her. She laid her head just under Dillon's collarbone.

Dillon felt the heat rush through her body. She missed the feel of holding Ashley close while they danced. Jan felt so nice pressed up against her. Dillon felt guilty.

"You're a great dancer Dill." Jan smiled.

"I had a great teacher." Dillon smiled back.

Jan looked up into Dillon's eyes. She could see the uncertainty in them. "You ever wonder why two people are brought together?"

"I guess it's just meant to be that way." Dillon said.

"I'm sure glad I found you again," Jan squeezed Dillon.

Dillon didn't know what to say. She was having some feelings that she knew she shouldn't be.

The song stopped. Dillon looked at Jan. "Thanks for the dance Jan. But I need to get going."

"Please stay for a little bit longer." Jan said.

"Sorry, I can't."

Jan stood on tiptoe and kissed Dillon on the lips. "Thank you. I had a nice time."

Dillon was flustered. Her body was trying to push her into some things her mind was warning her not to do. "Can you make it home OK, Jan?"

Jan smiled. "Do I look like I can?"

Dillon knew that she couldn't leave Jan stranded. "Let me make a call and I'll take you home." Dillon pulled out her cell phone and dialed home.

"Hello." Ashley said on the other end.

"Hey Doc. How are you?" Dillon tried to make conversion.

"I thought you said you would be home at ten?" Ashley's toned changed.

"I'm on my way, but Jan is still here and, well, she's in no shape to drive. I was going to drop her off, then head home."

"How convenient for Jan." Ashley could see what was happening now.

"What?" Dillon asked.

"Oh come on now Spit. I wasn't born yesterday."

"It's nothing like that." Dillon said.

"Really... let me guess, she gets tanked, her friends leave, she asks you for a ride home and you end up in her bed! And if that's where you're headed Dillon McCabe, then don't bother coming home!"

The line went dead in Dillon's ear.

"Well?" Jan looked at Dillon.

"Let's get you home."

* * *

Dillon pulled up in front of Jan's condo. She got out of the car and opened the door for Jan who was still wobbly.

"Nice." Dillon said trying to make small talk.

"Wanna come up?" Jan asked.

Dillon didn't know what to think or what to do. Yes, she did want to go up. She longed to hold a woman in her arms again and make love to her all night long. She was starting to have feelings for Jan. She made her laugh and smile, the way Ashley used to. Dillon's heart sank. She thought about Ashley and their daughter Zoë.

"Come on, Dillon. I know you want to." Jan looked her in the eye. She took Dillon's hand and led her to her condo. She fumbled for the keys and finally unlocked the door. She smiled at Dillon. "Come on in."

"Jan..... I...I...can't." Dillon said.

"Can't or won't?" Jan asked.

Dillon was silent.

"I see the way she treats you, Dillon. You deserve better." She moved to Dillon and put her arms around her. "I can give you better."

"Jan.... you're sweet and beautiful. You deserve everything your heart desires."

"My heart desires you." She pulled Dillon's head down and kissed her. "Think about it." She walked inside and saw Dillon turn and walk away.

Dillon drove down to the beach, tears streaming down her face. She needed to talk to her best friend right now. But that was Ashley. She picked up her cell phone and dialed.

"Hi, Mom?" Dillon's voice cracked.

"Dillon honey, are you OK?"

"I'm sorry to call so late. I hope I didn't wake you."

"No dear, not at all. What's the matter?"

"I don't know anymore. I don't know what to do." Dillon cried.

"I'm sorry, but I don't know what you mean." Mary said confused.

"It's Ashley. I can't get it through her mind that I still want to be with her. She's pushed me away. And tonight................." She choked on her words. "Oh God, I almost..........."

"Dillon, settle down. What can we do for you? Do you want me to talk with Ashley?"

"I don't think that'll help. But do you think you and dad can come and stay for a while and help with Zoë?"

"Of course, dear. But why?"

"I think I need to leave."

For the next forty minutes Dillon told Ashley's mother everything. Mary was a godsend to Dillon. She listened and never judged. She reassured Dillon and told her that they would call Ashley and be down in the morning.

Dillon drove down to Long Beach. She went to the lifeguard tower where she and Ashley had sat and looked at the ocean. She sat there all night thinking about Ashley and Zoë. She cried and laughed until the sun started to rise. She was exhausted and her head hurt from all the thinking she had done. She got home at 8:30am. She slowly unlocked the door. Zoë came running over.

"Spit! Spit!" she flew into Dillon's arms.

"Hey little bit, what are you up to?"

"Eating." Zoë giggled.

"Zoë Noel! Come back and finish your breakfast please!" Ashley called from the kitchen.

Dillon carried Zoë into the kitchen and sat her down at the table.

"You look like crap." Ashley said.

"Feel like it too." Dillon poured herself a cup of coffee.

"Mom and Dad called. They're coming down."

"Cool, it'll be great to see them." Dillon sat down at the table.

"Mommy, I done." Zoë giggled.

"One more bite." Ashley said.

"No mommy full." Zoë pouted.

"C'mon Little Bit, one more." Dillon took the fork and made like an airplane. Zoë quickly gobbled her pancake up.

"Mommy, done now." Zoë looked at Ashley.

"OK baby" Ashley said.

Zoë got down off her chair and ran to watch T.V.

Dillon took her dish and started to clean up.

"So?" Ashley looked at her.

"What?" Dillon kept cleaning.

"Don't . Where were you all night?"

"At the beach." Dillon answered. There was silence as Dillon continued to clean the kitchen.

"Did you sleep with her?" Ashley's voice cracked as she watched Dillon throw down the dish and walk away. She started to cry.

* * *

Dillon took a long hot shower. She was tired and her head was spinning. She knew she had to tell Ashley everything. It was the only hope she had of saving their relationship. She got out of the shower and found Ashley sitting there.

"Whoa Doc. Ya startled me." Dillon grabbed a towel.

"Dillon. Look, I'm sorry for what's happened to us, but I know you want more than I'll ever be able to give you."

"What?" Dillon looked confused.

"I think it best if we go our separate ways." Ashley choked out.

Dillon looked at her, her heart falling into her stomach. "Is that what you want?"

Ashley looked at Dillon. Tears started to stream down her face. She turned and wheeled herself out.

Ashley's parents came in about 11:30am. They could feel the tension in the air. Dillon was in the backyard walking Zoë around on the pony.

Ashley was in the gym working out. She was having such bad pain in her legs now that she couldn't stand it. She called the doctor with concerns that Jan may be overworking her. Instead, the doctor reassured Ashley that the pain was a good sign, that she was feeling things again and would be walking soon. He thought Jan was a great therapist for her and she should stick with it. She didn't care anymore. Dillon didn't want to be with her. Mary walked in startling Ashley. "Oh Mom, hi. I didn't hear you come in."

Mary walked over and gave Ashley a kiss. "How have you been?"

"OK, thanks."

"Don't lie to your mother. I know you've been crying."

Ashley knew she couldn't keep things from her.

"I've lost Dillon." Ashley's voice cracked.

"What?"

"It turns out that my physical therapist is an old school friend of Dillon's."

"Well, that's nice."

"Mom, no, you don't understand. Last night Dillon went to play pool with Jan and her friends."

"Oh, and they didn't invite you along?"

"Yes, I was invited."

"Did you go?" Mother asked.

"No." Ashley looked at her mother. "Mom, you're missing the point. Dillon didn't come home last night."

"Did you ask her about it?"

"It's too late now."

"Only if you let it be." Mary got up and walked away.

Dillon led Zoë around on the pony. Bill snuck up behind them.

"Hey! When is it my turn?" He smiled.

"Papa! Papa!" Zoë screamed.

"How's my girl?" Bill kissed Zoë.

"Papa. Ride, Ride!" Zoë squealed.

"How's my other girl?" He smiled and hugged Dillon.

"Trying to hang in there."

"Papa, pull Blaze." Zoë giggled.

Dillon handed the lead rope to Ashley's father.

"Did you two talk?"

"More like not talking now." Tears started to fill Dillon's eyes.

Bill pulled Zoë off of her pony. "Sweetie, go on in and find Grandma. She has a present for you."

"Gran! Gran!" Zoë yelled as she ran inside.

Bill put his hand on Dillon's shoulder. "Let's talk."

That night was silent. Zoë and Bill played while Dillon and Mary cleaned up. Ashley went to her room to rest.

"That's everything." Mary smiled wiping her hands on the dishtowel.

"Thanks, Mom. I appreciate the help."

"Dillon? When was the last time you slept?"

"I had a few hours a couple of days ago."

"This is getting ridiculous." Mary's voice rose.

"I know Mom. I love Ashley. But I can't go on like this anymore."

"Then do something about it." Mary looked at Dillon.

"I am. I'm gonna go to the cabin and try to work things out. I...I just don't know what else to do." Dillon was surprised how fast the tears came to her. Mary grabbed her and held her."

"It's OK." Mary rubbed Dillon's back.

Ashley finished her book and put it down. She was going crazy just sitting around. She had been working out a lot. She felt the energy coming back to her, not to mention her body was starting to show off the results. She pulled herself over the side of the bed resting her feet on the floor. She wasn't sure, but she thought she could feel the carpet under her feet.

Zoë came running in and bounced on the bed. "Mommy, come play."

"Well, look at you all clean and pretty." Ashley smiled.

"Gram and Papa had bubby bath."

"They did? Well, that was sure nice. Did you remember to thank them?"

"There's the escapee." Bill smiled as he came into the room.

"Papa, sit here!" Zoë pounded on the bed next to her.

"Grandma said to come on back and brush your chops young lady."

"Brush chops! Brush chops!" Zoë giggled as she climbed off the bed and ran out.

"She's getting so big." Bill smiled.

"Yeah. Seems like yesterday when Spit and I..." Ashley stopped herself.

"Speaking of, where's Spit going?"

"What do you mean?" Ashley looked at her father.

"Well, she asked if we could stay here with you for a while. I didn't know she was still fighting fires."

"She's not "

"Hmmm. Well, she's got her bags packed. Maybe it's some academy training."

Bags packed were all Ashley heard. It hit her hard. Her heart sank. She couldn't believe that Dillon was actually going to leave.

Bill leaned over and kissed her. "Get some rest pumpkin." He smiled and left the room.

Ashley was stunned. Tears started to roll down her cheeks.

* * *

That night Dillon couldn't sleep. Her heart was broken. The sadness overtook her. She sat in Zoë's room and watched her beautiful daughter sleep soundly. She got up twice hearing a noise coming from the hallway. She saw the light coming from under the door of their bedroom. Her memory flew back to the first night Ashley was in her room. Again Dillon wished she could tell Ashley how she felt. But all hope was gone now.

Ashley thought she heard something. She listened for a moment. She couldn't sleep. She was having pain in her legs, but it was nothing compared to the pain of the loss she was feeling in her heart. All her dreams were about to walk out the door and she was the one holding it open. It just hurt so much to think that Dillon was with another woman. Mother was right. Gia, yes. Dillon, never!

She had to talk to Dillon, though she knew it was too late. She turned the light off and slid down into her covers. She wept until sleep overcame her.

* * *

The next morning Mary and Bill were already up when Dillon dragged herself to the shower. She joined them at the breakfast table. Ashley could tell Dillon hadn't had any sleep either.

"Ah.... I wanted to tell you...I have to go away for awhile." She looked at Ashley. "I don't know how long I'll be gone."

Ashley set her fork down and wheeled herself away.

Dillon looked at Ashley's parents. She got up and went out back.

The doorbell rang. Mary went to answer it.

"Hello. I'm Jan. Ashley's physical therapist."

"Come in." Mary tried to smile.

Jan smiled and stepped in. "You must be Ashley's mother."

"Yes."

"Jan! Jan!" Zoë ran up to her.

"Hey there, Zoë. How are you?"

"I fine." Zoë smiled.

"Ashley's in the gym." Mary said.

"Great. Thank you." Jan smiled.

"Me take you." Zoë grabbed Jan's hand and led her to the gym.

She found Ashley already lifting free weights. "Wow, look at you." Jan smiled at her. "You're winning this battle, Ashley."

Ashley looked at her. "I guess we know who the real winner is."

Jan looked at Ashley. "Excuse me?"

"Zoë. Why don't you go get grandpa and go feed your pony."

"Pony food!" Zoë yelled as she ran out of the gym.

"Oh please, Jan. I know all about you. I know you can't wait to sink your teeth into Dillon. Well, now it looks like you'll have your chance."

"What are you talking about? There's no way in hell Dillon would ever leave you." Jan looked at Ashley.

"Guess again." Ashley's eyes were on fire. "I know Dillon didn't come home the other night."

"Well she wasn't with me. I got drunk at the bar and Dillon took me home. Don't get me wrong, she's pure sex and I did try to seduce her. Dillon is awesome, but she's way too much in love with you. She got me to the door and left."

"Are you telling me the truth?" Ashley asked.

"Unfortunately, yes. That's what happened."

"Oh my, God. Dillon," Ashley said as she wheeled herself out of the gym. She had to stop her.

She caught Dillon at the front door. Zoë was pulling on her pant leg.

"Spit no go!! No go!!"

Tears were streaming down Dillon's face as she scooped Zoë up into her arms. "I know, Little Bit, but I have too."

"Read story to me!" She handed her book to Dillon.

"What ya got there?"

"Siderrender."

"Huh? Oh Cinderella."

"Ever happy end Spit."

"Yeah. Happily ever after." Dillon tried hard to control her tears.

"Why you cry, Spit?" Zoë looked at Dillon.

"Spit has a boo boo right here." She pointed to her heart.

"I get mommy, she fix boo boos."

"Your mommy is a great doctor Zoe, but I don't think she can fix this one."

"Here, I kiss and make all better." Zoë leaned over and kissed Dillon's heart.

Dillon chuckled. "You're smart like your mommy. Beautiful like her too."

Ashley was in the hallway listening. She was crying.

"Heart all better, Spit?" Zoë asked.

"It's getting there." Dillon tried to smile.

"Then Spit stay wif mommy." Zoë said.

"I wish I could baby, but mommy doesn't want that right now." She kissed Zoë. "Maybe, when she feels better." She kissed Zoë again and put her down. Tears were now streaming down her cheeks as she picked up her bags. She never thought in her wildest dreams that she would be leaving Ashley and their relationship. It hurt so bad. She slowly reached for the door.

"Spit, wait.... Please." Ashley called to her.

Dillon froze.

"I'll try.......... just please, don't go." Ashley said.

Dillon stopped. Did she hear her correctly?

"Mommy walking! Mommy walking!" Zoë screamed.

Dillon spun around to Ashley standing, sliding her feet inches on wobbly legs.

Dillon dropped her bag and ran to Ashley taking her in her arms. "Doc, you're walking!" Dillon smiled.

Ashley smiled. "Please, don't go." Ashley looked into Dillon's eyes.

"Kiss! Kiss! Kiss!" Zoe squealed.

"We can't disappoint her." Ashley smiled.

Dillon took Ashley's face into her hands. "Are you sure?"

"Our family is the only thing I'm sure of."

Dillon kissed Ashley passionately.

"You'll stay?"

"Just try and make me leave." She kissed her again.

"Happy ever end!" Zoe giggled with delight.

"What?" Ashley looked at Zoe, then at Dillon.

"They lived happily ever after."

"Oh."

"Can't disappoint our daughter." Dillon grinned.

Right there, at that very second, Dillon and Ashley fell in love all over again.

TO BE CONTINUED

Printed in the United States
210081BV00016B/52-87/P

9 781440 108464